WHAT LIES
CAN DO

WHAT LIES CAN DO

To Donna and Jim,

all the best,

Erick

ERICK LEITHE

ISBN-13: 9781545009543
ISBN-10: 1545009546

To my family,
With love

False words are not only evil in themselves,
but they infect the soul with evil.

- Plato

1

It was a question Matt Beringer would never forget.

"Did you hear about Pete Rockwell?"

"No," Matt said, joining his classmate for breakfast.

"He died early Friday morning in a car accident."

"What? That's awful. How'd it happen?"

"He rolled his car heading north on Interstate 80," the young man said. "I read about it in yesterday's *Chronicle*. I couldn't believe it!"

"I'm stunned," Matt said. "Wasn't he a youth minister in Sacramento?"

"Yeah. He must have been heading home."

"Anybody with him?"

"No. By himself. It was after midnight, near Vacaville."

"Other cars involved?" Matt asked.

"No. Kind of late, don't you think?"

"Not if he was single. But maybe, if he was married."

"Wasn't married."

Matt sipped his coffee. "Probably returning from the city."

"On a work night? It's a three-hour round trip. I'd drive that far to see a baseball game, but the Giants and A's weren't in town on Thursday."

"Maybe he had a date in Berkeley," Matt said. "Any witnesses?"

"Nope."

"He could have fallen asleep at the wheel."

"That's what the California Highway Patrol reported."

"What a sad story," Matt said. "Remember when he spoke to our class during orientation week?"

"Yeah. He was excited about starting his internship."

"Hard to believe it was two years ago."

"The article said Pete was 26. He graduated last year and was hired at the church in October."

"So much ahead of him," Matt said.

"It said his car left the road at a high speed because it traveled 50 feet and flipped. Landed upside down in an irrigation ditch. What a horrible way to die!"

"I hear you."

"If you fell asleep at the wheel, wouldn't your foot automatically relax on the accelerator, slowing the car as it left the highway?"

"Possibly. Never thought about it." Matt paused. "Was someone chasing him? Maybe that's why he was going so fast."

"Good question. I'm a little spooked by his death. There are some things that just don't add up."

"You're interning in Sacramento, aren't you?"

"Yeah. I've already made a few trips on 80 to my church. If Pete fell asleep at the wheel, the same thing could happen to me."

"We'll probably never know the answers."

"I saw Dean Carlson at the library yesterday. He said there will be a memorial service for Pete in the Chapel on Friday."

"Okay, thanks. Can we change the subject?" Matt asked.

"Yeah. Sorry."

"When do you start your internship?"

"In two weeks. How about you?"

"A week from today," Matt said.

The other seminarian leaned forward. "I want to rent an apartment near the church. Commuting from here to Sacramento would be crazy."

"The less time spent on the freeway, the better." Matt finished his scrambled eggs and stared at his empty plate.

"You got a lucky break on your internship. Quite a few in our class applied for the San Lucas position."

"You're right," Matt said. "Playing college basketball may have helped. The job description included organizing basketball leagues for the middle school boys and girls, including the other San Lucas churches."

"Someone upstairs was looking out for you."

"Without a doubt. I'm heading over to attend the nine-thirty worship service and check out my office. Want to come along?"

"Thanks, but I'm taking a date to Paradise Park in Marin."

"Sounds like fun," Matt said. "You should have good weather over there. Don't forget the sunscreen."

"Yeah, yeah," he said, grinning. "I appreciate your concern."

"Tell me about your internship," Matt said.

"It's a small congregation. I'll be leading the high school group, teaching an adult ed class, and preaching once a month. How about you?"

"Supervising the middle school kids will keep me busy. It's a large church. About a thousand members. I'll be a small fish in a big pond."

"You mean a tall fish in a big pond. The basketball program was made to order for you."

"Yeah, like you said, someone's looking out for me."

"I have a few things to do before my date," he said, rising from his chair. "I'll see you later."

"May the Force be with you," Matt said, smiling.

He sat alone for a few minutes, staring out the windows at the fog that blanketed San Francisco and hid its skyline. The cafeteria was nearly empty on this Sunday morning in late August. However, when students returned in mid-September to start classes, the breakfast crowd would fill the room. Matt glanced at his watch. It was seven-thirty, and he had a half hour before he would begin his leisurely drive to the East Bay. He could easily reach his destination in an hour. Starving because he had stayed up late the night before, trying to finish a *New York Times* crossword puzzle, he wanted something more to eat. Returning to the cafeteria counter, he refilled his coffee cup and added a couple of cookies to his tray. Seated again at the table, Matt yawned as he glanced at the *Chronicle* sports section he found on a nearby chair. His crossword puzzle addiction sometimes distracted him from more important activities, like sleep. However, he relished doing battle every day with the puzzle editor.

A few more seminary students straggled into the cafeteria as Matt headed for the exit. Walking toward the parking lot, he began to feel butterflies in his stomach, like he did before suiting up for a varsity basketball game in college. He'd initiated the internship experience at the San Lucas church, so he wanted to embrace it and make it a success. Starting a new job, he'd be interacting with a congregation of strangers. Now that he thought about it, he was more than a bit anxious. In contrast with his optimism during the application process, he suddenly had mixed feelings about the next nine months.

During his senior year in college, Matt's world caved in when the dean of students called him to his office on a Friday afternoon in April and informed him that his parents had been killed in an automobile accident. After an hour with the dean, Matt walked across the Princeton campus to the athletic fields, where he could spend time by himself. He roamed the length and width of the grassy surfaces, moving from one field to the next, remembering the hours of watching baseball, soccer, and lacrosse competitions. He sat in the empty stands, gazing across the fields to the trees beyond. Tears ran down his cheeks. Finally, he walked to the crew house on Lake Carnegie. He didn't want his roommates to see him cry; he needed to gain control of his emotions, including waves of anger and fear.

When he told his three roommates about his loss back in the dormitory, they took him to dinner at a restaurant off campus in an attempt to comfort him. Grateful for their companionship on the worst day of his life, he let them carry the conversation during their meal together. As they sat at the table, Matt felt surrounded by loneliness. Never to hear his parents' voices again. There would be no more hugs. His home as he had known it no longer existed. As an only child, Matt had become an orphan overnight.

Two days later, he flew home from New Jersey to Seattle to plan his parents' mid-week memorial service. After the service, attended by over 100 of his parents' friends, Matt spent just a few days securing the house. He needed to be back at Princeton to complete his senior thesis for the history department. Graduation, then, was a blur. He didn't remember much of it. He shelved his plans to attend business school and enrolled instead at Calvin Seminary in San Francisco, his pastor's alma mater. He needed some theological answers to why his parents had been taken from him—part of the larger subject of human suffering. Returning to Seattle, he sold the house and most of its contents, and put what he wanted to keep in a storage unit. The tragedy had crushed him, but he had to lean on his faith and move forward with his life. Like many young adults, Matt had possessed the arrogance of invincibility. He believed his life's journey would be peaceful and positive. However, losing his parents had introduced him to the unexpected consequences that can follow false assumptions.

It was now eight in the morning. He drove from the parking lot and left the seminary campus that sat perched on a hilltop, west of the city's business district. As he passed the University of San Francisco just a few blocks away, a dark sedan closed in behind him. He'd noticed it in his rearview mirror. During his descent to the freeway, he cracked the windows of his Honda, admitting some fresh air. Matt eased his car down Turk Street, through the neighborhood to Oak Street, which pointed him toward Highway 101 and the San Francisco Bay Bridge. Periodically, he checked his rearview mirror. The sedan was there, tailing him, but he couldn't see the driver through its tinted windshield. Was he imagining things? Was he being followed? Or was it simply a seminary neighbor heading in the same direction?

Reaching the freeway leading to the Bay Bridge and the East Bay, Matt couldn't help but think about Pete Rockwell's death. The fog began to clear, revealing large patches of blue sky. As he merged onto Highway 101, he encountered light traffic approaching the bridge. The car no longer followed him. He breathed a sigh of relief and opened the windows all the way. A cool breeze rushed through the car as he sped across the seven-mile bridge, divided into two sections by Yerba Buena Island halfway across the span. He loved this drive. Sailboats dotted the surface of the cobalt blue bay as he glanced northward toward Marin County. Crossing the bay under the shade of the upper deck, he relaxed and let his mind idle. In the summer months, he relished how the pace of life shifted down a notch or two without the responsibilities of class work. His summer job as a coach at a high school basketball camp in San Rafael, across the Golden Gate Bridge to the north, provided an enjoyable respite from the seminary's academic schedule. In nine months, he would graduate and could pursue a career as a minister, if he wanted, although he had some reservations. He hadn't entirely given up his earlier plan to attend business school.

At the end of the bridge, he saw a fog bank nestled against the Oakland hills. Later, the bright sun would burn through the mist. In no hurry to reach his destination, he chose the far right lane as he cruised along the Nimitz Freeway.

Reaching over to change the radio station, he noticed the lights of a semi in his rearview mirror. The growl of the advancing truck's engine had interrupted his reverie. His back stiffened as he watched the image of the big rig grow larger, so he stepped on the gas. When the semi had closed the distance to less than two car lengths, Matt swerved left one lane to allow the truck to pass. To his surprise, the semi followed him into the same lane. "What's going on here?"

He veered left again to another lane, and increased his speed. The semi charged after him. His adrenaline flowing, Matt squinted to see what the truck driver looked like. However, the cab's dark glass obscured his visibility.

Moving his car left once more to the inside lane, the truck driver continued his pursuit. Matt accelerated to gain some separation from the menacing semi. When his car reached 85 miles per hour, Matt thought the truck driver would give up and slow down. However, the chase continued past the Oakland business district and Jack London Square. The air pouring through the car was no longer soothing, and instead heightened his agitation. That and the noise of cars and his own tires whirring on the cement surface. As he raced along the freeway, he hoped a California Highway Patrol car would appear, siren blaring, and pull them both to the side of the road. Receiving a speeding ticket in this case might save his life. While being questioned by the police, he'd also be able to come face to face with his stalker.

Matt decided to take the next exit into the residential neighborhoods of San Leandro where, he believed, the big truck would be unlikely to follow him. He sped south to the Davis Street off-ramp. Once he ditched this crazy man, he'd continue his drive to San Lucas.

When the semi didn't trail him down the ramp, Matt's body relaxed. He lessened his grip on the wheel and wiped beads of perspiration from his upper lip. "What a jerk," he yelled. "What was he trying to do? Kill me?" He slowly pulled to the curb and opened the door to stretch his legs and clear his head. Walking around the front of the car, he leaned against the fender next to the curb with his arms crossed, staring at the house in front of him, oblivious to the cars moving up and down Davis Street. Continuing to reflect on what had just happened, he asked himself, "Was that idiot drunk?!" His morning was going from bad to worse. First the news of Pete Rockwell, then the sedan, and now the mad 18-wheeler forcing him off the road. Things could only improve.

After a few minutes, Matt returned to the driver's seat, only slightly less agitated. The back of his shirt damp, he started the engine and turned on the air conditioning. "Why didn't I get the license number?" he asked himself. Frustrated that he had nothing to report to the police, he grabbed the steering wheel and checked his rearview mirror. No truck in view. Seeing no other traffic, he made a U-turn to return to the freeway. He continued south on the Nimitz for three more exits to the affluent community of San Lucas. Taking the exit, he came to a stop and crossed over the freeway, heading east, away from the bay. No sign welcomed him as he entered residential neighborhoods, protected by tall, tan-colored stucco walls lining both sides of the boulevard. The wealthy suburb took pride in maintaining its privacy. Reaching the San Lucas village at the base of the East Bay hills, he continued through the main street of small shops that led to Buena Vista Drive, which would take him up the slope to Hacienda Presbyterian Church. With no information about the truck, he had no choice but to forget about his encounter and move on.

Arriving at the church campus at the top of the hill, Matt drove into the parking lot and chose a spot facing the large sanctuary, with its adjacent bell tower, and the two-story administration building. A green lawn and mature plantings framed the property, dotted with oaks, lindens, and oleanders. Gathering his blazer from the back seat, he slipped it on as he crossed the concrete pavement. He'd visited the church once before, so he knew the church office was located in the two-story quadrangle whose open side faced the sanctuary and parking lot. The courtyard included a mosaic fountain in the center and a surrounding lawn that looked like a putting green. He heard the water splashing as he approached the building entrance.

Opening one of the double doors, Matt headed down the hall. Finding the office door, he ducked his head slightly and stepped inside. He surveyed a room clad in a palette of earth tones, muted by weak overhead lighting. A long, bare counter to his left divided the space. At the far end, curtains covered a large window and blocked the bright morning sunshine. A framed print on the wall to his right reminded him of the Sierra foothills in Calaveras County. The woman standing beside the receptionist stepped forward.

"You're a week early, Mr. Beringer."

"Good morning. I don't believe we've met," he said. "Are you Pastor Boyle's secretary?"

"No. I'm Evelyn Kirby, administrative assistant to the senior pastor, Reverend Staley. I know who you are, though. I've started a file on you."

"I see. Well, I'm just visiting today. I called this week to ask what time the worship service started and if I could take a look at my office."

"You didn't speak to me. I can assure you of that. We have volunteers during the week to help with the phones."

"If it's not too much trouble, I'd like to see my office before the service."

"Didn't they show you around after your interview?" Small in stature, she wore a navy blue jacket, white slacks, and pale green scarf. Her gray hair was pulled into a tight bun.

"No. Do you have a key?"

"I think I can find one for you." She turned and walked into her office behind a large glass panel. After writing something in a notebook, she reached into her center desk drawer. Returning to the counter, she dangled two keys on a short chain. "I'll give you another one for the building. The smaller key is for your office." Setting the chain on the surface, she slid the keys toward him. "They're yours for the year." Pointing toward the door, she said, "Turn right and go down the hall. Take the stairs to the second floor. Room 21."

"Do you find it a little dark in here? If you opened the curtains, you could turn off the lights and save some electricity."

"Our utility bill is the least of my worries. The lighting is just fine. Direct sun is too bright for me."

"Fair enough," he said, reaching for the keys. "Hmm, does she have a crown to go with her imperial manner?" he mused.

"You're taller than I expected," she said. "How tall are you?"

"Six-five," he said.

"Well, I guess basketball players are supposed to be tall," she said, adjusting the strand of pearls around her neck. "Pastor Staley expects you to be in his office next Sunday morning at eight-thirty. Don't be late."

"Not a chance," he said.

"That's a very confident answer. We'll see how you do this year. You may have some surprises."

"Such as?"

"Your internship may be more difficult than you think. Working here isn't like the ivory-tower existence you've had at the seminary. Our members have high expectations."

"So do I."

"That's what all the interns say. However, they quickly discover how challenging it is to perform at this church. We've had some good ones and some bad ones."

"What's your idea of a bad one?"

"Someone who's late to meetings. I wonder what problems you'll bring to us this year?"

"No need to worry. Dull is my middle name."

"Our members want more than dull, Mr. Beringer. We have a church full of successful people. They want to be impressed."

"We'll see what happens."

"Pastor Staley has some sad news to share with the congregation this morning about one of our previous interns."

The office door opened, and an attractive woman appeared. She had brown hair, lightly frosted, a golden tan, and wore sunglasses. Matt recognized her.

"Hello, Evelyn," she said. "I'm dying for a cup of coffee."

"Help yourself, Liz," Mrs. Kirby said. "You know where it is." Her manner was just as curt as it had been with Matt.

The woman turned, smiled, and extended her hand. "Hi there, Matt. You may remember, I'm Liz Canfield. I'm on the Education Committee that interviewed you last spring."

"It's good to see you again," Matt said, taking her hand.

"You were our *favorite* applicant. We're looking forward to having you on our staff," she said. "Have you moved to the East Bay?"

"As a matter of fact, I hope to find a place tomorrow."

"Don't forget to give your new address to Mrs. Kirby, so we can mail you the monthly newsletter." She patted Matt's arm as she moved passed him toward a coffee machine on a table in the corner. Filling her cup, she turned toward Matt and took a sip. "You're well-dressed for a seminary intern. The last young man showed up wearing jeans. Do you have any plans for lunch?"

"No."

"My husband's a pediatrician and is on call today, so he stayed home. Are you going to the service?"

"Yes."

"Let's talk about lunch at the coffee hour after the service." She wheeled and left the office with her cup of coffee. Her perfume sweetened the air.

"Don't feel special, Mr. Beringer," Mrs. Kirby said. "Liz likes to flirt."

Matt remembered that during his interview, Liz Canfield had asked him some questions, including one about his father's employment history, which had nothing to do with his internship qualifications and seemed peculiar. She also inquired about his health. He suspected her unusual and awkward questions were those of an inexperienced interviewer, and he'd given her the benefit of the doubt. In his ninety-minute interview, he'd been peppered with questions from eight committee members. Neither of his two interviews at the other Bay Area churches had taken more than an hour.

"See you next Sunday, Mrs. Kirby," Matt said, as he moved toward the office door.

"I understand your parents died a couple of years ago," she said.

He stopped and turned to face her. "Yes."

"Was it a car accident?"

"Yes."

"Losing your parents must be rough," she said.

"You're right about that. I'm still dealing with it."

"Are you sure you're ready to be a minister?"

"I hope to answer that question this year."

"You mean you don't feel called to the ministry?" she asked.

"I feel called to serve, but I'm not sure how or where. I plan to put 100 percent into my work here."

He felt her stare as he reached for the door knob.

2

Matt climbed the stairs at the end of the hall and found his office. He unlocked the door, stepped inside, and located the light switch. The air smelled stale. A dated ceiling fixture cast a pale-yellow glow over a desk and assorted furniture. He walked across the tan carpet, raised the blinds, and opened a leaded-glass window. Brilliant sun rays flooded the room. He looked down on the cloister with its perfect lawn and azure-colored tile fountain in the center. Its delicate spray of water droplets sparkled in the morning light. Across the courtyard, he saw the mission-style sanctuary and its adjacent bell tower. Cream-colored stucco walls supported terra cotta tile roofs that sheltered the interiors from the intense summer sun. People had started arriving for the worship service.

He eased himself into a comfortable swivel chair behind a large mahogany desk needing polish. Looking past two upholstered chairs in front of the desk, he noticed a couple of faded posters with curled edges tacked to the walls. An empty bookcase faced him from across the room. An old leather sofa sat against the wall to his left. Finally, his eyes were drawn to a crimson Bible, standing at the front of the desk between other books and two bookends, just beyond the writing pad.

Sliding his chair forward, he reached for it and cradled it in his hands, fingering the gold engraving on the leather cover and admiring the way the gilt-edged pages bestowed homage to the powerful truths within. As he set it down on its spine, the pages fell open to a large bookmark placed in the middle of the volume, at odds with the fragile, translucent pages with their Gothic script, interspersed with decorative letters and colorful ornamentations.

The bookmark, resting on the right-hand page, had writing on it. The neatly-printed words, all in black capital letters, focused his attention like a splash of cold water. *"A THIEF IS IN OUR MIDST."* He stared at the words.

Deaf to the sounds of people walking past his office, he closed the Bible and decided to forget about the bookmark, disinterested in dealing with anything job-related on this particular morning. His encounter with Mrs. Kirby and now the bookmark had added to his morning's frustrations. He looked up from the Bible and watched the shadows pass by the opaque window in his office door. "They could be Sunday school teachers preparing for classes," he thought. His mind wandered back to the message on the bookmark. "Almost comical."

He then thought about the previous intern from Calvin Seminary. Richard Finley struck him as a quiet, studious person, but perhaps he was a comedian. They'd never become acquainted, since they lived in different dormitories on campus and had never taken a class together. However, in his March interview with Hacienda's Education Committee, Matt learned about Richard's expert sailing skills and the sailing classes he'd taught for the middle school youth. "Is Richard playing games with the bookmark?"

A key in the lock startled him, and then the door swung open. A tall woman, with golden hair and broad shoulders, stood in the doorway.

"Oh! Hello there, Matt. I'm Sally Rowland, chair of the Education Committee," she said in a smooth, confident tone. "I didn't mean to barge in on you, but I thought the office would be empty, I'm taking inventory of our school supplies. I didn't expect to see you for another week."

"I came over to attend the worship service," he replied. "How's everything with you?"

"Pastor Boyle never tells me if we're short of materials until the day Sunday school classes begin. I need to let Mrs. Kirby know this week what things to buy. I watch *everything* at this place. My husband, Larry, and I are both on the Session, the board that governs the church. Has Boyle been in touch with you?"

"Yes. I'm supposed to help with the worship service next Sunday. He wants to meet with me a few days after that. I'll have a week to do some planning before the middle school program starts."

"Sounds good. Things are kind of quiet around here during the summer months," she said. "In two weeks, we begin a busy fall schedule. We return to having two services—at nine-thirty and eleven. Right now, we're in the lull before the storm," she said, smiling. "How was your summer?"

"Very enjoyable. I worked at a basketball camp in San Rafael." Matt liked enthusiastic, positive women.

"Sorry to be in such a hurry, but I need to make some notes and be on my way." She turned to open the cupboard doors and catalog the items on the shelves.

His eyes returned to the Bible on the desk. He pulled the bookmark from its pages, and put it in the inside pocket of his blazer while Sally Rowland still had her back to him.

Completing her survey of the supplies, she turned to him. "Did you say you're going to join us for the worship service?" she asked.

"Yes," he replied. "I'll be there."

"Maybe I'll see you at the coffee hour afterwards. It's in the Amigos Room, next to the church office." As she opened the office door, she paused and looked at him again. "I might mention one other thing to you about Pastor Boyle. You don't want to cross him. Last year, he and the Director of Children's Ministries locked horns, and she left Hacienda as a result of it. You might proceed with some caution. Keep him informed. He doesn't like surprises."

"Sounds like he has a short fuse."

"Just don't cross him."

She closed the door behind her, leaving Matt further irritated about the morning's unbroken chain of distressing events at the church—the cool welcome from Mrs. Kirby, his discovery of the bookmark, and what he had just heard about his future supervisor, Reverend Charles Boyle. He needed to learn more about the man's idiosyncrasies. After a few minutes, he left his office and descended the stairs, heading to the church office one more time.

Mrs. Kirby sat at her desk, holding the phone to her ear. When she saw him, she raised her index finger. Hanging up the phone, she walked to the counter. "Mr. Beringer, I've been keeping a letter for you. I forgot to give it to you earlier." She handed him the envelope.

"Thanks," he replied, slipping the envelope into his inside blazer pocket. "Can you give me the name and phone number of the woman who was Director of Children's Ministries last year?"

"You mean Jancy Nichols," she said. "She left in May after spending just one year with us. She came from Hayward First Presbyterian. Now she works at Montclair Presbyterian."

"Mrs. Rowland mentioned that she and Pastor Boyle had a disagreement."

"Oh, is that what they call it these days?"

"I'd like to speak with her. Can you give me her phone number?"

"No, I can't," she said. "That information is confidential."

"Okay," Matt said. "I understand." He left the office and walked out to the courtyard. He called Montclair Presbyterian on his cell phone and left a message on Jancy's voicemail, asking her to call him. Before going to the service, he wanted to read the letter. The back of the envelope listed a Sacramento address. He opened it, and the letter said:

Dear Matt,

I left a message for you on a bookmark in the Bible on the desk in your office. I apologize for being so brief. I was called home suddenly last May due to a family illness, and I left Hacienda in a hurry. Now that I've returned to Sacramento to begin my new job at Oakdale Presbyterian, I'd like to meet with you sometime soon to discuss some disturbing findings I made. Please call me at your earliest convenience. My cell phone number is 916-522-7030.

Peace,
Richard Finley

Matt stood in the courtyard, holding the letter, when a couple walked by him having a lively conversation. His eyes followed them toward the sanctuary. He heard the organ, so he put the letter in his pocket next to the bookmark and headed to the service. Knowing who had written the message on the bookmark settled the authorship issue. Now he wanted to understand its meaning.

Climbing several steps to the sanctuary entrance, he took a bulletin from a greeter at the door and entered the narthex. Once inside the nave, Matt found a seat toward the back and noticed that the pews were more than half full. "Not bad for a Sunday in late August." The white stucco walls created a sharp contrast with the dark beams supporting the high ceiling. Stained-glass windows on both sides admitted radiant sunlight, making the windows glow and casting patterns across the worshippers, as if they wore mantles of fine silk in hues of red, blue, and yellow.

The service began with the procession of choir members followed by the two ministers and two worship leaders, whom Matt assumed were members of the congregation. He had met both ministers after his interview with the Education Committee in April. Once in front of the congregation, Senior Pastor James Staley and Associate Pastor Charles Boyle sat next to each other on the left, behind and to the right of the pulpit on the elevated altar, where they could see and be seen. The other two men sat on the right side, near the lectern and also in full view.

Staley and Boyle differed in appearance. Tall, gray-haired, and slender, with sharp facial features, Staley reflected the serious, confident manner of the person in charge. His gaze seemed to be directed over the members' heads, somewhere toward the back of the sanctuary. Short, balding, and overweight, Boyle shifted in his seat and smiled at parishioners he recognized in the front pews. Waiting for the service to begin, he wiped his brow with a handkerchief and patted the arm of his chair.

The early part of the service consisted of prayers and hymns, performed by the congregation both standing and seated. About a third of the way through the program, during a time for Announcements, Pastor Staley rose from his chair and walked to the front edge of the altar. He paused and looked down at the Bible in his hands before addressing the congregation. The minister wore a frown.

"This morning, I'm afraid I have some very sad news that I must share with you. It is especially difficult for me to discuss this because it has to do with one of our own. This past Friday morning, our intern from two years ago, Pete Rockwell, died in a car accident on Interstate 80. An article on the accident appeared yesterday in the *Chronicle*, which perhaps some of you saw. It is believed the accident occurred shortly after midnight, as he was returning to Sacramento. According to the Highway Patrol, Pete fell asleep at the wheel, and his car left the highway and rolled over. It said he died instantly."

Matt's breath caught in his throat. "Pete Rockwell interned at this church?" There were moans from the congregation, followed by the murmur of members speaking to one another, and finally silence. Matt slowly exhaled. His thoughts swirled while absorbing the news.

Staley continued. "From all I've heard, Pete seemed to be doing well as assistant minister at his new church in Sacramento. It's a tragedy that a young man of such promise has been taken from us, with so many years of productive ministry ahead of him. This is a devastating loss, both for Pete's family and for our congregation. We must keep him in our prayers this morning. Pastor Boyle and I will be available at the coffee hour following the service and in the days ahead to help you work through this loss. May God continue to be with us as we mourn the death of our good friend, Pete Rockwell."

The rest of the service passed quickly. Matt didn't hear much of the sermon because he kept thinking about the bookmark, the letter from Richard Finley, and the extinguished life of Pete Rockwell. At the end of the service, a little after ten-thirty, he decided to skip the coffee hour. He'd speak with Liz Canfield and Sally Rowland another time.

Matt quickly left the sanctuary after the benediction and went to his car, thinking about the morning events as he returned to the seminary. His trip to Hacienda had unfolded so differently than he'd expected. On his first visit, he'd wanted to be an observer, disengaged from the life of the church. Instead, what had happened made him realize that his internship had already begun, for good or for bad.

3

The next morning, Matt returned to the East Bay to look for an apartment. He'd found three online listings near San Lucas that fit his criteria and scheduled appointments at each property. At eleven, he toured his third apartment, a vacant, one-bedroom unit in San Leandro. Walking from one room to another with the manager, he stopped in the bathroom to check the flow of water from the shower spigot. Located on the second level of a three-story building, the unit included a small balcony, facing west, accessible from a sliding glass door in the living room. After Matt inspected the refrigerator and oven in the kitchen, he and the manager stood facing each other.

"How does it look to you?" asked the bald, middle-aged man with a round face and olive complexion. He wore a baggy gray cardigan over a t-shirt, faded jeans, and black tennis shoes. The apartment manager stood a foot shorter than Matt. "If you want it, you'll have to sign a rental contract, and I need the first and last months' rent. You can move in tomorrow."

"I'll take it," Matt said, "and I'll bring my stuff over in the morning. I like the unit and the building, and I'm looking for a quiet street. I think I'll be happy here." Living closer to his work would allow him to avoid the rush-hour traffic on the Bay Bridge. Affluent San Lucas offered relatively few apartment buildings and sky-high rents, so Matt focused his search on adjacent communities. Situated between Oakland to the north and San Lucas to the south, San Leandro offered a convenient location, numerous apartments, and reasonable prices.

"Make your check payable to the company listed on my business card," which he handed to Matt. "Tomorrow, you can pick up your keys to the building, your apartment, and your mailbox. I'll show you your parking space in the garage on the way out."

Matt set his checkbook on the kitchen counter and wrote his check. Then he signed the rental agreement the manager handed him.

"How many units do you have?" Matt asked.

"Thirty-two," the man replied.

"How long have you been the manager?"

"Twenty years."

"That's impressive! Do you have much turnover?"

"No."

"When was the apartment built?"

"Hey, why do you care?! It's a solid building!"

"Just curious," Matt replied. "I had a couple of summer jobs building apartments. I've always had an interest in construction. This property looks very well maintained." He offered a compliment, hoping that it would calm the older man's irritation.

"You're right about that! My wife and I are like detectives. We don't miss a thing around here. We've been here so long, we've seen three different rug colors—brown, gold, and now tan."

Matt smiled at the history lesson and walked over to the sliding glass door in the living room, opened it, and stepped onto the balcony. Facing a eucalyptus grove by the creek in front of him, he appreciated the view of trees rather than another apartment building.

"Will I be able to see the sunsets?" Matt asked.

"Probably. I don't have time for that kind of thing."

"I'm not sure I will, either."

"You're not a bad-looking guy," the manager said with a scowl. "Will you have a lot of girlfriends visiting you here?"

"No. I don't have a girlfriend right now."

"Well, that's good. If you want a place to party, this apartment building isn't for you. All the folks who live here are working people."

"I'll be a youth leader at Hacienda Presbyterian Church in San Lucas, so I won't have much time for partying."

A slight smile appeared on the older man's face, as if his new renter had passed the test.

Matt glanced at his watch, which said eleven thirty. "I'll rent this apartment, but on one condition."

"Yeah? What's that?" the manager asked, frowning.

"That you and your wife have dinner with me here in my new home. If I'm going to be living in San Leandro, maybe you could give me some background on the community."

The man started to grin. "My wife and I could tell you a thing or two about this town. Years ago, it was just a bunch of cherry orchards."

"Choose a couple of Saturdays in the next month that work for you and your wife, and let me know."

"I'll check with her and leave a note in your mailbox."

"Do you and your wife enjoy wine?"

"Yes, we do. We'll bring the wine," he said. "Some Chianti. It goes with everything."

"It's good to meet you, Mr. Vitale," Matt said, looking at the manager's business card.

"You can call me Leo," he said. "My wife's name is Mary."

Matt followed Leo to see his parking stall in the basement garage. Before leaving the building, he arranged to pick up his keys at ten o'clock.

He'd scheduled lunch at noon with Jancy Nichols, the ex-Hacienda employee, during a conversation with her the night before. They agreed to meet at a Mexican restaurant on San Leandro Boulevard. He took just a few minutes to drive there.

Right on time, Jancy pushed through the door at El Sombrero. She told him she had dark brown hair and would be wearing a blue blouse. He waved, and then rose from the booth to greet her. He guessed she stood about five-eight, taller than he expected. After shaking hands, they slid onto the cushioned benches, facing one another. She had large green eyes, a slender nose, and full lips.

"Okay," she said. "My father's name is John and my mother's name is Nancy."

"You read my mind. It's an unusual name, and I really like it."

"And you're the new intern at Hacienda. How are things going?"

"A little differently than I expected," he said.

"In what way?"

"Yesterday, Mrs. Kirby gave me a letter from the previous intern, Richard Finley, who wants to tell me about problems he uncovered. Also, I learned that Pete Rockwell, who died last Friday, had interned there. I didn't know about his connection to Hacienda."

"I see what you mean," Jancy said. "I agree with you that working at Hacienda can have its share of surprises."

"Were you there when Pete was the intern?"

"No. His internship ended just before I was hired. I worked at Hacienda during Richard's internship. I was shocked to hear about Pete's accident."

"Me, too. I only learned about it yesterday morning at breakfast, when a classmate told me," Matt said.

"Did you know Pete?"

"No. He was starting his internship when I arrived at the seminary. He spoke to our incoming class, but I never got to know him."

"How is the congregation taking the news?" Jancy asked.

"Everyone is really stunned."

"The newspaper said he fell asleep at the wheel. I feel so sad about it."

"I agree. He was just getting started." Matt thought about his parents and their untimely deaths, which seemed so unfair to him. His conversation with Jancy stopped for a few moments, while his mind drifted. Focusing again on his guest, he changed the subject. "How did you like Hacienda?"

"My job was very frustrating," Jancy said, "which I didn't expect, given the church's excellent reputation. I wish I had done some research on the church before joining the staff. Maybe that's why I'm meeting with you. I think you're smart to ask some questions before you start."

"What questions would you have asked?"

"I would have tried to learn more about your supervisor."

"Pastor Boyle?"

"None other."

A waitress arrived with two glasses of water, along with a couple of menus. She said she would return to take their orders.

"It sounds like you have some misgivings about him," Matt said. "On that discouraging piece of news, maybe we'd better decide what we're going to eat."

After several minutes, the waitress appeared again and took their orders.

"I heard from Sally Rowland that you had a conflict with Boyle," Matt said. "What happened?"

"He wasn't a supportive supervisor. Boyle doesn't care one iota about youth ministry. He'll tell you that he does, but he spends very little time on it."

"Are the church leaders aware?"

"I believe the Education Committee knows. Four or five years ago, the Committee decided to recruit a seminary intern like you each year to help with the middle school program. They also have a volunteer who works with the high school group."

"So Boyle supervises the people who run the youth programs, but that's about all."

"Exactly. The four of us would have monthly meetings, but they were pretty much a farce. I can't recall that Boyle ever visited any of my activities. I'm sorry I can't be more positive."

"I appreciate your honesty."

"Are you being asked to do anything besides leading the middle school program on Sunday morning?"

"Yes. Organize basketball leagues for the boys and girls that will include the other San Lucas churches."

"A basketball program sounds great! You'll be using the gym, which is a fabulous asset."

"That's the plan," Matt said.

"You must have played basketball in college, and I'll bet those are the skills they wanted in their intern this year. Richard was an excellent sailor. The Education Committee wanted to have a sailing program, and he fit the bill."

"Yeah, I played basketball in high school and college. However, I hoped I was chosen because of my intellect and sense of humor."

"I don't want to sound too cynical about Hacienda. It's a pretty impressive church. I met a lot of wonderful people there."

"Tell me more about Boyle."

Jancy paused for a moment. "For example, I noticed that the gym was never used, so I spoke to the Education Committee about it. I wanted to start a weekday program in the gym for grades three through five, including dinner. I had mothers all lined up to help, but Boyle wouldn't approve my idea."

"What was his reason?"

"He didn't want the kitchen messed up the night before the morning committee meetings. I assured him that our cleanup would be thorough, but he wouldn't budge. I don't think he wanted to risk ruffling the feathers of certain big givers to the church."

"What attracted you to the job at Hacienda?"

"I was happy as a youth leader at my home church, First Pres of Hayward, but when you're offered a fifty-percent salary increase to join one of the top churches in the Bay Area, it was hard to say no. I'd met Sally Rowland, Education Committee chair, at some Christian education seminars around the Bay Area, and she'd heard about my work in children's ministry."

Jancy's green eyes mesmerized him, and her voice had a warm, soothing quality to it. He liked the way she communicated--a no-nonsense approach to her work that resonated with him. He knew he wanted to see her again.

During their conversation, he hoped she hadn't noticed how much he liked what he saw. A tiny, pale birthmark on her right cheek interrupted a flawless complexion. Her arching, dark brown eyebrows and long eyelashes created a stunning contrast to her green eyes. She wore soft red lipstick that didn't compete with her other features. And her long brown hair cascaded to the top of her shoulders, where it swirled in gentle curls. "I wasn't expecting her to be so attractive," he mused. Then he asked, "Did you speak with anyone about your job frustrations?"

"Not until after I resigned. I had an exit interview with Sally Rowland and told her how difficult it was to work with Boyle."

"Was she sympathetic?"

"To a degree. She admitted that youth work isn't his strength, but it isn't a big enough weakness to threaten his job. He also calls on the members, especially the older, larger givers, and oversees adult education. Maybe my recommendation to her about using the gym made an impact because of the basketball program they want you to organize."

"It sounds like it did. How did you get along with Richard?"

"Just fine. I haven't spoken to him recently, but I heard he was hired at a church in Sacramento, not far from Pete's church."

"It appears he found some problems at Hacienda," Matt said.

"I wonder what he's thinking,"

"I'm interested to know. How did Richard get along with Boyle?"

"He had a few bumps along the way," Jancy said, "but he wasn't the only one."

Matt wondered if she liked to go on picnics. Had she guessed he was interested in her? "Did Richard have any conflicts with Boyle?"

Jancy hesitated for a moment. "Richard and Boyle had an argument over money. Richard wanted a budget for the middle school program, and Boyle refused. He hates to spend money. Richard took his request over Boyle's head to the Education Committee, and they voted to give each supervisor a budget. I think Boyle considered Richard's act to be a sign of disloyalty, and their relationship was strained the rest of the year."

"Was Richard's sailing program a success?"

"Yes, I think so. With Lake Chabot so close, having a sailing program made a lot of sense. Richard had ten to twelve regulars who would go sailing once a week, as I recall. They'd meet at the church and he'd drive the church bus to the lake."

The waitress arrived with their orders. After sliding their plates and beverages onto the table, she departed quickly. Customers stood at the entrance, waiting to be seated.

"You know, Jancy, I'd like to return to Boyle for a moment. I've had a few supervisors who weren't the greatest, but I stuck with the jobs because there were other positives. It sounds as if you had some problems, but Boyle left you alone to run your own program."

"That's true."

"Was resigning your only alternative? Couldn't you have worked with the Education Committee to accomplish your goals?"

"I was sorry to leave Hacienda after one year, but something happened that made it impossible for me to stay," she said, staring out the window. "Matt, I'm going to share something with you that I haven't told anyone except my parents and my minister. I'm not sure why I'm telling you my secret. Maybe it's because you're a seminarian and I trust you. Will you promise to keep to yourself what I'm going to tell you?"

"Sure," Matt said, nodding to her.

"I wasn't enjoying my work with Boyle, but I probably could have stayed another couple of years," she said, and then took a deep breath. "The main reason I left is because a member of Session made a pass at me. I thought if I took the matter to Boyle or Staley, it wouldn't go well. It would be the Session member's word against mine. Since the other person is an important leader at the church, I decided it would be better for me to leave. I worried that my career could have been jeopardized by rumors if the story ever surfaced. I'm not a flirt, but I could have been labeled as one or worse. It was a difficult decision to leave, but I think it was the right one."

"Can I ask who it was?"

"It was Larry Rowland, head of the church's Finance Committee. He's pretty full of himself. I think he fancies himself as a ladies' man. I really like his wife, Sally. I feel bad that he would dishonor their marriage by propositioning me."

"That's terrible. I'm really sorry to hear about it." Matt paused. "Tell me about your current job."

"I'm director of children's ministries at Montclair Pres. It's the same position I had at Hacienda, but it's a better situation for me. My supervisor is very supportive."

The conversation turned to their early years, with Jancy sharing stories about growing up in the Bay Area, while Matt recalled boyhood memories from Seattle.

"What do you like to do in your spare time?" he asked.

"I've become hooked on mysteries. What do you like to read?"

"U.S. history," Matt said, "especially the nineteenth century. How about outdoor activities?"

"Bike riding with friends."

The waitress left the bill and gathered their plates.

"Thanks for having lunch with me," Matt said.

"I've enjoyed meeting you," Jancy said. "I hope you have a good experience at Hacienda."

He didn't want their conversation to end. Looking at the couple in the adjacent booth, he tried to think of something else to say. "You have a great smile."

"Thanks."

"I'd like to see you again."

Jancy smiled. "Give me a call," she said, sliding from the booth.

"Would you like to have dinner with me sometime?"

"Sure."

"I'll call you next week."

4

Leo Vitale was waiting when Matt arrived the next morning to pick up his keys. His fully-packed car allowed no room for a passenger, and he was able to transport all of his belongings from the seminary to unit #206 in just one trip. The same day, his rented furniture arrived, and he took several hours to organize his new home.

As he began his fourth day in his apartment, Matt still felt like a stranger. Staring into the bathroom mirror while shaving, he heard his cell phone ring in the bedroom. His watch on the vanity counter read a little after seven. He set down his razor, rinsed his face, grabbed a towel, and hurried to answer the call.

"Good morning, Matt, this is Jancy Nichols. I hope I'm not calling too early."

"No," he said. "I'm up. How are you?"

"Just fine, thanks," Jancy said. "T.G.I.F. Right?"

"Yeah. It's been a busy week."

"Are you going to Pete Rockwell's memorial service today? If you are, I wonder if I could ride with you."

"Yes, I'm planning to go, and it would be great to see you," Matt said.

"I'd like to honor Pete's life by attending, and I'd enjoy seeing you again, too."

"It's depressing to think about a memorial service for someone our age," Matt said, "and I'd appreciate your company. The service starts at eleven. Shall I pick you up at Montclair Pres at ten?"

"Sure. Do you know where it is?" Jancy asked.

"It's just off the MacArthur Freeway. I'll meet you in front at ten."

He ran several errands in San Leandro, buying some supplies for his office. When he arrived a few minutes early, Jancy was waiting on the sidewalk. Matt reached over and opened the passenger door for her, and she slid onto the front seat. "Too bad," he thought, "we're heading off to a sad affair. Not an ideal first date."

"Hi, there," Matt said. "I'm glad you called this morning. I was planning to call you next week about dinner."

"I beat you to the draw," Jancy said, smiling.

"Since this Sunday is my first official day at Hacienda," Matt said, "could we plan something for next week? How about Wednesday?"

"Sounds good to me. I'll be visiting my parents in Hayward that afternoon. On my way back to Berkeley, I could stop at Hacienda and meet you in the parking lot."

"Okay. I'll see you there at five o'clock. Can you recommend a good restaurant?"

"There's Angelo's in San Leandro, if you like Italian food."

"Perfect. I'll make reservations. At least our next date will be under happier circumstances," Matt said.

"For sure," Jancy said.

From the Montclair neighborhood, located near the crest of the Oakland hills, Matt headed down Moraga Avenue on his way to I-580 and the Bay Bridge.

"Will there be many people at the service?" she asked.

"I don't think so," Matt said. "Classes don't start for another two weeks." He fell quiet.

"I'm glad the seminary is having a service for Pete," Jancy said.

"Yeah. I've attended a few memorial services in the past couple of years, and they don't get any easier." He looked at her briefly, turning to catch her eyes, and continued. "My parents' service was really tough."

"Matt, I'm so sorry. What happened?"

"They were killed in a car accident two and a half years ago in Seattle by a drunk driver heading the wrong way on a one-way street."

"That's heartbreaking."

"You can say that again. I really miss them. My parents had kind and generous hearts. I keep wondering why it happened to them. Their deaths are what caused me to attend Calvin Seminary."

"We have to believe they're in a good place."

"I agree. I'm counting on seeing them again someday. On another subject, I wonder if Richard Finley will be at the service. He wants to talk to me. Something about problems at the church. I hoped it'd be under more pleasant circumstances."

"He never mentioned any problems to me."

"I'm looking for positives during my internship, *not* problems to solve."

The grounds of Calvin Theological Seminary had been groomed for the students arriving in mid-September. Traces of grass clippings covered the lawns and white spots on some tree trunks indicated the removal of low-hanging branches. While walking with Jancy across the leafy campus, Matt's mood darkened. Attending a memorial service for the young minister was discouraging. Life is so fragile. They moved in silence under tall elms that lined the slate pathways. Nearing the Chapel, a handful of mourners converged with them. Matt took Jancy's arm as they climbed the steps to the double doors. Inside, the pews sat nearly empty. Matt recognized a few faculty members, who had already returned to campus to start prepping for classes.

Halfway through the service, seminary President Cameron J. McAlister gave a eulogy about Pete Rockwell. With brown hair and a perpetual tan, McAlister looked younger than his fifty-eight years. He mentioned that

Pete was an only child who'd grown up in southern California. Pete had served as student-body treasurer at his high school, where he'd also been a member of the wrestling team. Until he went away to college, he'd been active in his local church. Completing his undergraduate degree at U.C.L.A., he'd sold insurance for a year before deciding to attend seminary.

"Every Thursday evening while Pete attended seminary," McAlister said, "he'd drive to Oakland to tutor grade school kids. He was a very humble person, and few of us knew he was involved in this kind of ministry. The only way I learned about it was because the program director called me, when he learned of Pete's death, to say what an outstanding job he'd done in his three years there. Pete continued his tutoring even while interning at Hacienda Presbyterian in San Lucas."

President McAlister paused and leaned forward, resting his elbows on the lectern. "This seminary is blessed to have had Pete Rockwell among us for three of his twenty-six years. Based on what I know about him, Pete lived the Golden Rule. He followed Jesus' words, found in Matthew 7:12, about how we should treat others: 'So in everything, do to others what you would have them do to you, for this sums up the Law and the Prophets.' Serving others is what Pete tried to do every day, and I hope you find inspiration from the life he led, as I have."

Following McAlister's remarks, a woman in her long choir robe entered from a side door, faced the people in the pews, and sang "The Lord's Prayer," accompanied by the organist. After the solo, the printed program called for the participants to sing "A Mighty Fortress Is Our God." Finally, President McAlister offered a benediction, asking for God's blessing on the gathering, and the service was over. Before they stood up to leave, Jancy put a Kleenex back in her purse.

Matt and Jancy eased out of the pew toward the center aisle and made their way to the exit. Their eyes met as they moved toward the door, offering silent comfort to one another.

Richard Finley stood in the foyer, speaking to someone. They caught his attention, and he approached them with a warm smile. "Jancy, it's great to see you," he said, giving her a hug. "What a surprise! I didn't expect to see you here. So you two know each other?" he asked.

"We're just beginning to," Matt said.

"Wonderful!" Richard said. "May it be the start of a beautiful relationship." He paused. "I had hoped you'd be here today, Matt. Did Mrs. Kirby give you my note?"

"Yes, and I was glad to learn that you wrote the words on the bookmark."

"Let's go outside to talk," Richard said. "I hardly know you, Matt, but I need to speak to you about Hacienda." They descended the chapel steps and walked a few yards along a slate pathway. "I left that message on the bookmark last spring," he said, "just before I finished up. It was all I could think of doing because I left quickly. I needed to go home because my mother was ill. I'm relieved that you were the one who found the bookmark and not someone on the Education Committee."

"Is your mother all right?" Matt asked.

"Much better, thanks."

"What's going on at Hacienda? I'm almost afraid to ask."

"The church looks great from the outside," Richard said, "but it has problems on the inside."

"Tell me more," Matt said.

"Someone's stealing from the church. I reviewed the recent annual reports and found some very suspicious numbers. I'm talking about thousands of dollars."

"Who is it?" Matt asked.

"Sadly, I think it might be your supervisor, Charles Boyle, but I can't prove it. I ran out of time. He acts very strangely when it comes to money. He won't spend any money on new programs."

"I can attest to that," Jancy said.

"He brags about attending theater performances all over the country, and he drives a Lexus," Richard said.

"How can a pastor afford that kind of lifestyle?" Jancy asked.

"The Finance Committee reports to Boyle," Richard said. "He controls the church's purse strings."

"Very interesting," Matt replied, putting his hand on Richard's shoulder. "I'll do some research of my own and let you know what I find out. Maybe I can visit you at Oakdale Pres."

"I'm seeing some friends in San Lucas tomorrow around two, and I plan to go sailing on Lake Chabot later in the afternoon. Why don't you two join me? I'll pack a picnic basket. We can continue our conversation."

"Unfortunately, I have to take a rain check," Matt said. "I need to prepare for Sunday's worship service, but why don't the three of us have dinner together after your sail?"

"I'd enjoy that," Jancy said.

"Sounds good!" Richard responded. "Come to the dock around five o'clock. It will be fun to have dinner with you before heading back to Sacramento. I'm really glad to have seen you both today, but I'm sorry it had to be at Pete's service."

They said their goodbyes, and Richard walked to his car in a nearby parking lot. He waved at them as he drove away from the campus.

"Jancy, how about going over to the cafeteria for a cup of coffee?" Matt asked. "I'm not quite ready to leave this place."

"Sure," she said.

Matt reached for her hand as they headed across the campus. She looked at him and grasped his hand in response. They exchanged smiles and continued walking.

"I wonder if any of Pete's family attended the service," she said. "I'm surprised that President McAlister didn't mention them. You'd think his parents would have been here."

"Maybe they couldn't attend because of their jobs," Matt said.

After having coffee, he drove Jancy back to the East Bay and dropped her off at Montclair Pres. It took him a half hour to return to Hacienda. He arrived around three o'clock. Sunday would be his first official day at the church, and he wanted to make sure his office was ready for visitors. The old posters had to go, and he needed to locate the church's vacuum.

He counted five cars in the church parking lot when he arrived, and he'd soon learn which staff members owned them. The white Lexus belonged to Pastor Boyle because he'd told Matt the first time they met what kind of car he drove. He guessed the Ford pickup might belong to the custodian, Carlo Barone.

In his office, Matt hung a few framed Van Gogh prints, plugged in a new table lamp, and added some books to the empty bookshelves. He placed a framed photo of his parents on his desk. Looking around, he felt more at home, but by five-thirty his stomach told him it was time for dinner.

As he left the building and walked past the sanctuary toward his car, he thought about Richard Finley's earlier comment that Boyle might be stealing from the church. That possibility cast a dark cloud over Matt's feelings about his internship.

5

Fresh air flowed into the apartment through the open balcony door on a bright, sunny Saturday morning. At the kitchen table, Matt reviewed the next day's worship service from a printed program Mrs. Kirby had given him. Then he paid some bills and did his laundry. He looked forward to having dinner with Jancy and Richard that evening. They would have a chance to discuss Richard's suspicions about Pastor Boyle. At four-thirty, Jancy was waiting for him in the Hacienda church parking lot, and he drove them to Lake Chabot, nestled in the hills that ran parallel to the shoreline of the East Bay.

"I'm sorry we didn't go sailing with Richard," Matt said, "but I have too much on my plate. I'm working tomorrow."

"Maybe we can schedule another time with him," Jancy said.

"I'm sure he could teach us a thing or two. Let's ask him when he can return to Lake Chabot."

The leaves of the trees along the road to the lake were bathed by the fading afternoon sun. Nature's beauty had a relaxing effect on Matt as they left the residential neighborhoods and entered the park district tucked away in the suburb of Castro Valley.

"I'm interested to know what Richard saw in the annual reports," Matt said.

"If he's right about Boyle," Jancy said, "it could be serious."

Trees surrounded the lake, located above the San Leandro commercial district. Picnic tables dotted the shoreline. In Matt's first year at seminary, he attended a party there to celebrate the retirement of a faculty member. He never expected to find such a jewel in that location.

Pulling into the parking lot near the lake, Matt scanned the grounds. The area looked about the same as he remembered it. He found an empty slot close to the long dock. At the far end of the dock stood a kiosk where boat rentals could be transacted.

Shadows appeared as the sun began to sink, and a slight breeze created ripples on the lake. "Not the best day for a sail," Matt thought. He saw only one sailboat.

As he and Jancy closed the car doors, Matt noticed several people running down the dock toward the kiosk. A person pointed toward the sailboat in the middle of the lake. Reaching the dock, Matt heard someone yell to the attendant, "Call 911!"

Walking faster on the wooden planks, Matt tapped a teenage boy in front of him on the shoulder, "What's going on?" His heart started to race.

"There's a guy in the water."

"How long has he been there?" Matt asked.

"I don't know," the boy responded.

A small group of onlookers stood at the end of the dock, staring at the body face down in the water beside the sailboat. The attendant hurried toward them from the nearby kiosk, holding a cell phone to his ear. "The police and medics are on their way," he said. Matt and Jancy worked their way to the front of the cluster of people.

"Why hasn't someone gone after him?" Matt asked. "We can't wait."

"I thought he was taking a swim," the attendant said, "but he isn't moving."

"I'll get him," Matt said, starting to unbutton his shirt.

"Do you have his name?" Jancy asked the attendant. "He may be our friend."

The attendant ran back to the kiosk and looked inside his desk. "I have his driver's license," he yelled. "Richard Finley."

Matt quickly removed his shirt and shoes. He handed his wallet and keys to Jancy, and then dove into the lake, still wearing his long pants. The cool water shocked his system. He swam toward the body, estimating the distance to be about thirty or forty yards. Water-logged slacks hampered his kicking and slowed his progress. Richard needed help, and every second mattered.

He finally reached the body and turned it over. His heart sank. Richard looked unconscious. His face was pale, and his body felt as cold as the lake water. "Why isn't he wearing a life preserver? Maybe he doesn't like them. How does an expert sailor end up face down in Lake Chabot?" Wrapping his right arm around Richard's chest, Matt kicked and pulled his way with his left arm back to the dock. He estimated Richard weighed about 150 pounds. Not a heavy load. However, his swim with the limp body seemed to take forever. When Matt reached the dock, several young men pulled Richard onto the surface.

Breathing heavily, Matt scrambled up the nearby ladder and rushed to Richard to begin CPR. The crowd on the dock had grown to a couple of dozen people. They remained frozen in place, like statues. He glanced at Jancy, whose hand covered her mouth.

"I need one helper!" Matt shouted. "The rest of you please step back."

A young man stepped forward.

"Let's turn him over on his chest. I'll force out the water he's swallowed. Get a sweatshirt or something to put under his head. Quick!"

On his knees, Matt pushed hard on Richard's back to clear his lungs, but nothing happened. After several attempts, he turned the body over on its back.

"I'll start CPR," Matt said. He leaned on Richard's chest, pumping furiously, trying to shock his heart into beating. After several minutes, he stopped and felt his friend's cheek. His skin was cold. "Check his pulse."

The young man reached for Richard's wrist, while Matt continued his straight-armed downward thrusts. He looked at Matt and shook his head. In the distance, the sound of a siren could be heard. Matt's arms felt like lead weights.

He willed his body to maintain the rocking motion, applying and withdrawing pressure to his friend's rib cage. He wouldn't stop until help arrived. Behind him, Matt heard multiple footsteps running down the dock. Suddenly, he felt a hand on his shoulder. He turned to see a policeman in a dark-blue uniform. Two medics in white appeared moments later.

"Let us take over now," a medic said.

Matt rolled away and sat on the dock. The medics moved in with their equipment. Jancy stood beside Matt, draping his shirt over his shoulders. He felt the cool evening air for the first time.

The police officer leaned over to speak to him. "Did you recover the body?"

"Yes," Matt replied. "He's a good friend."

"How long have you been doing CPR?"

"I'm not sure. Maybe six or seven minutes."

"Thank you for your efforts. The medics will try to save him."

The medics hovered over Richard's body, and the officer asked the crowd to retreat.

"His eyes are fixed and dilated," a medic said. "No pulse." He placed a mask over Richard's mouth and nose and pumped air into his lungs. After several minutes of working in silence, he spoke again. "I can't find a pulse. His skin is cyanotic. Let's put the paddles on him." Following several jolts of electricity, the medic said, "I have no reading on the paddles. There's no electrical activity."

Then they started an IV, and the other medic stood over Richard, holding a bag containing epinephrine. "I hope this works," he said. The two medics worked on him for thirty minutes. Finally, they agreed there was no pulse. One of them called the station to ask for the deputy coroner to come investigate the death and take the body to the morgue.

The group of bystanders had watched the medics try to revive the young minister. Jancy put her hand on Matt's shoulder. He hung his head. A second policeman arrived and conferred with the other officer.

Matt had never been involved in a rescue before and had never seen death so close. Richard was full of life at Pete Rockwell's memorial service, but now his body lay still and lifeless. Grief seized Matt, as he recalled his mother and father being so happy, having celebrated their twenty-fifth wedding anniversary a few months before the car accident. Then their lives were unexpectedly snuffed out. Thoughts of his parents, Pete Rockwell, and Richard Finley swirled through his mind as he and Jancy stood together, staring at their friend lying on the dock.

Wanting to do something, Matt approached the first policeman. "Can't they work on him a little longer?" he asked. "I don't understand how this could have happened. He was an expert sailor."

"They can't get a pulse," the policeman said. "They've worked on him for a half hour."

Jancy had followed Matt and stood close to him.

"I'm sorry to say your friend didn't make it," the policeman said. "I think it's the first drowning we've had this year." Turning to the crowd, he asked, "Did anyone see him go into the water?"

Nobody in the group could say they had. They shook their heads.

"I rented him the sailboat an hour ago," the attendant said. "It was the only sailboat on the lake this afternoon. Here's his driver's license. When we saw he was in trouble, this guy goes after him." The attendant looked at Matt.

Taking the license, the policeman studied it for a moment, and asked the attendant for the sailboat rental application. "Who did he list to contact in case of an emergency?" The attendant went to the kiosk to find the application. The policeman asked Matt, "Do you know his next of kin?"

"No, I don't. We were going to have dinner with him. He's currently an assistant minister at Oakdale Presbyterian Church in Sacramento. They'd know." The policeman made some notes in his journal.

The attendant returned with the rental application. When the policeman looked at it, he said to Matt, "Carol Finley, mother, Coeur d'Alene, Idaho."

"That's close to my aunt and uncle," Matt said. "They live in Spokane, Washington."

"What will happen to him?" someone asked.

"The coroner's office will send a deputy coroner to confirm the death of the young man," the policeman said. "He'll take the body to the morgue, identify the victim, and inform the next of kin."

The other policeman said to his partner, "I'll get the attendant to row me out to retrieve the sailboat. Maybe there's some stuff on board that belongs to him." He motioned to the attendant, and they walked toward a rowboat.

The policeman who stayed behind turned to Matt. "You say he was an expert sailor?"

"Yes. He'd been sailing for years. He taught a class at Hacienda Presbyterian last year. Could he have had a heart attack? He seemed really healthy to me."

"An autopsy would tell."

The policeman took the names, addresses, and phone numbers of a handful of witnesses. Then the officer asked if a few of them could stay to speak to the deputy coroner. Everyone else, he said, could leave.

"I can't believe this," Matt said, looking at Jancy.

"Neither can I," Jancy replied.

"How does an experienced sailor drown?"

"I don't know," she said.

"I wanted to get to know him better."

"We just saw him, and now he's dead? It doesn't make sense."

"I agree."

The policeman confirmed that the coroner could perform an autopsy, as early as Monday morning, if Richard's death looked suspicious. If requested, he would have a completed toxicology report within twenty-four hours. The next of kin could be informed about the autopsy findings by the end of the week.

The other policeman and attendant returned in the rowboat, towing the sailboat. Climbing onto the dock, the policeman held a life preserver, duffel bag, and a partially eaten sandwich in a plastic container. Richard's driver's license and the other items would be given to the deputy coroner.

The medics put a tarp over Richard's body. As they packed their equipment, the deputy coroner arrived with an assistant, who was pushing a gurney. The medics gave the deputy coroner a copy of their report, and returned to their ambulance. He spent a few minutes examining the body, and then interviewed witnesses. After their interview, Matt took Jancy's hand, and they started walking slowly toward his car. When they reached the beach, Matt looked back at the policemen still conversing on the dock. The deputy coroner and his assistant had lifted Richard's body onto the gurney and were pushing it toward the van. The duffel bag sat on a shelf below the body.

Shivering, Matt suggested they return to his apartment, where he could change his wet clothes. It was after six o'clock, and shades of pink and orange began to color the sky.

Jancy offered to drive his car to the apartment while Matt huddled in the passenger's seat. He reached over and turned up the heater. Both of them rode in silence for a few blocks.

"This is unreal," Matt said. "Am I dreaming or did another Hacienda intern die today?"

Jancy glanced at Matt. "I know. It's awful. Two deaths so close together. Kind of scary."

"Richard's drowning doesn't seem possible," he said.

"It seems rather suspicious, if you ask me."

"Yeah," Matt said. "Unless the boom hit him in some freak accident or he had a heart attack, I don't understand how he could have fallen into the lake."

"An autopsy might provide some answers."

When he'd had a warm shower and emerged from the bedroom in dry clothes, he poured himself a glass of Kahlua from a bottle in a kitchen cupboard. He asked her if she'd like one as well.

"Yes," she said. "I think I'll join you."

Matt still couldn't believe the young minister was dead. Richard's drowning, coupled with Pete's death, shocked him. He'd wanted to learn more about Richard's investigations at the church, but that door had closed.

Jancy noticed an unfinished crossword puzzle on the coffee table. "Why don't we work on this?" she said. They sat close together on the sofa, spending considerable time trying to finish the puzzle, but eventually they set it aside. Matt turned on the TV, while Jancy heated a couple of frozen dinners she found in the freezer. Uncomfortable with the blaring sounds, he turned off the TV, and the two of them ate quietly together. He appreciated Jancy's company that evening.

After dinner, Matt called Pastor Staley and left a message about Richard's death on the minister's home voicemail.

"I wonder if Boyle knows that Richard suspected him of stealing from the church?" he asked.

"Do you think Boyle wanted to harm Richard?"

"Your guess is as good as mine."

"What can we do?" Jancy asked.

"If they perform an autopsy, Richard's mother should hear the results in a week. I'm visiting my aunt and uncle in Spokane for a few days next weekend. I'll try to meet with Mrs. Finley and ask her what she learned."

Matt stared outside at the eucalyptus trees beyond the sliding glass door and wondered, "Who's next?"

6

They had faced a disastrous situation together, and it had brought them closer to each other. After coming to terms as best they could with Richard's death, Matt drove Jancy to her car at the Hacienda parking lot at around ten o'clock.

"I'm sorry you had to be involved in all of this," Matt said. "Dinner with Richard sounded like a great idea, but it turned into a real disaster."

"It's like a bad dream."

"I'm blown away by the deaths of Pete and Richard. One right after the other. Interning at Hacienda doesn't seem to be the pathway to a long life. Do these deaths say something about my future?"

"No, of course not. All I know is I saw a very brave guy try to save a friend."

"Having you with me tonight meant a lot, Jancy."

They left Matt's car and stood close together in the empty parking lot. Darkness surrounded them, while in the distance millions of lights outlined the San Francisco Bay. Matt reached for Jancy's hand, and he pulled her into his arms. She didn't resist as he lifted her chin and kissed her, gently at first.

"M-m-m-m," moaned Jancy. "What took you so long?"

"I wanted to kiss you when we met five days ago."

They smiled at each other and hugged. He buried his face in her fragrant hair and closed his eyes. His spirit soared as he held her close and felt her arms around him. Then they kissed again, longer this time, as their lips expressed a new intensity. Minutes later they parted, slowly. His hands cradled her head and they stared into each other's eyes. After a final embrace, Matt opened Jancy's car door for her, and then reached for her shoulders.

"I don't want to say goodbye, but I start my job tomorrow," Matt said. "I should get some sleep. We're having dinner on Wednesday."

"I'm already looking forward to it."

They could do nothing more about their dead friend, and Matt needed rest before his introduction to the Hacienda congregation the following morning. He planned to wake up at six-thirty to review the worship program again and wanted to arrive at the church a few minutes before the eight-thirty meeting in Pastor Staley's office.

After one more kiss, Jancy drove away and Matt returned home. He didn't want to let her go, but he needed to focus on the next day.

Soon after entering his apartment, his cell phone rang. Staley expressed his shock at receiving Matt's voicemail.

"Richard and I were planning to have dinner after his sail," Matt said, deciding to leave Jancy out of the conversation. "I don't understand how an expert sailor drowns. The whole thing really bothers me."

"His death certainly changes the complexion of tomorrow's service. Having to announce the death of another former intern is unbelievable. How are you doing?"

"I haven't had time to think about it. If I did, I could start to worry. Hacienda's two previous interns are dead. It's not a good trend."

"I've never heard of anything like this in over thirty years of ministry. We'll get through this, Matt, but I'm sorry your internship is beginning on such a somber note."

"Thanks. Me, too."

Late as it was, Matt felt wide awake after talking to Staley, so he picked up the unfinished crossword puzzle he and Jancy had worked on earlier that evening. However, he couldn't concentrate on it. His back muscles ached, and his mind felt frayed at the edges, so he took two ibuprofen tablets and went to bed. He spent the night tossing and turning in spite of his exhaustion.

——

When his radio alarm sounded the next morning, Matt awoke with an anxious feeling. He wanted to stay in bed, but he had to rally. In three hours, he would be sitting in front of the congregation as a worship leader for the first time, waiting to be introduced to the members. However, his first day as a staff member would be clouded by the death of Reverend Richard Finley. The service was going to be anything but upbeat and happy, as he'd envisioned.

Matt ate some toast and chugged a glass of milk while standing at the kitchen counter. Preoccupied with the events of the past twenty-four hours, he didn't even notice the blue skies outside his window. He looked at the worship bulletin on his nearby table and, beside it, his Bible open to the New Testament scripture he would read at the service. It was from Jesus' Sermon on the Mount in the Book of Matthew, chapter five, verses three through sixteen. He didn't want to flub his part in the worship service, so he sat down at the table to read the passage aloud: "Blessed are the poor in spirit, for theirs is the kingdom of heaven. Blessed are those who mourn, for they will be comforted...."

He checked his watch. It was seven o'clock. He'd have time to work his *New York Times* crossword in the church parking lot. That would calm him. He left his apartment on schedule at seven-thirty.

As he drove through the San Lucas village, Matt encountered little traffic on his way up the hill to the church. He glanced at the price of gas on a sign in front of the service station. On the other side of the street, a waitress wiped the outdoor tables in front of El Primero. He felt the sun's warmth through his front window. Puffy white clouds accented the skies overhead. A postcard kind of morning, and he thanked God for another day.

"Good morning," Pastor Staley said when Matt entered in the minister's office. He had arrived before Pastor Boyle. Staley was sitting behind his desk with a worship bulletin in his hands. He didn't look like he had slept much. His face looked paler than usual.

"This won't be the kind of service I had hoped for on your first day. It will be a very difficult experience for the congregation, with two death announcements just one week apart, but I'm glad you're here. Ministry is full of the unexpected, and death is part of the mix. Yesterday must have been a very stressful day for you. Are you okay?"

"I didn't sleep well last night."

"Well, you're not alone, my friend," Staley responded. "I can't remember having such a concentrated dose of sadness in my entire ministry. Let's try to cope with it and maintain our composure. Before Pastor Boyle arrives, go over to my closet and find a black robe that fits you. They may be a little short for you, but I'll have a longer one for you next time."

Minutes later, Boyle appeared at the doorway. Staley motioned for him to enter.

"Jim," Boyle began, "I must tell you that *Meet Me in St. Louis* was marvelous last night. The cast was superb and the music...."

Staley had raised his hand, stopping him in mid-sentence. "I have some bad news to share with you. Yesterday, Richard Finley drowned while sailing on Lake Chabot."

Boyle slowly took his seat beside Matt in front of Staley's desk. The associate pastor nodded at Matt, but didn't smile. Matt noticed his flushed cheeks and watched for a reaction to Staley's message, but none surfaced. "I'm sorry to hear about it," Boyle said, as he crossed his arms and shifted in his chair.

"Matt went to Lake Chabot to meet Richard for dinner, but when he arrived Richard was face down in the lake, next to his rented sailboat. Matt swam out to get him and brought him back to the dock. The medics were unable to revive him, and he was pronounced dead at the scene. After Pete Rockwell's recent death, we have another piece of very sad news to report to the congregation. Let's offer a prayer for Richard." Then Staley bowed his head. After the prayer, he turned to Boyle.

"Sorry to cut you off, Charles. I'd enjoy hearing about the play later in the week, but just not today. I hope you understand. This morning, I'd like you to read the Old Testament passage. Matt will follow with the New Testament scripture. I'll tell the congregation about Richard's passing during Announcements. Then you can ask the members if they have any news to share during the Joys and Concerns portion of the service. After the news about Richard, you may not hear much from them."

"They'll be in a state of shock," Boyle replied.

Staley continued. "This is Matt's first day, and I wish the service didn't include such painful news, but ministry involves dealing with adversity. I know it will be a challenge for us to lead the congregation through this time of loss, but that's what we're called to do."

"Do you want me to stay for the coffee hour?" Boyle asked.

"Yes, I think the three of us should be there, in case our members want to speak with us about Richard."

"How long does the coffee hour last?" Matt asked.

"People usually stay about a half hour," Staley said. "By the way, I have an additional job for you today besides the New Testament reading. I'd like you to handle the offering rather than Pastor Boyle. When the ushers come forward with the offering plates, you move to the front of the altar and lead us in prayer before they collect the offering. It doesn't have to be a lengthy prayer. After the collection, the organist will pause and play a different piece as the head ushers walk toward the altar with the plates. That's your signal to return to the top of the steps and receive the offering. Then you set the plates on the Communion table. Do you follow me?"

"Yes," Matt replied. He wished he had been given more time to think about an offertory prayer.

"One more thing, Matt," Staley said. "I'd like you to help us occasionally at future worship services. When I introduce you to the congregation, I want them to associate you with the role of a pastor who leads worship services, in addition to your work with the young people. You were featured in an article in our church newsletter last month, but today is the first time our members will see you in person. I'll ask them to greet you at the coffee hour after the service. Okay? I think we're ready."

Staley rose to lead them to the sanctuary. Wearing black robes, the men walked down the hall toward the building exit. No words were spoken as they walked across the courtyard to the steps leading to the entrance.

The three worship leaders stood with the choir in the spacious narthex. After the choir entered the sanctuary, Staley motioned Boyle and Matt forward with a sweep of his hand. The two pastors, followed by Matt, walked behind the choir members in their crimson robes to the front of the church. Near the altar, the choir members turned right and climbed a few steps to their loft, while Staley and Boyle turned left and climbed to their upholstered chairs near the pulpit. Matt trailed the two pastors, but at the top turned right and walked to one of the two chairs behind the lectern.

Matt surveyed the pews, which appeared to hold about the same number of people as the week before. The organ music reverberated throughout the sanctuary, introducing the first hymn. Sunlight poured through the stained glass windows. Sitting for the first time in front of this group of strangers, he felt tense and uncomfortable thinking about Richard's death, which Staley would announce at any moment.

When the hymn ended, a woman from the choir came forward and sang a solo. Boyle then read the Old Testament verse and, after another hymn, Matt followed with the New Testament text. A minute passed before Staley stepped to the pulpit. The senior pastor rubbed his temple with his right hand and removed his glasses.

"This morning, I'm pleased to introduce to you this year's seminary intern, Matt Beringer. We profiled Matt in the last newsletter, and I'm delighted that he'll be working with the middle school group this year as he prepares for the ministry. I hope each of you will get to know Matt and make him feel welcome during his time with us. Please greet him at the coffee hour after the service."

Staley folded his glasses and set them on the pulpit. He scanned the congregation, and then cleared his throat.

"The past two weeks have included more sorrow than I have experienced in all my years in the ministry. As we gather in worship after a summer of rest and recreation, I am eager for us to enter into our dynamic fall activities here at Hacienda, which begin next Sunday. Both adult education classes and Sunday school will start at nine-thirty. However, today my heart is heavy for the second week in a row because I must share with you another loss in our church family. Death is a part of life, part of the life cycle that God has ordained in nature and in the human community. Seldom does a week pass without my participating in a funeral service for either one of our members or for someone else in our East Bay community. At the same time, I don't know how to prepare you for this announcement," Staley continued, "because I can't believe it's true myself. With great sadness, I must tell you that Richard Finley, our intern last year, drowned yesterday afternoon while sailing on Lake Chabot." A hush settled over the now stunned congregation. Matt slumped in his chair, caught his breath, and tried to stay focused.

Staley waited to let the congregation digest the news. After a few moments, the audience stirred as people spoke among themselves. Eventually, Staley interrupted the whispers. "I can't remember the premature death of a single young minister I've known personally, and in the past two weeks we've lost not just one, but two. These deaths are a shock to all of us. We must pull together as a congregation and support one another, for these two young men touched so many lives in positive ways. Richard and Pete had many years of service ahead of them, and it's such a loss that their ministries have been cut short. Why these servants of God have been taken from us is a mystery. However, we must carry on for them and take comfort in knowing that they are with their Creator in heaven. Before this morning's sermon, please join me in prayer as we remember the lives of both Richard Finley and Pete Rockwell."

Matt leaned forward in his chair during Staley's prayer, with his elbows on his knees, staring at the pale green carpeting. His stomach felt queasy, and he wanted to take a long walk.

Boyle didn't ask for joys and concerns from the congregation following Staley's prayer, and simply remained in his seat.

The senior pastor seemed to struggle in delivering his sermon. He rushed his words, as if he wanted to end the service as quickly as possible. A heavy, gloomy atmosphere descended over the sanctuary.

Matt collected his thoughts before the offertory prayer. After the congregation sang "Be Thou My Vision," he rose at the organist's musical signal and the ushers came forward with the offering plates. He glanced at Staley, who nodded in return. Matt walked forward and gave the offertory prayer. After concluding it with "Amen," he returned to his seat, and the ushers made their way toward the people in the pews.

As members passed the offering plates, the organist played a Bach cantata, which the bulletin said had premiered in 1723. The piece reminded Matt of his walks across the seminary campus, where hymns and works of the masters floated through the air, compliments of the chapel organist.

The offertory music ended, and Matt returned to the front of the altar to receive the offering. He felt as if he were moving in slow motion and had a heavy backpack strapped to his shoulders.

After taking the plates, Matt placed them on the Communion table. Before the closing hymn, a stillness had settled over the members in the pews. The singing of the hymn lacked energy, and Staley's benediction sounded mechanical and distant.

The sanctuary cleared quickly. Before attending the coffee hour, Matt accompanied Staley back to his office to return his robe. While not in the mood to exchange small talk with the members at the coffee hour, Matt had no choice as the guest of honor. Before he could leave the senior pastor's office, Staley said, "Our worship service wasn't very good today. It's my fault. My heart wasn't in it."

Moments later, Matt and Staley joined Boyle in the Amigos Room, just down the hall. Staley recommended that Matt stand near the table in the center, where members could help themselves to coffee and punch, along with an assortment of cookies. Members greeted him, and during their conversations several persons offered assistance if he needed it. He hoped he could remember their names. Despite the encouraging comments, Matt wanted to be alone.

Driving back to his apartment after the coffee hour, Matt's thoughts returned to the worship service. "Was I supposed to take the offering plates to the office after the service? Is there a locked cabinet where the plates are stored? When is the offering counted?" Nobody had told him. Next week, he would find the answers. As he pulled into his parking space, he couldn't remember a more distressing worship service.

7

The next morning, with the Sunday worship service still weighing on him, Matt arrived at the church at around ten-thirty, later than he'd intended. Neither the two pastors nor Mrs. Kirby worked on Mondays and Saturdays. Eventually, he might imitate them, but right now he was in a steep learning curve. He needed to prepare for his first middle school worship service and classes in a week. Walking down the hall toward the stairs, he entered the church office to check his mailbox and saw Mrs. Kirby standing by the filing cabinets.

"I didn't expect to see you today," he said.

"The only reason I'm here is to complete a specific project. I had a new filing cabinet delivered on Friday, so I'm in the process of transferring all of the files from the old one to the new one. They're coming to pick up the old one tomorrow."

"Let me do it for you. That looks like some heavy work. I'll move the files. You sit in a chair and supervise."

"I'd appreciate it. I have some arthritis in my hands and back, so this job could take me all day."

"Should I keep the files in the same order in the new cabinet?"

"Yes. That would be perfect."

Matt worked quickly, and soon finished.

"Now I can go home and enjoy the rest of my day," Mrs. Kirby said. "It was very thoughtful of you, Mr. Beringer."

"Happy to help. I'd prefer that you call me Matt."

"I'll try to remember."

He left the office, grateful for a project that distracted him from thinking about Richard Finley. Continuing down the hall, he slowly climbed the stairs to his office and sank into his desk chair, wishing he were someplace else.

He spent an hour reviewing the Bible lesson for his first class the next Sunday. It took another hour to generate a rough draft of the chapel worship service. Mrs. Kirby had given him some programs from the previous year, which gave him an idea of how Richard had organized the services he led. Boyle had predicted that twenty middle school students would show up. However, based on Matt's positive telephone conversations with the parents, he expected a better turnout. After making progress on the lesson and worship service, he decided to call it quits. The events of the past two days distracted him, and he wanted a break. Putting the papers in his upper-right desk drawer, he locked his office door and headed to his car. He had the rest of the week to wrap things up.

Reaching the parking lot, Matt opened his car door, intending to drive home, but spotted his athletic bag and basketball on the back seat. "No time like the present," he thought. He grabbed his gear and returned to the quadrangle, walking toward the gym on the opposite side of the cloister from the building entrance. He'd been puzzled that he hadn't been shown the gym during his internship interview with the Education Committee, but never mind, he was looking forward to shooting some baskets in the facility he'd been hired to use. He entered the building and walked down the hall to a set of double doors leading to the gym. Opening one of the doors, Matt surveyed the basketball court, with its wooden floor glistening in the sunlight flooding the space from high windows above the fold-up bleachers that ran along the outside wall.

He sat down on a folding chair near the doors and removed his shoes. Reaching into his bag, he found his athletic socks and basketball shoes.

After lacing them up, he walked to the free-throw line, dribbling his basketball, and took a shot. The ball didn't even make it over the front rim. Shaking his head, and laughing out loud, he retrieved the ball and returned to the free-throw line. The second shot dropped through the rim, touching nothing but net. "That's more like it," he said to himself.

After fifteen minutes of shooting a variety of shots, he stopped at the center of the court and imagined it was halftime at a Golden State Warriors' basketball game. By holding the lucky ticket in a lottery, he'd been chosen to shoot a basketball from the midcourt line. If he made the shot, he would win $50,000. Matt crouched and launched the ball toward the basket. The jackpot slipped through his fingers as the ball hit the rim and bounced away. Smiling, he put his basketball next to his bag by the doors and decided to inspect the rest of the gym.

At the far end, he opened a door that appeared to be a storage room. He stepped inside and turned on the light. The large room, about thirty feet by fifteen feet in size, held folding chairs on six carts with wheels. Matt wondered how often the chairs were used.

Another door opened into a second smaller room that stored athletic equipment. On one wall the floor-to-ceiling shelves held a wide array of items, from baseballs to badminton racquets. Two volleyball poles leaned against the opposite wall, with the net attached. The amount of equipment impressed him, although some of it appeared worn and in need of replacing. However, the four basketballs looked barely used, confirming that the court hadn't seen much recent traffic. He would use them instead of buying new ones, which he suspected would be a relief to Pastor Boyle.

On the top shelf sat a faded blue athletic bag. As Matt pulled it down from its ledge, he saw patches of dried mud on the bottom, crumbling now, drop to the floor. He unzipped the bag and found a short-sleeve shirt, jeans, and leather sandals. Inside the side pocket, he discovered a wrinkled journal, full of notes, with Pete Rockwell's name on the cover. On page one, Pete had written: *Pastor Staley is reported to have come West from North Carolina in his early twenties to become a Hollywood actor, but then decided to return to the East Coast to become a minister.* Matt smiled to himself, well aware that success in both professions involved an ability to entertain. "These words must have been written during Pete's internship," Matt thought.

He thumbed through the journal, scanning the entries. Another of Pete's comments was, *Ricky Rowland said that Pastor Staley was often at their house in the afternoon, talking to his mother, when he arrived home from school.* A nearby statement said, *Julie Canfield mentioned that Pastor Staley had been to their house on numerous afternoons to meet with her mom.* Pete's innuendos suggested Pastor Staley spent considerable time visiting women in the congregation. "Is he a womanizer?" Matt wondered.

He read comments focusing on Pastor Boyle's preoccupation with the church's appearance: *Boyle appears to enjoy supervising the crew of the landscape company, like he owns it! He spends a fair amount of time outside, overseeing their work, whether it's weeding or planting a shrub. He acts more interested in the way the campus looks than in my middle school activities.*

Another note had to do with seeing numerous bills from the landscape company on Boyle's desk. Pete wrote: *Given Boyle's reluctance to spend money on such items as films and speakers to improve the middle school program, why is he so committed to spending the church's money on planting and maintaining flowers, plants, and trees? Is he receiving kick-backs from the landscape company for the work he requests?*

The last entry Matt read described Pete's attendance at Session meetings to observe how the church officers functioned. He reported, *All of the committee chairs are new appointments, except for the Finance Committee chair, Larry Rowland. He is beginning his third year in that position, which doesn't seem right. In his position, it is easier to embezzle funds because of the absence of security checks and balances found in a corporate setting. The chair of the Finance Committee should be rotated on an annual basis, just like the other committee chairs. I also haven't heard about an annual audit of the church's finances, which I believe should be a requirement.*

As Matt closed the journal, a piece of paper dropped to the floor. Picking it up, he saw that it was a neatly-folded newspaper article from a Sunday edition of the *San Francisco Chronicle*, dated in April of the previous year. The headline was *Three Youths Drown in Canoeing Accident*. Matt continued to read: *Three middle school youths from San Lucas died Saturday in an accident on the Russian River in Sonoma County, while on a church-sponsored canoe trip. The victims belonged to a group from Hacienda Presbyterian Church. Their canoe became separated from the others and, when it was found, it had capsized and trapped the youths underwater. Attempts to revive them were unsuccessful. The names of the victims are being withheld for the duration of the investigation.*

"The middle school group?" Matt said to himself, surprised by his discovery. He slipped the article back into the journal and put it in his pocket. That evening at his apartment, he would read Pete's notes in greater detail. "Why did he leave his bag and journal behind?" he asked himself. He then returned the bag to the top shelf and left.

Walking to the church office to check his mailbox, he passed the custodian's office and noticed the door was ajar. Carlo Barone was the only staff member he hadn't met, so he decided to introduce himself. Pushing open the door after knocking, Matt saw him sitting in a chair behind his desk. With a full head of silver hair and a tan face, he wore a gray sweatshirt over a green polo shirt. A green Oakland A's baseball cap, with its yellow bill, sat on his desk. Matt guessed he was in his seventies.

"Mr. Barone, I'm Matt Beringer, the new intern who'll be working with the middle school kids this year. I wanted to say hello."

"Hey, Matt," the older man said. "Call me Carlo. How are you doing?"

"I didn't expect so much bad news during my first week on the job, but I'm trying to deal with it."

"Both Rockwell and Finley were good guys, and losing them is a real shame."

"I'll bet you have a lot of stories about this place."

"I have a few," Carlo replied. "I've been the custodian here for seven years."

"I'd like to hear them."

"Stop by anytime," Carlo said. "I'm usually around the church from nine to five, Tuesday through Saturday. I came in today to do some yard work. They allow me to shift my hours as necessary."

"Should I schedule an appointment?"

"Naw. Just stop by. But if I'm not here, that's the way the ball bounces. Don't take it personally," Carlo said, grinning.

"Do you have time for a question?" Matt asked.

"Sure."

"I just finished shooting a few baskets in the gym. In the closet, I found a duffel bag that belonged to Pete Rockwell. It had a journal with a newspaper article from last year about a canoeing accident. It said three middle school kids from Hacienda had drowned. What happened?"

"We lost three kids on the Russian River. Very sad. Their canoe capsized, and they were underwater too long. The church was devastated, and Pastor Staley was concerned about how the accident could affect the church. He told the staff to refer members with questions to him. He wanted us to concentrate on our jobs."

"He's probably right. I can see how it could be harmful if it became the main topic of conversation."

"I think the church has worked its way through that calamity," Carlo said, "and things have pretty much returned to normal."

"That's good to hear," Matt said. "Thanks for the explanation. I'm glad to finally meet you."

At the church office, he found the September issue of the *Bell Tower* newsletter in his mailbox. As he closed the office door and headed to his car, he bumped into Sally Rowland.

"How are you, Mrs. Rowland?" Matt asked.

"Just fine, but how are *you* doing?

"To be honest, I'm stunned that Pete Rockwell and Richard Finley are dead. I can't believe it."

"I was very involved in recruiting those two young men to Hacienda," she said, "so I feel like I've lost members of my family. It's terrible. I'm having trouble sleeping at night."

"I'll be attending Richard's memorial service at the seminary later this week," Matt said. "That's two services in a week."

"You didn't know Pete and Richard as well as we did because they each spent nine months with us. I hope you won't become overly distracted by these events. Keep your eyes on the ball because you have important responsibilities around here."

"Two deaths so close together. It's a real shock. But I'll be okay."

"We think you'll do a good job, Matt. That's why we chose you. If you ever have any concerns or need to bounce an idea off of someone, please don't hesitate to call me."

"I appreciate your support, Mrs. Rowland. My internship hasn't started the way I thought it would, but I think the middle school kids will have a good year."

"I need to leave a note for Mrs. Kirby, so I'll see you later," Sally said, turning toward the office door.

"What was Sally Rowland doing at church today?" Matt wondered, as he left the building. "Neither of the pastors are around. Did she see me shooting baskets in the gym? Was she checking up on me?"

8

He was swimming furiously toward a man in the water, but he couldn't close the distance and save him from sinking. Matt awoke with a start, his pajamas soaked with sweat. It was still dark outside. After his nightmare, he arose and took a shower. He was ready to start the day and leave his terrifying dream behind. Projects at his office awaited him, such as studying Sunday's lesson and putting the finishing touches on the order of worship for the chapel service.

The sky was growing lighter as Matt pulled into the church parking lot. He was glad to have some time to himself to work without interruption, so he appreciated the deserted church campus. Arriving early, he hoped to be more productive than the day before.

Walking toward the quadrangle, he looked up at his office on the second floor. The blinds were raised, although he usually lowered them before he left for the day. He had been so preoccupied with the discouraging Sunday service and thoughts of Richard Finley that maybe he had forgotten to lower them. But his light was on, and he was sure he had turned it off. When he reached his office, the door was unlocked. "Who's been in my office?" he wondered.

Unsettled by these discoveries, he put them aside and sat down at his desk. He opened the lesson book and turned to the table of contents, which contained thirty class sessions, each focusing on one of Jesus' parables. Every lesson had questions to stimulate class discussions. He wanted to review all of them before the middle school program began in five days. Around eleven-thirty, after completing the first ten, he decided to get something to eat. Before he left his office, he finalized the agenda of the chapel worship service.

On his way to El Primero in the village, he stopped at the church office and asked Mrs. Kirby if she would type the worship program for him. Ever the optimist, he asked her to make fifty copies, hoping for a large turnout. She told him they would be in his mailbox by Friday morning.

When he returned to his office after lunch, he called the three volunteer teachers from last year who said they'd return for another year. He wanted to know if they had any questions about the first lesson. Satisfied that they were prepared for Sunday, he had one more project—to find a guitar player from the high school group who could lead songs during the chapel worship services. Matt wished he played the guitar because it tends to increase the energy and participation of the singers. Sally Rowland had given him a boy's name, so Matt called him to discuss his idea. He agreed to help. Next Sunday's middle school program was falling into place. Before leaving for the day, Matt called the five middle school leaders at the other San Lucas churches and scheduled another meeting to discuss the basketball program.

Satisfied with what he had accomplished, Matt left his office and walked to his car. The late afternoon sun on his face felt good. Mrs. Kirby waved as she drove out of the parking lot. On his way home in light traffic, he stopped at the neighborhood supermarket to buy some groceries. Then he went to McDonald's for a hamburger and shake, while he perused the sports section of the *Tribune*. He had a basketball game that evening at the Hayward YMCA.

It was after seven when he arrived at his apartment building at the end of the cul-de-sac on Chumalia Street. The three-story structure dominated the block lined with houses. The eucalyptus grove across the street bordered San Leandro Creek, which started at Lake Chabot in the hills above, descended into the city of San Leandro, cut through the northern neighborhoods, and continued north on its way past the Oakland International Airport to the San Francisco Bay. During his first week at his new home, he had seen the neighborhood kids playing in the street when he returned to his apartment, but tonight it was empty. Several houses were dark, except for their porch lights. The street seemed unexpectedly quiet.

The previous evening, he had played touch football in the street with some fathers, including Ed O'Neil and John Hansen, and their teenage sons. The men had invited him to a spaghetti feed at the Hansens' house on Saturday. In return, Matt planned to invite these neighbors to his apartment for tacos sometime before Halloween. He was settling into the neighborhood.

Reaching the end of the street, he made a U-turn, and pulled up to the curb in front of the apartment building. Since his basketball game started at nine, he decided to leave his car outside. As he walked to the front door, he smelled the pungent eucalyptus trees. No music drifted through the air from open doors or windows. Not a single dog or cat wandered around, looking for something to do.

Once inside the apartment lobby, he checked his mail. His next-door neighbor, Harold Leviton, slight of build, stood beside him at the mailboxes. He was wearing a robe over his pajamas.

"The neighborhood feels like a ghost town. Where is everyone?" Matt asked.

"Beats me," Harold replied. "I've been on my sofa for most of the day. I came home from work this morning with an upset stomach," he said, rubbing his hand across his midsection. "I've been trying to get some rest. I sure wish the lady on the other side of me would turn down her TV," he whined. Matt wondered if the stress in Harold's job as an insurance adjuster caused his indigestion.

"I hope you feel better," Matt said.

"Thanks. I can't afford to miss any work," Harold said, as he punched the "up" elevator button to return to his apartment.

Matt continued to sift through his mail. The junk-mail marketers had found him, but he also received a letter from his Aunt Ellen in Spokane and an invitation to a wine tasting party at the Canfields' condo in San Francisco. It would be a change of pace to interact with members of the congregation away from the church, and he looked forward to seeing the Canfields' second residence. He would RSVP tomorrow. He took the elevator to his apartment, set the mail down on the living room coffee table, and opened the sliding glass door to his balcony. A soft breeze flowed into the room.

He brought his clock radio into the living room and set it for eight. A half-hour nap would help him relax. Then he could tackle his crossword puzzle and maybe call Jancy before he left. He flopped down on the sofa to read his aunt's letter. It ended with, "We're looking forward to seeing you in a week. Love, Aunt Ellen and Uncle Cal." Dropping the letter on the floor, Matt closed his eyes. He didn't remember where he was when he awoke to the sound of bossa nova music.

Rising from the sofa, he thought about the basketball game. It would be smart to shoot a few baskets before it began, so he decided to leave right away. He would call Jancy later, and the crossword puzzle could wait, as well. Grabbing his athletic bag, he hurried to his car for the fifteen-minute drive to the Y. The evening was warm enough. He didn't need a jacket.

A full moon shone with a silver hue, its light fanning across the sky like a shimmering curtain. Branches bobbed and swayed in the evening breeze and cast shadows that looked like cats on the prowl.

As Matt reached for the driver's door, he heard tires squeal behind him and turned to see a dark-colored car emerge from the shadows and head toward him, its lights off. Matt froze, but then felt his adrenaline surge. The car rushed straight toward him. He leaped onto the hood of his car, intending to roll off on the other side. But the car struck the edge of his rear fender with a loud bang. The impact threw Matt off the hood and onto the sidewalk, as the advancing car scraped along the side of his vehicle. The car sped away as Matt lay on the sidewalk. In a matter of seconds, silence settled once again over the cul-de-sac.

He stayed on the ground for a minute, trying to make sense of what had happened to him. Then he struggled to rise to a kneeling position. Time suspended as his body felt the after-effects of the physical threat he had just avoided. He had no energy, and his arms and legs seemed weak. "Someone wanted to kill me!" he thought to himself.

Raising his head, he looked at his car and realized he'd had a very close call. He heard noises in the background—doors opening and closing, footsteps, and voices. After some moments, he felt an arm on his shoulder.

Ed O'Neil was bending over him, looking down with a worried expression.

"Are you okay?" he asked.

"Yeah," Matt mumbled.

"You almost got hit. I heard the crash and saw you roll across your hood from my living room window. Jumping out of the way was quick thinking on your part. I've called the police. They're on their way."

"Thanks," Matt said. "Did you see the license?"

"No. It happened so fast. I couldn't even tell the make of the car, but it was either dark blue or black."

Ed helped Matt to his feet. His shoulders and knees aching, Matt leaned against the passenger door of his car and slowly raised his arms. They felt sore, but he didn't think he had broken any bones. "I'm a little light-headed, but I think I'm okay. My shoulders took the impact when I landed, and I scraped my knees, but that's all."

"Let me walk you over to the bench by the front door," Ed said.

"Okay," Matt said. His left ankle also hurt. With Ed's assistance, he hobbled toward the seat like an injured football player leaving the gridiron. Still feeling dizzy, he welcomed the chance to sit down. He slumped against the back of the bench, resting on his right elbow. Ed sat down next to him.

"I've got to ask you something," Ed whispered, "before the police get here."

"Sure," Matt replied.

"Are you involved with drugs in some way?" he asked. "That car was playing for keeps. Are you in some kind of trouble?"

"No," Matt said, both amused and surprised by Ed's comment. He felt tired and wanted to lie down. "I have no idea who that might have been."

"Sorry for asking," Ed said, "but nothing like this has ever happened on our street."

A few more neighbors had gathered on the sidewalk beside Matt's car. Some apartment residents stood on their balconies and looked uneasily at the destruction below. The apartment managers, Leo and Mary Vitale, emerged from the lobby and stood by the front door, staring at the vehicle.

Matt's stomach churned, and he hoped he wasn't going to vomit. He could have been killed by the dark car, and what he'd just experienced made no sense to him.

A police car appeared and parked at the curb. John Hansen arrived with a cup of coffee he handed to Matt.

"Hey, John, where was your car tonight? Matt asked. "Don't you park it in front of your house? The street was vacant when I came home this evening."

"Yeah, I know," he replied. "We got a coupon book in the mail today with some restaurant discounts, so I took the family out for dinner at the China Palace."

"I had a strange feeling driving into the cul-de-sac tonight," Matt said. "I can't explain it. It was so quiet."

"The Mallorys' son had a high school football game tonight, so several neighbors went to see him play," John responded.

One of the two policemen approached Matt with a note pad in hand and asked, "Is this your car?"

"Yes," Matt said. "I was about to get in it when a car appeared out of nowhere and tried to run me down. Luckily, I jumped out of the way."

"Are you okay?" the policeman asked. "Do you need some medical attention?"

"I'm a little shaken and my knees are sore," Matt said, "but nothing serious."

"Did anyone get a license number or make of the vehicle?" the officer asked.

"I don't think so. It happened really fast," Matt said.

"That's unfortunate because it limits our investigation. We have some criminal activity in the East Bay, some of it drug-related, and I'm guessing a gang may have targeted the wrong guy in a deal gone bad. I think you were the wrong guy in the wrong place at the wrong time. This is a real clean part of the East Bay, so I don't know why they came to this neighborhood. We'll try to locate a dark blue or black car with some damage on the right side, but I'm not very optimistic."

"That's not encouraging news," Matt replied.

"I know," he said, "but without a license number or better description, we don't have much information."

"Okay," Matt said. "Thanks for responding."

The officer took Matt's name, address, and phone number. After the policemen spoke to a few more neighbors, they got in their car and slowly drove away.

By now the Vitales were sweeping up the glass in the street in front of the apartment. They rarely had their evenings in front of the TV interrupted by a disturbance in the neighborhood. Matt expected that Leo would knock on his door tomorrow and want an explanation.

Standing up, Matt turned to Ed and John. "Thanks, guys, for checking on me. I think I'll go lie down for a while."

Stressed and exhausted, he limped to the front door and rode the elevator to his apartment. His team at the Hayward Y would have to get along without him tonight. He would call the Y and report that he had become ill. From the way he felt, it wasn't entirely a lie. If his stomach hadn't felt nauseous from the attempt on his life, looking at the his damaged car might have cinched it.

———

The next morning, after a night of interrupted sleep due his aching body, Matt called Ben Miller, a friend and detective with the Oakland Police

Department, to fill him in on what had happened. Ben's younger brother, Sidney, had played basketball with Matt in college. After the hit-and-run attempt, his evening had taken on a surreal dimension. He couldn't help thinking about Pete and Richard.

"Detective Miller," the voice said. Matt knew only one person with a voice that deep.

"Ben, this is Matt Beringer."

"What's happening, Matt?" Miller asked. "Or should I call you Reverend?"

"I'm not quite there yet," Matt said, "and if someone has his way, I may not make it."

"How so?" Miller asked.

"I was almost run over last night," Matt said. "Do you have a few minutes to talk about it?"

"I have a little time before a meeting at ten. Go for it."

"There have been some troubling events at the church in San Lucas where I'm doing my internship."

"What's the name of the church?'"

"Hacienda Presbyterian."

"I didn't know you were working there," Miller said.

"I'm in my third year at Calvin Seminary, and we do internships in our last year. Hacienda's job description seemed like a perfect fit, and they selected me. They want me to organize basketball leagues for middle school boys and girls that include the other San Lucas churches. After seminary, I may want to become a youth minister, so this internship seemed to be right up my alley."

"Your Princeton basketball experience probably helped you."

"Yeah. They seemed to like that."

"What's going on over there?"

"I just started the internship, but in the past week the two previous interns have died in separate accidents. First, a guy by the name of Pete Rockwell died in a car accident on Interstate 80. Then last year's intern, Richard Finley, drowned last Saturday while sailing on Lake Chabot. He was an expert sailor, so his death is really disturbing. What are the odds of the two previous interns dying within a week of each other? Then last night, a car almost ran me down in front of my apartment. I don't know if these events are connected or not, but I feel like I'm in danger."

"I'm not aware of the guy who died on Interstate 80, but I read the short article about the drowning in Sunday's paper. Tell me more about last night."

"As I was getting into my car, another car tried to hit me. I escaped by rolling over the hood of my car, so I just got a few scrapes, but you should see my car. To be honest, I'm scared. I could have been killed. The San Leandro police think it's a case of mistaken identity—a drug-related revenge crime or something like that. They don't think I was the target. However, I'm not so sure. Unfortunately, nobody saw the license number or had a good description of the car."

"Matt, what have you gotten yourself into? Let me research these incidents. I'll try to get back to you as soon as I can."

"Thanks for listening. I haven't told my aunt and uncle, but I want a friend to know what's happened to me."

"I'm glad you called. Have you talked to Sidney lately? We haven't seen much of him? He says he's working hard at business school."

"I spoke with him a couple of weeks ago, and we talked about getting together. I owe him a phone call," Matt said.

"Well, I'd like to see both of you guys," Miller said. "I need to run to my ten o'clock meeting right now. Call me back in a few minutes and leave your phone number on my voicemail. You'll be hearing from me in the next day or two. These events are probably a coincidence, but if they're connected you could be in danger. Be careful, brother."

Matt ended the telephone call and leaned back on the sofa. He needed to arrange for a rental car. In no hurry to do anything, he reached for a new crossword puzzle on the coffee table. He would call Mrs. Kirby and say he was having car problems.

9

Matt arrived at Hacienda around eleven, and he tried not to limp as he walked to his office. His battered car had been towed to a garage in San Leandro, and his insurance company had provided a loaner. The ambush the night before had left him with sore shoulders, knees, and an aching left ankle. As he sat at his desk, his cell phone rang.

"Hi, Matt, this is Jancy."

"Hey, Jancy! Good to hear from you. Are we still on for dinner tonight?"

"You bet. Am I calling at a good time?"

"Sure." He decided not to mention last night's dance with danger.

"Have you read the *Tribune*?" she asked.

"No. Haven't had time." Matt replied. "Why?"

"There's an article on the front page of the second section about Pete Rockwell. The California Highway Patrol now says it may not have been an accident."

"What?" Matt asked.

"Over the weekend, someone discovered some yellow paint on the rear bumper of Pete's car that apparently had been overlooked. The original report mentioned broken glass on the car's path from the highway to the irrigation ditch. The glass came from Pete's tail lights. Someone connected the dots and concluded that Pete may have been rear-ended."

"Very interesting."

"You won't believe this, but they traced the paint to Hannifin Trucking because of the distinctive color. The color matches the signature yellow on Hannifin's trucks. That's Larry Rowland's company."

"Wow! Any comments from Rowland?" Matt asked.

"In the article, Rowland denies any knowledge of the incident, although he admits that one of his trucks had a scheduled trip to Sacramento the night of the accident. Rowland confirmed that the driver was a guy named Kenny Cole. He's worked for Hannifin for three years."

"Has anyone talked to Cole?" Matt asked.

"No," Jancy said. "The article said he's on a leave of absence he requested a few days ago. No one seems to know where he is."

"If Rowland isn't involved, why did Cole run Rockwell off the road? What was the motive?" Matt asked.

"The article suggests that Cole may have been high on drugs or alcohol and had no motive. Just a random act."

"So Rockwell didn't fall asleep at the wheel after all," Matt said.

"Right. His car may have been run off the highway by a Hannifin truck," Jancy said. "What a terrifying experience that must have been for poor Pete."

"Are they searching for the truck driver?" Matt asked.

"Yes, there's a statewide search underway," Jancy said. "Cole apparently lives in an apartment in Alameda. He's divorced, with two kids. His ex-wife and kids live in South Carolina. He moved to California after his divorce. There's a girl friend who lives with Cole, but she can't be located, either."

"Does the article say anything more about Rowland?"

"The *Tribune* sounds sympathetic toward him," Jancy said. "The article says he's a prominent resident of San Lucas and a church leader at Hacienda Presbyterian. It also mentions that his company is a major employer in Oakland. Rowland is naturally trying his best to distance himself from the incident. He claims he knows nothing about the accident. The article makes it sound like he's completely innocent, which I guess he is until proven guilty. He does acknowledge that the truck Cole drove that night needed some front-end body work."

"Jancy, thanks for calling," Matt said. "I really appreciate the update. Now I'm convinced there's a connection between Pete's death and Richard's drowning. I hope they find the truck driver and learn more about the accident. Are we meeting today at five o'clock in our parking lot? I'm looking forward to seeing you."

"I'll be there," she said.

"I've made reservations at Angelo's for five-thirty," Matt said, "and I'll drive us to the restaurant."

Matt returned to study the first lesson for his class on Sunday, but Jancy's call had distracted him. His thoughts kept returning to Pete and Richard.

The bell in the tower next to Hacienda's sanctuary rang three times, and he looked at his watch. He stood up, walked to the window, and stared at the fountain below. "If there is someone behind the deaths of Pete and Richard, who is it?" He could think of several candidates, but were they capable of murder?

He saw Pastor Staley walking to the parking lot, and his thoughts returned to his first meeting with his supervisor at four o'clock. "Will working with Boyle be as challenging as Sally Rowland described? Will I see firsthand his controlling and inflexible personality traits that Jancy mentioned? Even more worrisome, was Boyle connected to the deaths of Pete and Richard? Did he know that *both* of them suspected him of stealing from the church?"

Early last week, as he settled into his office, Matt had asked Mrs. Kirby if Boyle had a resume he could read before their first meeting. She had retrieved an article from an eight-year-old issue of Hacienda's monthly *Bell Tower* newsletter, announcing his appointment as the new associate minister. When Matt asked for a resume of the senior pastor, Reverend

James Staley, she shook her head, saying, "His resume hasn't been updated in years."

The article about Boyle included more information than a resume. The front page featured a photograph of a younger, somewhat thinner Charles Boyle, then age forty-eight, followed by a profile of his life history, including his comments about growing up in nearby Oakland. What interested Matt the most was the number of his various ministries. His tenure at the churches before Hacienda never lasted more than five years. In all, Matt counted seven different churches that he had served since graduating from seminary at the age of twenty-seven: Denver; Colorado Springs; Phoenix; Reno; Anaheim; Fresno; and San Lucas. He observed two possible themes: first, that Boyle liked warm weather, and second, that he had wanted to return to the West after attending seminary on the East Coast. Matt remembered a comment by one of his professors, a retired pastor, that it can take seven years for a minister to make an impact on a church. How should he view Boyle's work history in light of so many job changes?

In his eighth year at Hacienda, Boyle had finally achieved a level of stability that had eluded him in his previous ministries. Matt reminded himself that there may have been good reasons for each move. Boyle's brief employment stints may have been influenced by poor relationships with the senior pastors or by their departures. When a senior pastor leaves a church, the successor usually wants to bring in a new staff rather than keep the previous team. He could have been such a victim on more than one occasion because the senior pastor had taken a job at another church.

The article mentioned that Boyle was divorced, single, and had a daughter, Edith, age seventeen. Today, she would be about his own age. It said he enjoyed live theater and was a dedicated baseball fan who looked forward to attending Oakland A's games once he relocated to San Lucas.

Why hadn't he ever been a senior pastor? Either he didn't aspire to lead a church or hadn't been chosen for a senior position. Despite his numerous job changes, or perhaps because of them, Matt hoped to learn from his supervisor how to evaluate a ministerial opportunity. However, during their first meeting, Matt's top priority would be to build rapport and try to lay the groundwork for a positive relationship.

Shortly before four o'clock, Matt descended the stairs and walked toward Boyle's office at the end of the hall. His knees still hurt, his left ankle bothered him, and his palms felt damp. This meeting could set the tone for the rest of the year.

Located across the hall from Pastor Staley's corner office, Boyle's office looked east, across the rooftops of San Lucas. The door was closed, so Matt knocked a couple of times. He had arrived a few minutes early. After a few moments, he heard an answer: "Come right in!"

Boyle was sitting at his desk, with his arms crossed. A large window to the right offered a panoramic view. "Not bad for an associate pastor," Matt thought.

The room Matt entered was anything but orderly. Papers, books, and bric-a-brac filled every available space on his bookshelves and the surface of his desk. However, it reminded Matt more of a collector than a disorganized individual. A number of black and white photos of actors in costume sat on the credenza behind his chair. An Oakland A's pennant adorned the wall.

Boyle motioned for Matt to sit down. "You're the tallest intern we've had," he said with a smile. "No wonder you played basketball."

"I was recruited for my grade school basketball team because I was tall. I've been playing basketball ever since."

"Well," Boyle said. "if you were a baseball player, all you'd have to do to steal second base is lie down!"

"I've played a little baseball, and stealing second base was never quite that easy for me."

"I find that hard to believe," Boyle said.

Matt inventoried the man. Short and overweight, Charles Boyle had a shiny, balding pate. Jowls interrupted his round face. A couple of lines creased his forehead. His thick neck strained against his shirt collar, and his tie knot was too small to cover the gap between his collar flaps. His sports jacket hung over the back of his chair.

"Now about your work with me," Boyle began. "You're going to take a load off my shoulders this year by organizing the boys' and girls' basketball leagues and running the Sunday school activities. I have to tell you that the Education Committee came up with the idea for the middle school basketball program, over my objection. What does basketball have to do with Christian education? We don't use the gym very much, but that's going to change this year. I'm glad you'll be handling this because I don't want any part of it. As a reward for your help this year, I'll teach you Boyle's Ten Laws of Ministry. Stuff they don't teach you in seminary. Are you with me?"

"Yes," Matt responded. "I'm interested."

"Glad to hear it, Beringer," Boyle snorted. "What do you like to do in your spare time? What are your hobbies?"

"I enjoy sports, books, movies, and interesting food."

"Good for you!" Boyle exclaimed, pulling his chair closer to the desk, so he could rest his arms on its surface. "Ministers need outside interests to recharge their batteries."

"I never run out of things to do. I enjoy watching professional sports on TV, like Major League Baseball."

Boyle raised his hands off the desk as if he were having a religious experience. "So you're a baseball fan! That's good to hear. I like to sneak down to spring training in Mesa to see how the A's team is coming together. I have two season tickets along the first-base line for all of the home games, so I can look across to their dugout. You'll have to join me."

"That would be great fun," Matt said. "It sounds like professional baseball is one of your hobbies."

"The Oakland A's and theater are right up there at the top. I also like to drive a nice car. I've told you about my Lexus."

"You have."

"Thanks to my deceased aunt, who left me her car and some money a few years ago. The Lexus is three years old, but it looks like new. I couldn't have purchased that car on my salary. What else do you want to talk about?" Boyle brought his hands together, interlocking his fingers.

"Quite honestly, I'm losing some sleep over the deaths of Pete and Richard. It's shocking."

"I know what you mean," Boyle said.

"Do you think there could be some kind of connection?" Matt asked.

Boyle wrinkled his brow. "Connection?"

"They happened just a week apart. Could there have been some foul play?" Matt asked.

"What are you saying?"

"Could they have been murdered?"

"Beringer, you have quite an imagination," Boyle said. "I think they were random accidents, pure and simple. How do you link a car accident to a drowning?"

"Maybe they had information someone didn't want them to know."

"You've been reading too many mysteries."

"I learned today that Pete might have been rear-ended," Matt said. "One of Larry Rowland's trucks."

"I read the same article. That situation sounds like bad luck to me. Rowland had nothing to do with it. Rockwell was just in the wrong place at the wrong time. The truck driver may have been high on drugs or alcohol. He didn't know Rockwell from Adam."

Matt sensed Boyle's impatience and, sure enough, he changed the subject.

"Is there anything else you want to cover?"

"It would be interesting to hear about your various ministries," Matt said.

Boyle sighed and looked away, turning his swivel chair toward the window to his left. "In a nutshell, I've been at this church for eight years now," he said, "and before that I had ministries at churches in some western states. I grew up in the Bay Area and always wanted to return here. I attended seminary in Pittsburgh, but I was homesick much of the time. I was very happy to return to the West after graduation, when a job opened up in Denver. The seminary wants me to return for my thirtieth class reunion next June, but I won't be going. I'm not what you'd call a loyal alum."

"Did you ever consider attending Calvin Seminary?" Matt asked.

"My father didn't want me to attend seminary," he answered, "so I needed to get away. The East Coast seemed like a good place at the time." Boyle again changed subjects. "I'm glad you'll be with us this year. Of course, you already know about the Sunday morning worship service in the chapel and the classes that follow. You have the roster I gave you of the middle school kids. As I told you, I expect about twenty students will join your program this year, more or less. But don't judge your success by the numbers. The attendance will ebb and flow during the year. I've given you the curriculum to use. And you have a list of last year's teachers. See if they want to come back for another year. Be sure to keep me informed about what you're doing."

"Would you like to hear from me directly or would you prefer a note in your mailbox?"

"Let's start with notes. I check my mailbox daily. Now is a good time to tell you a few things that may help your career in ministry. I wish some-one had given me some tips early on because I had to learn the hard way through experience. We just covered my first law for ministers, which is 'Stay informed because knowledge is power and job security.' A lack of knowledge can get a minister fired, and I don't want to lose my job. Number two is "Give the members what they want.' By that I mean no political sermons or lectures on other religions. Deliver a positive message. That is, unless you want to alienate people and lose your job. I've seen too many ministers try to educate, and they end up offending people in the process."

"What about the prophets in the Bible, who told people some uncom-fortable truths? The Israelites repeatedly ignored God and the laws, and the prophets reminded them of their failings."

"If you want to share the truth," Boyle said, "hire a local seminary pro-fessor to teach a class. The members can learn the uncomfortable truths from someone else. For me, I want to keep my job. My third law is 'Know your biggest contributors and shower them with attention.' They're usu-ally the most influential members, so stay on their good side. I enjoy tak-ing the larger pledgers to dinner once a year—on the church, of course."

"One of my seminary professors suggested that ministers shouldn't know what the members give, in order to treat them as equals and avoid favoritism."

"That's why he's a professor and why I'm working in a church. Information is power, so why wouldn't you want to know who the big givers are? You should know who's paying your salary and who isn't."

"Okay. I'll have to think about that one."

"And Boyle's fourth law is 'Keep your sermons on a personal level, and leave national and international issues out of them.' " He leaned back in his chair.

"Recently, I read a survey of church members," Matt said, "indicating they want to hear about the Church's position on major issues like abortion; religious liberty and persecution; poverty; and the role of government. Can ministers ignore these issues that their members are struggling to understand? The theologian, Karl Barth, said we should read both the Bible and the newspaper, and interpret the newspaper using the Bible. Shouldn't ministers try to connect the stories of the Bible with the stories of their members?"

"You'll be penalized for discussing those subjects from the pulpit. Stirring up the members with sermons on controversial issues can divide a congregation. Again, if you want to stay employed, don't rock the boat."

Boyle stood up and walked toward the office window, scratching his head. "Well, Beringer, I don't want to share all of my jewels with you today, so we'll leave the rest for another time."

"Thanks, Pastor Boyle. I appreciate hearing your views. Will we have weekly meetings?"

"Maybe. Monthly, for sure." Boyle winked at Matt and grinned an elfish smile. "My job here at Hacienda is too much fun to let it slip through my fingers because you haven't kept me informed. If you'll keep me posted, I won't interfere with your work." Then he returned to his chair.

"Sometime, I'd like to hear about your favorite ministry, besides Hacienda," Matt said.

Boyle squinted as he responded. "Interesting question, Beringer. It was the church in Phoenix. I fell in love with professional baseball while watching spring training, and those retired folks in the church who followed baseball really knew how to enjoy life. It was a very relaxing time in my life. Even my marriage was working then."

Matt had hoped to learn something about Boyle's daughter. He didn't see a photo of her or any other family member.

Boyle straightened some papers on his desk and rose from his chair, signaling to Matt that he wanted to end their meeting. "Just follow the approved curriculum and you'll be fine. The congregation pays us to do the work, Beringer. Most of our members are too busy with their professions and families to volunteer much time to help around here."

Matt held a different viewpoint. "San Lucas parents may be more interested in what their kids are doing at church than you think," he mused, but decided to keep his opinion to himself.

"Should I start the basketball program in October or November?" Matt asked.

"It better begin in October," Boyle said. "This is a busy place between Thanksgiving and Christmas, so you should stop by the first of December. Then you can continue your schedule after January 1st."

Matt nodded in response.

Boyle glanced at his watch as if he heard an alarm ring in another room. "It's time to go. I have tickets for the theater tonight," he said.

"Thanks for the meeting," Matt said, as Boyle followed him out of the door. Retracing his steps to his office, he thought, "Boyle is a piece of work." Matt made a mental note to mention the A's on a regular basis. "Then we should get along just fine."

It was almost five. He cleared the papers from his desk, then locked the door behind him and headed for his loaner car in the parking lot. A brilliant orange sun was sinking toward the horizon. He looked forward to seeing Jancy. Spotting the shiny car in the parking lot, he opened the driver's door and slid onto the front seat. He would listen to the radio while he waited, so he turned his key in the ignition. Nothing happened. It sounded like a dead battery. Frustrated, he walked back to the church and cut across the courtyard toward the entrance near the custodian's office. The administration building was dark, but he hoped to find Carlo Barone.

As he entered the hallway, Matt saw that his door was open. He peered inside. The custodian stood by his desk, reaching for his jacket hanging on a wall hook.

"Carlo?" he said.

"Hi there, Matt," he said, turning to face him. "How's it going?"

"Not bad. Could I ask you for a big favor?"

"I'm on my way home. How can I help?"

"I think my car battery is dead. It's a rental car, if you can believe that. Can you help me jump-start it?"

"Sure," Carlo replied. "You caught me in the nick of time."

"I don't want to hold you up," Matt said.

"It's no problem," Carlo said. "I have jumper cables, Let's go start your car."

Carlo positioned his truck to face Matt's car, and attached his cables to the batteries of both vehicles. "My wife died a year ago and I'm just now getting over feeling sorry for myself." Matt told him about the loss of his parents. After Carlo started his engine, Matt started his own. With both motors running, Carlo removed the jumper cables.

"Before you go," Matt said, "could I ask you what you think about Pastor Boyle? He's going to be my supervisor this year. I don't want to put you on the spot, but I'd appreciate hearing your thoughts, if you know the guy. I met with him, officially, for the first time today."

"I've known Charlie for a long time. He grew up poor. Our families lived in the same neighborhood in Oakland. I'm 15 years older than Charlie, so I also knew his parents and older sister. He loves rubbing elbows with rich people. To me, people are people. Having money doesn't make you happier or better than other people. Charlie thinks having money is important, but he's not a bad guy once you get to know him. What do you think about him?" Carlo asked.

"I don't know him well enough to have any opinions," Matt said. "He seems to like working here at Hacienda. And he appears to be a big

Oakland A's fan. I've been told he's not a very flexible person, so that may present some challenges. We'll see how it goes. Thanks for sharing your thoughts."

"Anytime."

"I'm grateful for your help. I owe you one."

Carlo smiled, opened the door of his truck, and slid in behind the steering wheel. "Stop by and say hello sometime. You take care." Then he waved and drove out of the church parking lot.

Matt sat in his car, waiting for Jancy, with his engine running.

10

Jancy pulled into the Hacienda parking lot as Carlo left. She looked surprised to see Matt in a different car. He left the engine running and walked to her car. She opened her door and stood to greet him. After they kissed, he told her someone had dented his fender. She didn't need to know that the entire driver's side of his car had been destroyed or that he'd almost been killed. When he told her about his battery problem, they decided she would drive them to Angelo's. Before turning off his engine, he confirmed that she had jumper cables in her trunk.

At the restaurant, they chose to sit at the counter in swivel chairs with high, wraparound backs. While waiting for their glasses of Cabernet Sauvignon, they watched the chef and his staff in action in the open kitchen in front of them. For entrees, Jancy chose Fettuccine Alfredo and Matt ordered Chicken Marsala.

Jancy had turned her chair to face Matt when a man entered the restaurant.

"Hey," she said, "There's a familiar face."

Matt turned toward the door. "What a surprise."

Pastor Staley walked to a corner table, where he joined Liz Canfield. Staley wore slacks, a polo shirt, and a v-neck sweater. A waiter delivered two glasses of red wine to their table. They had an animated conversation for about fifteen minutes. At the end, he stood up and left the restaurant. Liz waited a few moments and then followed him outside.

Matt excused himself and went to the window beside the front door. He saw Liz catch up with Staley as he reached his car. They spoke for a few moments. After Staley got into his car, Matt returned to his seat.

"I wonder if Mrs. Staley knows where her husband is this evening?" Matt asked.

"I hope so," Jancy said.

"Staley's meeting with Liz Canfield seems a little unusual."

"Pastor Staley is a busy guy," Jancy said, smiling.

"Yeah," Matt replied. "Larry Rowland may not be the only womanizer at Hacienda Presbyterian."

The meeting between Staley and Liz Canfield, together with the notes about Staley in Pete's journal, raised all kinds of red flags for Matt. He mulled over this information during dinner. The profile emerging of the senior minister both angered and deflated him. If Staley represented the Church's example of the model minister, he wanted no part of it.

Matt told Jancy about Evelyn Kirby's rebuff when he asked for a copy of Staley's resume. Kirby had provided a comprehensive history of Boyle from the church newsletter, but referred Matt to the church's website for Staley's profile. It was brief and dealt mainly with his tenure at Hacienda.

"Mrs. Kirby has worked for Staley during all of his ten years at Hacienda," she said, "and she also worked for him at his previous ministry in La Jolla."

"Is she keeping secrets?"

They sipped a second glass of Cabernet after a leisurely dinner, before ordering dessert. Jancy produced the two newspaper articles about Pete Rockwell--the first one from the *San Francisco Chronicle*, describing his death after falling asleep at the wheel, and the second, more recent one from the *Oakland Tribune*, suggesting a possible homicide involving a driver at Hannifin Trucking. The second article had sparked considerable interest in the East Bay, and the news appeared in other Bay Area newspapers. The connection between the young minister's untimely death and a member of the East Bay's upper crust had ignited the fires of rumor and speculation, especially since the deceased had been an intern at Larry Rowland's church.

Jancy observed that the reopened Rockwell case had been conspicuously absent from the local television news. She and Matt guessed that the Rowlands' law firm had been providing damage control by trying to limit media coverage of the case. Even though Rowland had not been charged with any crime, the law firm wanted to protect his reputation.

"I read another article that cited Kenny Cole's history of drug use, including an arrest several years ago," Jancy said. "It suggested that Cole may have been high on drugs at the time of Pete's death. In the same article, Rowland argued that his company screens for users and doesn't hire anyone who's had any related convictions. And he added that Cole was clean and his record hadn't surfaced at the time of his employment."

"I'd say it's quite a coincidence that the boss of the guy who rear-ended Pete is a member at Hacienda," Matt said.

"I agree."

As Jancy drove Matt to his car after dinner, they heard on the radio that the California Highway Patrol had finally found Kenny Cole that afternoon. He and his girlfriend had rented a motel room near Jackson in the Sierra foothills, 120 miles east of Oakland. Police surrounded the motel and ordered him to come out of his room with his hands up. Cole answered by firing a gun through the window. Shots were exchanged by both sides until the police used tear gas. They discharged canisters through the windows, which filled the room with smoke. Just as the police prepared to break down the door, they heard two shots from inside. Cole and his girlfriend, later identified as Lisa Harkins of Vallejo, lay dead on the floor, victims of an apparent murder/suicide. They found drugs, guns, and ammunition in the room, as well as in his truck. In the report, Cole was connected to the death of Pete Rockwell. The young minister's death was described by the press as a random act resulting from the truck driver's use of drugs. The media conjectured that his drug habit had also clouded his judgment in deciding to battle the police.

In the news report, Larry Rowland issued a statement: "I've been informed by the California Highway Patrol that they found Kenny Cole. I'm sorry to learn that he took his own life, and that his kids have lost their father. While I had no involvement in Cole's murder of Pete Rockwell, Hannifin Trucking's reputation has been negatively impacted by these events. I vow to restore our good name and do a better job of screening our job applicants."

"Too bad they didn't capture Cole alive," Jancy said, "because now we'll never know the full story."

11

Sitting on his living room sofa the next morning, Matt tried to process all of the bad news that had come his way--the deaths of his two predecessors and his own brush with death in front of his apartment.

"At least I'm still alive. Pete and Richard weren't so lucky." Matt looked through the sliding glass door at the clear blue sky. "Could Kenny Cole have targeted Pete or was it simply a coincidence?" The connection between Pete's death and Larry Rowland's trucking company didn't appear to Matt to be accidental. He picked up a lined yellow tablet from the coffee table to make some notes to help clarify his predicament.

"Did Staley know that Pete suspected him of having affairs with women in the church?" The comments in Pete's journal confirmed frequent meetings between Staley and Liz Canfield, as well as with Sally Rowland. "Also, what about the rendezvous between Staley and Liz Canfield at the restaurant? Did Staley hire Cole to murder Rockwell to protect his amorous relationships and frame Larry Rowland at the same time?" If that was Staley's strategy, he had succeeded in focusing attention on Hannifin Trucking and Larry Rowland, in particular. Matt also held suspicions about his supervisor, Charles Boyle, as he continued writing notes. "Did

Boyle know that both Pete and Richard suspected him of financial tricks? Was Richard's drowning an accident, as the police believed, or would an autopsy reveal something else?"

Matt wanted to tell the ministers at the church about his hit-and-run incident, but at this point he didn't trust either of them. "Was Staley or Boyle connected with the person who tried to run me over?"

He found it difficult to believe that Pastor Staley chased women. It appeared so out of character for a man of the cloth to cheat on his wife. "On Sundays in the pulpit, he asks his parishioners to avoid the temptation to sin. He recounts Bible stories that show how destructive it can be to fall away from God's word and violate the Ten Commandments and Jesus' teachings, but is he a hypocrite?"

That afternoon, after spending the morning in his church office, Matt went to the Oakland Public Library, hoping to find anything about the senior minister's past in the *San Diego Union* newspaper prior to his being hired by Hacienda Presbyterian. Initially, he didn't find anything in the rolls of microfiche from eleven years earlier. However, reaching back a dozen years, he found an article titled: "Popular La Jolla Minister Resigns."

The article described Reverend James E. Staley, minister of First Presbyterian Church of La Jolla, who abruptly left his position after seven years at the church. The Session of the church had asked for his resignation after conducting an investigation of an allegation by a woman who claimed Staley had made several passes at her during counseling sessions. Matt sat back in his chair and looked across the room. "This guy has a pattern of predatory behavior. How can someone with his track record continue to find work in a church?" he wondered. "How can he fool so many people?"

In the article, Staley strongly denied the charges. His secretary, Evelyn Kirby, was quoted as saying that she'd been present in an adjoining office during the weeks of counseling sessions and never observed any unprofessional behavior. She said that Staley always left his door ajar when he was counseling, so she could hear much of the conversations.

Since the woman was married to a prominent business executive in San Diego, and both she and her husband had been church members of long standing, it appeared the Session sided with her against Staley's denials. A Presbytery investigation had upheld the Session's decision to terminate his employment. "If Staley had left La Jolla twelve years ago, what had he done during the two years between his departure and his arrival at Hacienda Presbyterian ten years ago?" Matt also wondered how the Hacienda church newsletter, introducing Staley to Hacienda members, had handled the La Jolla skeleton in his closet. Tonight would be a good time to visit the church and read that newsletter, and the sooner the better.

———

Matt drove to San Lucas just before midnight and parked his car several blocks east of the church campus overlooking the bay. It was a warm, balmy evening. He walked past large houses on Hermosa Street on his way to the church office. Overhead, a crescent moon confirmed a clear night, including a sprinkling of stars. Except for an occasional porch light, Matt walked alone in darkness. The affluent hillside enclave of San Lucas, ranked seventy-third on *Fortune* magazine's list of "America's Richest Towns," had rolled up its streets for the night. Matt wore black sweat pants and a dark polo shirt. Tennis shoes muffled the sounds of his steps. He took long strides and hoped he wouldn't meet anyone he knew or who wanted to know what he was doing at that hour.

At the end of the block, he turned left and headed south on Domingo Avenue that ran along the east side of the church campus. Even though he didn't expect any traffic on Buena Vista Drive, which fronted the church on the west side, he chose to approach the church from the rear. He walked to the middle of the block on Domingo, where he could see the dark shapes of the sanctuary, bell tower, and open quadrangle. Avoiding the street lamps on the corners, he crossed the street and entered the campus through an archway. The air was still as he made his way toward the lighted building entrance. He passed the fountain to his left, which was turned off at night. His heart was pounding. A small spotlight beyond the fountain at the far end of the cloister formed a small island of pale yellow on the stone walkway that ringed the inside of the building. On his right, another spotlight above the front doors of the sanctuary illuminated the steps below. Halfway across the courtyard, he stopped. He thought he heard a sound. Matt scanned the entire area to make sure he was alone. Convinced that no one else was there, he proceeded toward the familiar double doors. He fingered the flashlight in his pocket. His collar was damp with perspiration, and his mouth felt dry.

Matt had no trouble finding the keyhole, but his shaking hands made it difficult to insert the key. Finally, he opened the door, turned on his flashlight, and slipped into the stuffy hallway. He made his way down the hall to the church office, which wasn't locked. The room had retained heat from the late afternoon sun. Matt walked behind the counter and looked at three tall filing cabinets along the wall. He would work quickly and leave as soon as possible.

He pointed his flashlight at the filing cabinet on the left, directly behind the receptionist's desk. He would start there. Opening the middle desk drawer, he found some keys. Even though nobody would interrupt him at this hour, sweat ran in rivulets down his cheeks. His conscience told him that he shouldn't be there, but he needed more information about the senior pastor. "Why didn't Mrs. Kirby give me a copy of the newsletter introducing Staley to the congregation, as she had for Boyle?" He felt she had given him the brush-off by referring him to the church's website.

After several attempts, Matt found the key that opened the cabinet. In the second drawer from the top, he found the file he wanted, with the heading "Reverend James E. Staley." He opened it and pulled out the newsletter announcing his arrival as senior pastor. On the cover was a photo of both the pastor and his wife, standing beside the courtyard fountain. Matt didn't see any reference to children in the article. The narrative listed his ministerial positions: three years as a youth minister in Chapel Hill, North Carolina; ten years at Westminster Presbyterian in Wellesley, Massachusetts; six years at Second Presbyterian in Darien, Connecticut; and seven years at First Presbyterian in La Jolla. Matt noted that Staley had attended John Knox Theological Seminary in Richmond, Virginia.

The article mentioned that in between his position in La Jolla and Hacienda, Staley had earned a master's degree in pastoral counseling at the Graduate Theological Union in Berkeley. He earned the degree in two years, and the article said Mrs. Staley had taught in the Berkeley public school system while her husband completed his studies.

Near the end, the article added that Staley had given some well-received sermons at Hacienda as a guest preacher during the previous minister's vacations. When the senior minister at that time, Reverend Stanley Collingwood, announced his retirement after twenty years at Hacienda, Staley had been an early favorite to succeed him. After the pastor-nominating committee reviewed the files of applicants and interviewed a handful of them over a one-year period, Reverend James E. Staley was presented as the top candidate to the congregation, which elected him to be its pastor by a unanimous vote. Nothing was said about Staley's termination from the San Diego church. Hacienda Presbyterian had decided to give him a second chance.

Matt held the newsletter for several moments, remembering what he'd read about Staley at the public library. Finally, he put it back in the file and returned it to the cabinet drawer. About to close the drawer, he heard a noise behind him. The office door opened. Matt's heart rose to his throat. "Who could be entering the church office at this hour?!" Before he could dive for cover, someone shined a flashlight in his face. Matt's knees felt weak and his pulse raced as he waited for the holder of the flashlight to speak. He couldn't see a face behind the bright light. The beam cast a wide path, a little like a searchlight. He felt a wave of heat engulf his body, followed by a shiver down his back.

"Matt, is that you?" asked the man from the other side of the counter.

Matt breathed a big sigh of relief. The voice belonged to Carlo Barone.

"Carlo, I'm sure glad it's you. You really scared me," Matt said.

"What are you doing here at this hour?"

"I just read the *Bell Tower* issue from ten years ago when Staley was hired."

"Matt," Carlo said, "have you been drinking?"

"No, and I don't think Pastor Staley is all that he's cracked up to be."

"What do you mean by that?"

"I'm not exactly sure," Matt said, "because I'm still gathering pieces to the puzzle. But I learned today at the library that Staley was forced to resign from his last church in La Jolla because a woman accused him of making passes at her. Staley appears to have difficulty controlling his interest in the opposite sex."

"You're playing with fire, young man. You shouldn't be snooping around the church office at midnight."

"I can't argue with you, Carlo. Maybe it wasn't such a good idea, after all."

"I don't think Staley and Boyle would be impressed if they knew you'd been in here at this hour going through the office files."

"It doesn't look very good, but I didn't expect anyone else to be here. Isn't it a little late for you, too?"

"This is the night I play cards with some buddies. I live just ten minutes down the freeway, so it's easy for me to drive here after we're finished."

"I'd sure appreciate it if you wouldn't tell anyone I was here tonight."

"Well, you lucked out. I like you, Matt, so I won't tell anyone," Carlo said, "but you weren't planning on taking anything, were you?"

"No. I wanted to see if the newsletter mentioned Staley's ministry in La Jolla."

"Why didn't you ask Mrs. Kirby for the newsletter?"

"I asked her for a copy of Staley's resume, but she referred me to the church's website, which doesn't say much. On the other hand, when I asked for a copy of Boyle's resume, she gave me a copy of the *Bell Tower* from eight years ago that introduced him to the congregation and described his background. I thought she was trying to hide something in Staley's past.

I decided not to ask her for a copy of the newsletter because I didn't want her to think it was important to me."

"So you opted for a little late night adventure," Carlo said.

"I was curious about how the church reported Staley's background," Matt said, "and decided to do my own research. I find Mrs. Kirby to be rather pompous, so I try to limit my interactions with her."

Carlo smiled. "I know what you mean." The custodian's response helped Matt relax.

"I found Pete Rockwell's journal, with some notes that suggest Staley may be having some affairs with women at the church. He may be continuing the same behavior here that he followed at the La Jolla church."

"I find that hard to believe," Carlo said. "In my opinion, Jim Staley isn't what you'd call a ladies' man. I don't think you should spend your time trying to find the goods on Staley. This is a powerful church. The folks here are very proud. Digging up dirt is like playing with dynamite. Staley could end your internship if he learned that you were snooping through the church's files at this hour. I don't want to see you get hurt."

"I hear you loud and clear, but what should I do about stuff I see that doesn't look right? Ignore it?"

"Let's face it, Matt. You don't have any power at this church, so you're not going to be able to change anything in your short time here. I recommend that you do your job, learn about church work, and then take your wisdom with you."

"You make a lot of sense. Do you have a counseling degree?"

"Yeah," he said. "From the school of hard knocks."

"Thanks for the advice," Matt said. "Working in a church can be disturbing. Even scary. I didn't expect the two previous interns to die during my first week on the job. I think their deaths are very strange. Did you read that Pete may have been run off the highway?"

"Yes. I don't know what to think at this point, but I know how you must feel. You've had to deal with some tough news the past two weeks. It's warm in here. Let's go over in my office and have a Coke. It sounds like you have a lot on your mind. I'll bet you never expected someone to walk in tonight and shine a flashlight on you. Kind of worried you, right?"

"Big time! I didn't know who you were!"

After Carlo emptied three wastebaskets, he pulled his cart out of the office and pushed it down the hall as the two of them walked toward the custodian's office by the gym, on the other side of the quadrangle. As Carlo opened his office door, Matt saw that the overhead light was on. The older man motioned for him to sit in the padded easy chair in front of his desk, while he reached into a small refrigerator and pulled out two cans.

"What a good idea," Matt said. "I'm thirsty."

Carlo handed one to Matt and sat down behind the desk. "You're pretty lucky it was me who came in with the flashlight and not the cops. They patrol this neighborhood at night, you know. They have keys to the church like I do."

"I know I'm lucky," Matt said. "What I did was risky."

"As I told you, I don't usually do my chores at midnight. After we drink these Cokes, I want you to get out of here."

"Gladly," Matt said. They sat there in silence for several moments before he spoke again. "Richard Finley told me he believed someone is stealing from the church."

"Matt," Carlo said, "you seminarians think too much."

"I'm not kidding you. Richard suspected someone on the staff, like Pastor Boyle!"

"Listen," Carlo said, "Finley was a nice young man, but he was a small-town boy in a big-time church. To be perfectly honest with you, he was a fish out of water. He was a square peg in a round hole."

"Well," Matt said, "I believe he found something that troubled him. He suggested that we have dinner to discuss it, and the next thing I know he drowns in Lake Chabot."

"Finley preached a sermon last year about Satan that really stirred people up. Some members are still talking about it. They said he sounded like Elmer Gantry, some raving evangelist. Fire and brimstone. Hard to believe those kind of words could come from such a little guy."

"Maybe the church needed to hear a sermon like that. Richard was an excellent student at the seminary. I think he was passionate about his faith."

"I think the deaths of Rockwell and Finley have wound you up a little," Carlo said. "That's understandable. This church isn't much different from other churches, though. It's made up of people with feet of clay. The ministers aren't such bad guys. They don't walk on water, but they're both men with good intentions. Staley likes books and travel, and Boyle likes the theater and the A's. They're doing the best they can. Working here is like being in a pressure-cooker. It isn't easy. You'll see."

"You know the ministers much better than I do," Matt said. "I guess I was expecting them to be perfect, which isn't realistic or fair."

"You need to cool it. Do your job and do it well, get to know as many members as you can, and keep your opinions to yourself. Work at Hacienda for nine months, and see if your first impressions change."

"That's good advice," Matt said.

"Now take that last sip of Coke and be on your way. I won't tell anyone you were playing detective tonight, but you've got to promise me something. No more monkey business. You hear me?!"

Matt rose, walked around the desk, and put his hand on Carlo's shoulder. "Thanks. I really appreciate your friendship, and I'm glad we had this talk."

12

The next day was Friday, which meant an evening basketball game for Matt at the Hayward YMCA. A good workout would serve as a helpful distraction from the stressful events of the past week. Although he felt some residual soreness from the hit-and-run incident three days earlier, it wouldn't cause him to miss the game.

Playing basketball had always provided Matt with a welcome diversion from school and work, and he enjoyed getting to know the other players. Once the game began, time passed quickly, and Matt's team defeated its opponent with relative ease. He made a high percentage of his shots and left the court satisfied. Teammates congratulated each other in the locker room through friendly banter and harmless braggadocio.

"Hey, Matt," said a burly young man named Tom Dawson. "Want to go have a beer with some of us at the Green Parrot?" Standing six feet tall and built like a fire hydrant, he made up for his lack of finesse on the court with a fierce appetite for rebounding that had gained Matt's admiration. While most of the players on the team had little interest in rebounding, Tom Dawson thrived on it. From Matt's perspective, Tom would play an important role in competing for the league championship.

Having a drink together after a game allowed players to continue bonding with one another. It would also add some companionship to what remained of Matt's evening. His other option involved returning in his apartment by himself, which didn't appeal to him on a Friday night.

"Who's going?" Matt asked.

"Kevin and Sean will probably be there," Tom answered.

"Okay," Matt said. "Is someone driving or should we meet there?"

"I'm driving. You can come with me. The others will meet us at the Parrot."

"How long are you planning to stay?"

"No more than an hour, maybe an hour and a half. Have a few beers, shoot some pool, throw some darts. They have some real babes waiting tables. I'll bring you back to your car."

"Let's do it," Matt said. He and Tom left the locker room and headed toward the Y lobby. Once outside, Matt followed Tom to his Chevy pickup.

The men's basketball league had just started, but Matt relished the camaraderie among his diverse group of new teammates. They had just defeated another team by eleven points, and he now knew they had some talented players. The team's victory raised their spirits as the teammates exited the building. Kevin and Sean, the two starting guards, boasted to each other about how many points they had scored. Someone seeing the chemistry between the two players might have assumed they'd played together for a season or more. In reality, they and the others had never seen each other before the season began. Tom Dawson had been added to the team after the season started, missing the first game.

As he pulled out of the Y parking lot, Tom turned up the music on the radio while driving quickly through the central business district toward the silent streets of Hayward's warehouse section along the waterfront. Passing the low buildings, Matt thought about the diversity among his teammates. They represented a wide variety of work, from dentist and software designer to the construction trades. Tom told Matt that he built houses, and he had the right physique for it.

Matt simply wanted to keep playing a sport he enjoyed, and he liked his teammates. He possessed a proficient skill and had nothing to prove. Because the players had such a broad range of attitudes and abilities, he'd wondered as the season began if his team might have some difficulty jelling as a unit. However, tonight they had played with remarkable teamwork. As the team's tallest, Matt assumed the position of center, although he'd been a forward in college.

Night engulfed Tom's truck as they left the lights of downtown Hayward and reached the waterfront--the city's daytime center of commerce, where shipping and trucking converged to transport manufactured goods from northern California to other destinations. A noisy and bustling neighborhood from sunup to sundown, it became dark and deserted at night. As Tom's truck rounded a dark corner, a lime green neon sign outlining a parrot flashed from its perch over the tavern's door.

"Here we are," Tom said. "I'm ready!" Matt couldn't tell if his teammate's comment referred to drinking beer or ogling the waitresses, or something else. Matt gave him a sidelong look.

The Green Parrot Bar & Grill occupied a long, narrow building astride one of the piers reaching into the bay. It had a gray metal roof and faded, green wood siding. Before it had become the home of the Green Parrot, the building had been a warehouse that stored electronic equipment, such as computers and copiers, phones and fax machines, all imported from the Pacific Rim.

On the piers to the south, a row of darkened warehouses lay in shadows. A couple of piers to the north supported a large, crowded parking lot twice as wide as the Green Parrot. Tonight, the place appeared to be packed. Tom pulled slowly into the parking lot and stopped for a moment, looking for an empty slot.

"I'll drive around the loop. I'll bet I can find us a place."

As Tom drove the truck forward between rows of cars, he suddenly accelerated, heading toward the end of the pier.

"Hey!" Matt said. "You'd better slow down! You won't make the turn!"

Tom looked straight ahead and said, "Maybe not."

"What are you doing?!" Matt said.

The pickup burst through the picket fence bordering the parking area along the edge of the pier. Tom leaned forward and covered his face with his arms. Fear gripped Matt as he felt the front of the truck point downwards. His body stiffened as he pressed his feet hard against the floorboard.

As the front of the vehicle struck the water, Matt's head hit the dashboard and he lost consciousness. Tom quickly pulled himself through the open driver's window as the truck started to sink. None of the windows had shattered upon impact, but that didn't keep water from pouring into the cab through the driver's window. Darkness enveloped the pickup, except for glints from the headlights that sent tubes of light into the inky water. The surroundings became increasingly dark as the truck plunged toward the bottom of the bay. No plants or fish lived under these piers. The industrial waterfront of Hayward was not a friendly place for marine life.

Matt awoke a few seconds later, confused, icy water rising above his knees. He couldn't see anything. His heart raced, and terror gripped him. He wondered what drowning must have been like for Richard, and now it was happening to him! "Why did Tom do this?"

The truck started to roll on its right side. The total lack of light had disoriented him. He reached for the empty driver's seat and, like a blind man, touched the dash board and the passenger's window. Panicking, he pushed against his door, while raising the handle. The door didn't move. "How did Tom get out so quickly?" Matt extended his hand toward the driver's window to feel the water rushing into the cab, and he realized his best escape would be through the opening Tom had used. The water surging through the driver's window would make it difficult to exit that way, but it appeared to be his only choice.

By now the chilly salt water had reached his chest. He took a couple of deep breaths and unhooked his seat belt. Fighting against the water's force would consume his energy, so he decided to wait until the cab had filled with water. Once the water pressure outside the truck reached equilibrium, he reasoned, it might be easier to escape through the opening.

Waiting to make his move, he struggled to stay composed because with every second the truck sank deeper in the bay.

As the truck listed to the right, heading toward the bottom of the bay, Matt wondered how deep he had sunk. The longer he waited for the cab to fill, the farther upward he would have to swim to reach the surface. "Will I be able to hold my breath long enough?"

Grabbing the steering wheel, he pulled himself up toward the high side of the tilted truck, straining against the onrushing water. Standing on the passenger door with the water up to his shoulders, he held onto the driver's window frame. The water continued to flow into the cab, making it difficult to gain his balance. He needed to move now.

Too late to remove his shirt and jeans, he stepped on the backs of his tennis shoes to free his feet. With his body pressed against the listing truck's rear window, now perpendicular to the bottom of the Bay, he breathed a prayer, took a final gasp of air, and pulled himself upward through the open window and into the cold darkness.

Matt implored, "God help me!" He thrust his hands upward and then pulled them down to his sides, trying to propel himself through the water in his race to the surface. "I can make it to the top," he coached himself as he ascended, his arms continuing their sweeping motions, his legs moving like the blades of a pair of scissors.

Pulling and kicking his way upward against the drag of his clothes, he opened his eyes, searching for light above, but saw nothing but black. His lungs began to burn, his arms ached. He needed a breath of air. One more breath was all he needed. Legs pumping, he had to reach the air above with what he had in his lungs. Straining, after what seemed like forever, he started to expel his breath because he couldn't hold it any longer. He feared he was losing this race.

But he was wrong. Matt's hands and head finally burst through the water's surface, and he sucked in air, taking deep, frantic breaths. He'd been saved.

Shouting came from a small crowd on the pier above, but he couldn't understand what they were saying. A flashlight shone in his direction. A lifebuoy attached to a long rope landed near him. Matt floated lightheaded and weak on his back and filled his aching lungs with the cool night air. Numbness gripped him. His ears were ringing and he was losing consciousness when someone grabbed him. The rescuer put his arm around his chest and supported his head with his shoulder. Holding Matt firmly, he gripped the lifebuoy with his other hand. Others on the pier dragged them to a ladder. As they reached it, Matt could hear cheering, then a siren in the distance. Matt thought of the time he retrieved Richard, but tonight someone was rescuing him. The young man placed the lifebuoy over his head and lowered it below his shoulders to his chest, and Matt struggled to climb the ladder while people above used the rope to pull him up to safety. His rescuer followed, pushing him from below.

Reaching the top of the ladder, two medics laid him down on a portable stretcher and covered him with a blanket. After checking his vital signs to make sure he was stable, the medics took him to the aid car where they continued their examination, but Matt had passed out—from exhaustion, fear, relief, and exertion like he'd never known.

He woke up minutes later in the Emergency Room of Hayward General Hospital. The ER physician told him that he had a mild case of hypothermia, and a nurse mentioned the lump on his forehead. Besides his shock and trauma, Matt knew he'd almost died. He was grateful for having escaped from the sinking truck and for the people who'd rescued him. Apart from some cuts and bruises, he hadn't suffered any serious physical injuries. He had survived, but he asked himself: "Why had Tom done something so crazy?"

Eventually, two police officers appeared at his bedside. One of them held a sheet of paper. "According to the hospital, the name on your driver's license says Matthew C. Beringer. Is that right?"

"Yes," Matt responded.

"What were you trying to do tonight, Mr. Beringer?" the officer asked.

"I was going to the Green Parrot for a beer with a teammate, after our basketball game at the Hayward Y."

"How did your truck end up in the bay?" the officer continued.

"First of all, it isn't my truck," Matt said. "We turned into the parking lot, and then Tom, the driver, accelerated and crashed through the fence."

"So you weren't the driver?"

"No. I was riding with Tom. Tom Dawson. I told you. We play on a basketball team at the Y. I was in his truck."

"Were there any other passengers?"

"No, just the two of us."

"So you say the other guy was the driver?"

"Yes."

"Well, that's interesting because we think the truck may have been stolen today in Oakland. Tom Dawson is not the owner."

"What do you mean?"

"A guy in the parking lot got the license number as you drove off the pier. We've tracked it to a truck that was reported missing today by the owner."

"That's incredible."

"Where do you live?"

"San Leandro, but my car's back at the Hayward Y. You can ask my teammates. You can also talk to Roy Waite, who runs the Y."

"We'll do that."

"If this Tom Dawson was driving the truck," the second officer said, "what happened to him?"

"He got out right away, I think. I don't know. I never saw him again. I hit my head on the dash board and blacked out momentarily, I guess. When I woke up, he was gone."

"What do you do for a living, Mr. Beringer."

"I'm a student at Calvin Seminary in San Francisco, but this year I'm doing an internship at Hacienda Presbyterian in San Lucas."

"Witnesses have verified that there were two of you in the vehicle," the second officer continued. "Right now, we have you as the possible driver of a stolen truck. We'll leave it at that until we speak to Mr. Dawson."

Matt stared at the officer. The evening was taking on a weird quality.

"Well, I didn't steal the truck, if that's what you're suggesting. And I wasn't driving. I drive a Honda Accord," Matt said somewhat louder than he'd intended, "and it's parked at the Hayward Y right now. Go check. I don't know anything about a stolen truck. You can call the Y. Tom and I play on the same basketball team. Like I said, ask Roy Waite. You can also call Pastor Staley, the senior minister at Hacienda Presbyterian, and my friend, Detective Ben Miller of the Oakland Police Department. They'll verify my identity."

He sank back against the pillow and looked through the window on the opposite wall. He never imagined that his internship would involve any danger. He rather imagined it might become downright boring at times. Now he was suspected of driving a stolen vehicle. After the hit-and-run incident the other night and tonight's plunge into the bay, he'd had enough excitement to last a lifetime.

Before his internship, Matt had never been interviewed by the police, and this made it three times in two weeks—at Richard's drowning, the hit-and-run, and tonight.

During the police questioning, the first officer, the one taking all of the notes, had stepped aside to call Pastor Staley, who confirmed Matt's position at the church. When he returned, he said they would be leaving. The officers were satisfied for the time being, but he was informed they would have more questions once they found Tom Dawson. As they left his room, he was told he must not leave the San Francisco Bay Area.

The police said they had no proof that Tom Dawson had been the driver of the stolen truck. That alarmed Matt. On top of that, his character was being scrutinized.

The attending physician wanted Matt to spend a couple of hours in the ER before being released. Exhausted, he fell asleep. When he opened his eyes a few hours later, his supervisor stood next to his bed.

"Pastor Boyle," Matt said. "Fancy meeting you here."

"I admire your sense of adventure, Beringer," Boyle said. "Are you finding your work at the church a little dull?"

Matt laughed.

"They told me you took a wrong turn," Boyle said, "and wound up in the San Francisco Bay. If you keep this up, my next visit to see you might be at the morgue. It's too late to find a replacement for you, Beringer. I want you to complete your internship with us."

"One of my basketball teammates from the Y suggested going for a beer at the Green Parrot after the game. Instead, he drove off the end of the pier. He must have been on drugs or something. I almost drowned."

"I'm glad to see you survived," Boyle said, smiling. "Show me your friends and I'll show you your future. In light of your near-fatal mishap tonight, you might want to find a new group of friends."

"I didn't know the guy very well," Matt said, "and the swim in the bay wasn't my idea." He then recounted the evening's events to Boyle. The panic he felt in the sinking truck was still with him.

"You look like you'll make it, Beringer, and I'm glad of that. Take it easy tomorrow, but you have things to do on Sunday morning." As he left the room, he turned and said, with a slight smile, "The next time you try something like this, make it an evening when Pastor Staley's on call, will you?"

Two hours later, an ER nurse reported to Matt that he'd received his discharge from the hospital. She brought him his wallet, jeans, and other dry clothing, and he dressed in the bathroom. Matt's watch said a little after midnight. He had to return to his car two miles away in the parking lot of the Hayward Y. The nurse called a taxi for him, compliments of the hospital. After waiting a few minutes in the lobby, he left the hospital and walked to his chauffeur in the bright yellow car with the light on top, who drove away into the night.

13

Before starting his internship, Matt had arranged to take a few days off in September to visit his aunt and uncle in Spokane. Since the day at Lake Chabot, he'd wanted to add one more visit to his itinerary—a meeting with Richard's mother, Mrs. Carol Finley, who lived in Coeur d'Alene, Idaho, thirty-four miles east of Spokane on Interstate 90.

Matt had booked his Sunday flight weeks in advance, but he called the Hayward police the day after his incident at the Green Parrot to ask for permission to leave the area. He learned that they no longer suspected him of driving or stealing the truck. He was free to travel. During the conversation, he asked if they'd located Tom Dawson, and was told that they wouldn't disclose information relating to an ongoing investigation.

Then he called Jancy to tell her about his swim in the bay before she read about it in the *Tribune*. She was relieved to learn he was safe. He promised to call her when he returned on Tuesday afternoon.

Detective Miller also needed to hear about his incident at the pier, so Matt left a lengthy message on Miller's voicemail.

His fourth call was to Mrs. Finley. After introducing himself, he asked if he could visit her on Monday to express his condolences in person. She agreed to meet at ten in the morning, but he sensed she wasn't pleased to hear from him. She spoke in a monotone, and he could barely hear her. Had she received the results of the autopsy?

———

On Sunday afternoon, following his morning responsibilities, Matt caught an Alaska Airlines' flight on a Boeing 737 from Oakland to Spokane. It had been just over a week since Richard's drowning, five days since the hit-and-run incident, and two days since his plunge into the San Francisco Bay. He was ready for a change of scenery.

Renting a car at the airport, Matt drove to his aunt and uncle's home and arrived in time for dinner: barbecued, rib-eye steaks. His aunt had already told him what was on the menu. Since his parents' deaths, this was the second September trip Matt had made to visit his Aunt Ellen and Uncle Cal Beringer. They had reached out to him, trying to help fill the sudden void in his life, and he was grateful for their efforts.

Aunt Ellen had taken up golf in her early fifties and, after a couple of years, won trophies as a member of the Hidden Lake Golf & Country Club outside of Spokane. She freely admitted that her love of golf surpassed her interest in housekeeping, although to Matt's eyes the house looked perfectly tidy. Uncle Cal, age fifty-five and ten years away from retirement as a manufacturers sales rep, liked to talk about the day he would play more golf with his wife. Another of his passions was barbecuing on the backyard patio, and steaks were his specialty.

As a boy, Matt and his parents would spend a couple of weeks every August vacationing at Aunt Ellen and Uncle Cal's home. Matt would tag along with his older cousins, Roger and Paul, who liked to crank up the family's powerful Mercury outboard motor on a sixteen-foot boat for water skiing outings on nearby Lake Coeur d'Alene. The three of them spent long summer days under the sun, traversing the large lake. He missed those days.

When Matt knocked on the front door, his Aunt Ellen opened it with a big smile. "Hi there, Reverend," she said and held out her arms. Matt bent down to embrace her, kissing her cheek. As he glanced around the living room, he saw that nothing had changed from his last visit.

Aunt Ellen said. "I'm so happy to see you, Matt! Take your things to the back bedroom. Cal will be home in no time, and I know he'll also want a blow-by-blow description of what you're up to these days."

In no time, Uncle Cal burst in the door and gave Matt a big hug. "Hey, Matt, wait until you see the steaks I brought home. We're glad you could spend a few days with us."

"It's great to see you."

"There's an opening for a minister at a Presbyterian church just a mile away," Cal said, as he stood in the kitchen and prepared the marinade for the steaks. "I hope you'll think about Spokane when you start to look for a position."

"I'm about a year away from that step. Finding a church here would be perfect, but I'm not completely sure I'll enter the ministry. This internship year should help me answer that question."

The three of them enjoyed a glass of Merlot on the patio of the Beringers' comfortable home on Spokane's South Hill. Then Cal tied on his barbecue apron, brought the steaks outside, and started the gas barbecue. The patio temperature hovered in the mid-seventies, the gift of an Indian summer, so they could eat outside on the warm September evening.

"Since I'm not a good cook," Matt said, "I'm finding some interesting restaurants in the Bay Area. Everything from Mexican to Indian cuisine, but steaks are my favorite, and nobody does them better than you, Uncle Cal."

"Your uncle isn't a big fan of spicy food," Aunt Ellen said.

Cal smiled. "I judge restaurants by the size of their dessert menus."

"I have to hide the desserts around here," she said, smiling.

Shortly after dinner, Uncle Cal excused himself and went straight to bed. His uncle's disappearing act following an evening meal always amused

Matt. By contrast, his own parents had been night owls, staying up to hear the eleven o'clock news. Matt told Aunt Ellen about his morning meeting with Mrs. Finley, but didn't mention the recent death of her son or his own encounters with near misses.

As Matt helped his aunt clear the table, he wondered what he would learn once he arrived in Coeur d'Alene. If there had been an autopsy, he hoped Mrs. Finley might share the findings with him.

———

The next morning, he headed on the freeway toward his destination just over the Idaho border. The municipality where Mrs. Finley lived appeared occasionally in his crossword puzzles that asked for the name of a town with an apostrophe. Interstate 90 connects Seattle to Spokane, Coeur d'Alene, and Boston, covering a distance of 3,020 miles, making it the longest Interstate Highway in the U.S. Today, however, Matt had no interest in a road trip. Not long after entering Idaho, he saw the city-center exit.

Matt drove along a boulevard that guided visitors to the central business district on the lakeshore. From there Matt headed north, following Mrs. Finley's directions, away from the lake and shops, toward the residential neighborhoods. Mrs. Finley lived at 368 Cedar Street, a couple of blocks to the east of Government Way, the street on which his dad had grown up. It didn't take Matt long to find her modest home, which looked similar to the saltbox design of his grandparents' house. Everything felt familiar. A porch ran across the front of the two-story residence.

His watch said nine fifty-eight. Matt rang the doorbell and waited several moments until the door opened and a small lady with graying hair looked out.

"Mrs. Finley?" he asked.

"Hello, Mr. Beringer. I've been expecting you. Please come in."

Through the screen door, Matt saw a woman who looked much older than her age. Her eyes looked red, and her pale, hollow cheeks revealed deep creases. "Did the wrinkles confirm too many hours in the sun or a more serious health condition?" She wore her hair short. Her green cardigan harmonized with the colors in her plaid dress. She motioned him into the front hallway. As he opened the screen door, he noticed that she wore faded blue canvas deck shoes.

Stepping inside, he paused and then followed her into the living room. In one corner, numerous framed family photographs filled the top of a table, while others sat on the mantle over the fireplace. The upholstery on the furniture looked worn, and the walls needed a new coat of paint.

Mrs. Finley sat in a cushioned rocking chair directly in front of the television, and asked Matt to sit next to her on the sofa. Curtains covered the windows, so she had turned on a stand lamp by her chair to brighten the room. He glanced at *Sunset* and *Better Homes & Gardens* magazines on the coffee table in front of him, before he met her gaze.

"I heard you tried to save my Richard, Mr. Beringer," she said in a tired but steady voice. "The police told me."

"Yes, I did. Please call me Matt." He paused. "I feel so badly about your loss, Mrs. Finley."

"I'm still in a state of shock. It doesn't seem possible."

"I can't understand how it happened. There was hardly any wind that day. Richard was an expert sailor. Something doesn't feel right about it."

"It was no accident." She looked around the room and her eyes found Richard's photograph on the mantle, and she held them there for a long moment. "According to the coroner, my son was poisoned."

Matt felt the blood rush from his face. He tried to gather his thoughts.

"I wondered about that possibility. That's frightening news."

"The police asked me to keep the autopsy results to myself while they investigate Richard's death, so I probably shouldn't have told you."

"I'm grateful you did because it didn't make sense to me. Now I know how it happened."

"Every day since I learned of his death I cry here in front of the TV, looking at a black screen, and I can't stop crying. Why would anyone want to murder my Richard?"

She looked to Matt as if for an explanation.

106

"He said he was bringing lunch," Matt said, "and asked me and our friend, Jancy, to join him on the sail. We weren't able to go sailing with him, but we planned to have dinner that evening. I honestly can't imagine who would have poisoned his food. He said he was planning to visit friends in San Lucas before his sail…, but it seems unlikely that they would have added the poison."

"Who are the friends he visited?" she asked briskly.

"He didn't say," Matt said.

"Why would someone poison him? I'm overwhelmed." She twisted her hands together and softly pounded them on her lap as if to knock the thoughts away.

"I don't understand it, either."

Her voice raised. "What's going on at that church?" Her eyes pleaded with Matt to explain.

"This is what I know. Richard told me he suspected someone of stealing. We were going to discuss his concerns over dinner, after his sail."

"Richard thought it might be his supervisor, Pastor Boyle."

"He told me the same thing. Maybe Pastor Boyle or someone else knew that Richard suspected foul play, and he was murdered because he knew too much."

Mrs. Finley slowly shook her head.

"I know it's hard to believe," Matt said, "but it could be someone at the church." He studied Mrs. Finley's face for a moment. Her eyes filled with tears, and she reached for a Kleenex.

"Someone at the church would murder my son?" she asked.

"It's very troubling," he said. "I never dreamed something like this could happen," Matt said. "Did Richard talk about his relationship with Pastor Boyle?"

"He never felt very close to him," she said, "and his suspicions didn't help their relationship. Richard said Pastor Boyle seemed more interested in outside activities than in youth programs. They didn't have much in common."

"I also find it difficult to relate to Pastor Boyle," Matt said, "and if I believed he was stealing from the church, that would be very disillusioning."

"I hope the police can find some answers. Richard was troubled by the financial reports. He thought something was wrong with the church's money management."

"I plan to do some investigating as well, and I'll let you know if I discover something." He took her hand for a moment.

"Where did you grow up?" she asked.

"In Seattle…, but my parents were killed in a car accident two years ago. I'm an only child, so I decided to sell my parents' home because it had too many memories. Since then, I've been living at the seminary. My future home will be where I go after graduation."

"I'm so sorry to hear about your parents," she said. "You and I have suffered great losses, haven't we?"

"Yes, we have." He released her hand. They sat in silence for a few moments before he spoke again. "Losing Richard must be so hard for you. He was going to be an outstanding minister."

"He was my pride and joy."

"I attended Richard's memorial service at Calvin Seminary last Friday morning."

"I'm sorry I couldn't attend the service, but I just don't have the energy to travel these days. My health isn't what I'd like it to be."

"I really appreciate the opportunity to visit with you."

Mrs. Finley sat in her chair, hands folded in her lap.

"When I was younger," Matt said, "I learned to waterski with my older cousins on the lake. My dad grew up here, over at 152 Government Way, and I remember coming with my parents to visit my grandparents."

"Were you and Richard good friends at the seminary?"

"No, I'm afraid we didn't know each other very well. He was a year ahead of me. We didn't take any classes together and lived in separate dorms, so our paths never seemed to cross. However, we had a good conversation recently at the seminary and were fast becoming friends. I only learned a few months ago that he was an outstanding sailor."

"It's a shame you two didn't get to know each other," she said.

"Maybe I can help find his murderer. The congregation is devastated by what has happened."

Mrs. Finley dabbed her eyes with a Kleenex. "I knew your grandparents. My husband and I bought this house from them over twenty years ago."

"What a small world," Matt said. "I remember my dad saying that his parents owned a considerable amount of real estate here."

"Your grandfather was a fine man," Mrs. Finley continued. "He was a town leader, even mayor for a couple of terms. Your grandmother was quiet, but she was devoted to her three children and was a good neighbor, too. We rented this house from them for several years and then asked if they'd sell it to us. It was a very happy day for us when they agreed to our offer."

Matt remembered the day his dad returned home to Seattle from his father's funeral in Coeur d'Alene. He came walking along the sidewalk from the bus stop several blocks away. Unclear as to why his father had been away from home for a couple of days, Matt saw a sadness in his eyes as he came closer. Surprised to see him walking instead of driving the family car, he had simply waved at him and continued playing football with the neighbor kids.

He didn't know what to do that day at age nine, but, with more maturity, he would have rushed to his father's side, put his arm around his waist, and walked home with him. Later, when he asked his mother about his father's return, she told him about his grandfather's passing. Matt felt small and helpless in the face of such an overwhelming event from which his parents wanted to shield him.

"What drew Richard to the ministry?"

"Richard became close to our pastor, and I think that friendship influenced his interest in becoming a minister. I lost my husband when Richard was eleven, and our pastor filled an important void in my son's life. I was very pleased when Richard told me he wanted to attend seminary. He majored in accounting in college. His dad was an accountant at the local lumber mill, and Richard was very good at math."

"He definitely had an interest in church finance," Matt said. He sat there looking at this frail woman who had lost her husband and now her son. "Did Richard enjoy Calvin Seminary?"

"He loved it," she said. "He liked the class work and felt that ministry was what God wanted him to do. But he was on the quiet side, and Hacienda Presbyterian may not have been the right place for him. Richard grew up in our small neighborhood church around the corner. He was very good with people, one-to-one, but was more reserved in large groups. However, the Education Committee at Hacienda wanted Richard to give sailing lessons to the middle school students, and he jumped at the chance. He thought an internship that included sailing would be a wonderful experience."

"I felt the same way when I read they were looking for an intern to organize a basketball program for the middle school kids," Matt said.

"Richard thought his interview at the church didn't go very well, but they chose him anyway. He was surprised, but happy."

Matt and each of his forty-six classmates could apply for three internships at Bay Area churches, and he had ranked Hacienda Presbyterian as his first choice. The Education Committee had chosen him from among twelve other classmates who had applied for the position. It appeared that the church had recently favored seminarians with athletic skills.

"Did you ever talk to Richard about his sailing program?" Matt asked.

"Yes," Mrs. Finley said with a faint smile. "He told me that ten to fifteen kids would attend his weekly sailing classes, and he felt good about their progress. I believe they sailed on Wednesday evenings. I think the church was pleased with his work. At the end of his internship, I received a very nice letter from Pastor Staley."

"I thought Richard's drowning was suspicious, given his sailing skills."

"Richard loved sailing, especially the mental side of it. Man against nature. Racing competitively in college was a thrill for him. He'd calculate how he could get his boat to perform to its maximum potential."

"He had a positive impact on those middle school kids, and I think he would have been a wonderful pastor."

"When you asked to meet with me, I didn't understand why you were interested in my son," she said. "But you've shown me that you care about people."

"I liked your son," Matt said, "and I'm so sorry he was taken from us."

"Richard wasn't happy at Hacienda Presbyterian, but he was determined to finish his internship. I think he would have been happier in a smaller church." Mrs. Finley leaned forward. "I wish you luck with your investigation. And I pray the police can find the person who murdered my son."

"Could I call you again if I have a question?"

"Call me any time," she replied. "And thank you for caring about Richard. I'm so weighed down by losing him that I've run out of strength."

"I'll be working for both of us to find some answers."

"I'm glad we had this conversation," Mrs. Finley said. "You take good care of yourself. I'll be praying for you."

"Thanks."

"I love remembering my Richard. He's never far from my thoughts. His murder is so shocking. I want to help the police, but I don't know what to do. If you learn anything, will you please call me?"

"I will."

"You'll be a good minister. I can see that about you."

"We'll see where God leads me this year. Thanks again for meeting with me," Matt said. "You are not alone in losing your son. The members at Hacienda and the seminary community grieve with you."

Matt slowly rose from his chair. As they walked toward the front door, he put his arm around Mrs. Finley's shoulder. He hugged her in a way he hoped conveyed his deep concern for her well-being.

14

After returning to Oakland on Tuesday afternoon, Matt called Detective Miller and told him Richard Finley had been poisoned. The autopsy results confirmed to Miller that both murders were planned. He thought the deaths of Rockwell and Finley, so close together, were more than a coincidence, and he told Matt to be careful. Matt's second call was to Jancy to invite her to have coffee with him the next morning. They agreed to meet at nine-thirty in Berkeley.

———

Jancy was waiting in a corner booth when he entered the bakery. He gave her a kiss, and then settled into the seat facing her. "Do I have some news for you," Matt said. "Mrs. Finley told me Richard was poisoned."

"Wow!" Jancy said. "That changes everything, doesn't it? Pete's death doesn't look like such a random event, and it increases the odds that the two deaths are connected."

"And it means we have a murderer running loose in the East Bay."

"You were definitely a target in the truck last Friday night, and I'm worried about your safety."

"So am I."

After an hour's conversation over coffee, they agreed to have dinner together the following evening. Matt had heard about a restaurant in Walnut Creek featuring Spanish cuisine, and they both thought it sounded interesting. Outside on the sidewalk, they parted with a kiss, and Matt drove south on the Nimitz Freeway to his apartment. He was happy to be back in the East Bay, spending time with Jancy, but he worried about how and when the killer would strike again.

Nobody from the Hayward Police Department had called him about Tom Dawson and their investigation into the incident at the pier. He also wondered if the San Leandro Police had learned anything about the hit-and-run accident in front of his apartment. His life had been threatened twice.

Staring at the traffic in front of him, Matt thought about the lesson he had to prepare for Sunday. He felt his work at the church was having positive results, recalling the first worship service he led three days before. Thirty-nine students packed the chapel, almost twice the number Boyle had predicted. Matt was pleased with the turnout, since he worried that the deaths of his two predecessors might reduce interest in the middle school program. On the other hand, the upcoming basketball leagues may have stimulated interest. Matt reminded himself that he shouldn't equate program success with attendance, but the level of student participation was encouraging. In the days preceding, Matt had called the parents of the fifty-five students on his roster to introduce himself and discuss the Sunday school curriculum for the year, as well as his plans to organize the boys' and girls' basketball leagues.

After the chapel service, four different classes had met upstairs, in rooms down the hall from his office. Matt taught one of them, using the new curriculum. The three volunteer teachers seemed pleased with the way their kids had responded to the first lesson.

As he sped along the freeway, Matt's thoughts returned to the attempts on his life. "Does someone think I know too much? Reviewing the church's financial records needs to be my next priority," he said to himself. He would ask Mrs. Kirby for the past ten annual reports. His goal would be to prove or disprove Richard's belief that there was a thief at the church. Perhaps he would uncover a clue, such as a suspicious pattern or trend in the numbers. By comparing and contrasting figures in the budgets, along with expenses and receipts, he might identify a smoking gun. Finding a problem would expose a sensitive, even criminal issue.

Before going to the church, he paid a quick visit to his apartment to check the mail. Matt had a fifteen-minute commute to and from Hacienda. It was a wise choice to move to the East Bay and eliminate the long trip from the seminary in San Francisco. Pastor Staley, on the other hand, had a shorter commute. He lived in lower San Lucas and needed only a few minutes to reach the church. Matt had heard from a church member that the Session wanted Staley to live in the community where he worked, not in an adjacent town. Perhaps the Session had arranged the financing to make that possible. Living in San Lucas would not be affordable for most ministers. He learned that Pastor Boyle lived in a garden apartment in nearby San Lorenzo.

Matt parked his car in the church parking lot and walked toward the office. Autumn brought a coolness to the air in the Bay Area that signaled a change of seasons. He preferred the warmer summer months. Approaching the doors to the building, he waved at Carlo Barone, who was mowing the lawn around the fountain.

Opening the door, Matt looked into the long, dimly-lighted hallway. After his eyes adjusted to the corridor, he walked toward command central. As he entered Mrs. Kirby's domain, he saw a wave of natural light filtering into the office from the bank of windows. Because of the overcast sky, Mrs. Kirby had dared to open the curtains. He was stunned that she had taken his earlier suggestion.

Matt leaned on the office counter. "How's your day going, Mrs. Kirby?"

She sat in her office, with the door open. "Just fine. I'll bet you're surprised I've opened the curtains. The sun isn't so bright today."

"Your views are spectacular. They could distract you from your work."

"Not when the curtains are closed."

"I have a favor to ask. I'm trying to get acquainted with the church, so I'd like to borrow the last ten annual reports. I won't need them for more than a week."

"You should try to focus on today and tomorrow, Mr. Beringer. The past won't help you in your work here." She rose and walked to a filing cabinet outside her office. Pulling out a drawer, she explained, "I type all of the committee summaries and find time to assemble the annual report during the month of December. You may see a typo or two along the way, so don't expect perfection. I know you were an English major." Mrs. Kirby dropped the stack of annual reports on the counter.

"Actually, I was a history major, and there's a lot of imperfection in history. I'm sure they'll be easy to read."

"Recommended for bedtime reading," Mrs. Kirby said. "Guaranteed to put you to sleep."

"I haven't been sleeping that well," Matt said. "Maybe they will help."

"With so many great books to read, I'm surprised you'd waste your time with our annual reports, but there they are."

Matt headed to his office with the reports. Putting them on his desk, he sat down to start his review. Selecting the most recent one, he looked at its table of contents. He found the financial report at the very end, after the ministers' statements, committee summaries, and articles on various church activities.

After examining all of the financial reports, he noted that the total budget had almost doubled. Total revenues had grown steadily year-over-year. Both check and cash receipts increased until five years ago, when Larry Rowland became chair of the Finance Committee. Since then, check revenues had continued to grow, but cash receipts had remained flat. In fact, they had declined during Rowland's first year. "*This* is when it happened!" Matt could now see what Richard had discovered. For the past five years, someone might have been stealing money from the Sunday offerings. The Finance Committee chair reported to Pastor Boyle, so either Rowland and/or Boyle could be guilty.

In addition, he observed that each committee chair had changed from one year to the next, except for the chair of the Finance Committee. Turnover in leadership can bring fresh ideas to the table. Especially in the area of finance, security procedures call for rotating responsibilities.

Matt had seen Larry Rowland at a recent Session meeting, since he was one of twenty elders elected to lead the church. The Session also included the chairs of the other eleven church committees: Buildings and Grounds; Community Life; Education; Foundation; Long-Range Planning; Missions; Nominating; Outreach; Pastoral Care; Personnel; and Worship. Rowland didn't say much at the meeting, but when called upon to discuss the upcoming fall stewardship campaign, he spoke with enthusiasm and confidence. He sounded like an athletic coach, using phrases such as "hard work and focus" and "team effort." Matt had heard that Rowland, now rather portly, once played guard on the U.C.-Berkeley football team.

The previous week, Matt had asked Mrs. Kirby about the procedure for handling the Sunday offering, one of the tasks of Rowland's committee. She said it was counted by Finance Committee members following the service and then placed in canvas bags that were locked in a cabinet. Every Wednesday afternoon, Rowland took the offering to the local bank, where it was deposited into the church's account.

After completing his first review of the annual reports, Matt left the church for a one-thirty meeting. Lunch would have to wait.

———

Matt had called a faculty member at Calvin Seminary to ask for a referral to a C.P.A. in the East Bay. Elliott S. James was a partner at James & Swearingen. Matt rode the elevator to the tenth floor of the Kaiser Building in downtown Oakland, across the street from Lake Merritt, a small lake in the heart of the central business district.

Matt opened the office door and introduced himself to the receptionist. The waiting area included a couple of leather sofas, facing a circular table covered with magazines and several newspapers, including the *Wall Street Journal*. Matt looked at the view and noticed that a single sailboat breezed across the surface of the lake below. He sat down and started to look at the newspaper. Moments later he looked up to see a man standing in front of him.

"Mr. Beringer," the man said, peering through thick glasses. "I'm Lee James. Won't you come back to my office?" Matt rose to greet him.

James' corner office overlooked the lake. Matt eased into a leather chair and eyed some framed professional accounting certificates on the wall behind the desk.

"You've caught me at a good time," James said. "I'm usually swamped from January 1st to April 15th, but my schedule is lighter in the fall. I understand Professor Walters gave you my name. How can I help?"

"I'm looking for an accountant to do my annual income tax return. I've been working with my family's C.P.A. in Seattle where I grew up, but he's close to retirement."

"I understand," James responded. "I've been a C.P.A. for twenty-six years, and my partner and I started our firm fourteen years ago. Do you live in the East Bay?"

"I lived on the seminary campus in San Francisco my first two years, but now I have an apartment in San Leandro. I'm doing an internship at Hacienda Presbyterian in San Lucas."

"I live just up the hill in Piedmont," James said. "What will you be doing after seminary?"

"Probably trying to find a job as a minister, but I'm not sure. My internship should help me figure things out."

"We have a wide variety of clients, including some companies that have complicated tax returns. I assume yours is straightforward."

"I have earned income from coaching at a basketball camp during the summers. Also, I inherited a small stock portfolio from my parents, with some dividend income. And I'm sitting on a fair amount of cash from the sale of my parents' home."

"Your tax return doesn't sound complicated. I'd be happy to help you with it."

"Let's plan on it, and I'll bring you all of my tax information in early March, if that works for you."

"That would be fine. The earlier, the better."

Matt shifted in his chair. "Is there time for a few more questions? I'd like to ask about...a...church accounting."

"Go right ahead. I have a few minutes. By the way, I won't be charging you for this introductory meeting."

"Thanks. I've been reviewing Hacienda's financial reports. Do you know how a person could steal money from a church?" Matt asked.

"That's an intriguing question. I hope you're not thinking of ways to supplement your income," James said, smiling.

"I'm not, but I recently read in the newspaper about an employee at a San Francisco company who stole thousands of dollars from his employer over a multi-year period. I'm curious to know if the same thing can happen in a church."

"Yes, it can, and it does. Generally speaking, churches don't audit their books as diligently as corporations, so there are opportunities for theft due to a lack of oversight. However, it probably occurs less frequently than in a corporate setting, where the numbers are larger. In addition, most churches that discover theft are reluctant to report it because they don't want the publicity."

"Have you ever audited a church?" Matt asked.

"Yes, but not recently."

"Did you uncover theft?" Matt got up from his seat to look out the window to see where the sailboat had gone, and then sat down.

"Are you all right?" James asked.

"Yes, I will be. A sailboat on the lake distracted me. Go on, please."

"I've never found theft in a church, but I've uncovered criminal activities at some companies. For example, a bookkeeper depositing money or checks into a secret bank account, or paying phony bills."

"I wish I could say that I'm shocked," Matt said, "but I'm beginning to suspect something similar at the church."

"It's hard to believe that someone in a church would do that."

"I agree. I hope I'm wrong."

"Sometimes churches fail to implement proper security policies and procedures. We audited a church and learned that a member would enter the room where the offering was being recorded and tell the counters he was short of cash. They agreed to exchange cash from the offering for his check, made payable to the church. They eventually questioned his motives and suspected he may have been claiming the checks as tax-deductible donations when in reality he was being reimbursed. Fortunately, they stopped this activity. He should never have been allowed in the counting room, but it's an example of lax security measures."

"That's amazing!"

"Some churches simply aren't aware of standard security practices, such as dual control, where two persons are required to complete a specific task, such as signing checks. As you can understand, it would require a greater level of corruption to violate dual control procedures."

"I need to learn more about the security system that Hacienda uses. Thanks for sharing your thoughts with me. I have another appointment, so I'll be on my way. You'll be hearing from me in early March about my tax return."

"Very good. I look forward to working with you. The earlier, the better."

Matt was about to say something about possible theft at Hacienda, but smiled instead and left. First, he needed to prove it. Pastor Boyle and Larry Rowland were his prime suspects.

———

Matt returned to his office and waited for Larry Rowland to pick up the canvas bags that afternoon, as was his custom on Wednesdays. He appeared a little after three o'clock. Matt watched from his window as he approached the quadrangle, heading toward the church office, and then emerged minutes later, sauntering across the courtyard carrying a full briefcase. Matt closed his door and walked down the stairwell. At the bottom of the stairs, he looked through the leaded windows into the courtyard and saw Rowland moving toward the parking lot. Matt walked quickly down the hall and exited through the double doors.

He didn't want Rowland to notice him as he followed him to the parking lot. Before getting into his car, Rowland opened the rear door, took off his suit jacket, tossed it onto the back seat, and set the briefcase on the floor. Then he slid into the driver's seat of his black Mercedes at the same time that Matt opened his car door.

Rowland headed down the hill on Buena Vista Drive, with Matt a block behind him. He expected Rowland to drive to the Bank of San Lucas in the village. Instead, he drove to the freeway and turned south, finally taking the exit to the Fremont business district. He pulled into the parking lot of the Fremont Community Bank, and Matt saw him carry his bulky briefcase into the bank building. Minutes later, when Rowland returned to his car, the briefcase looked thinner.

The Bank of San Lucas had to be Rowland's next stop. Matt followed him as he retraced his steps, watching from a block away as he entered the bank in the village through a revolving door. "Had Rowland deposited money into a Fremont Community Bank account?"

———

The following day, Matt returned to the bank in Fremont to speak with the branch manager. He presented his church business card to the balding man with wire-rimmed glasses seated behind a large desk with nothing on its polished surface. Matt explained that the church had misplaced its last statement and asked if he could have a copy. The statement he received read "Hacienda Presbyterian Church, P.O. Box 632, Oakland, CA 94612." Clearly the wrong address, he observed. Matt guessed that it was Larry's personal post office box, which might surprise a few people. The account showed a balance of slightly over $30,000, and it had been open for five years. Matt wondered about the purpose of a separate church bank account.

Thanking the bank manager for his assistance, Matt asked for his business card and left the bank with a copy of the account statement. Had he just uncovered a secret strategy to steal money from the church? Richard's suspicions about theft had been on target. However, the thief appeared to be Larry Rowland rather than Reverend Charles Boyle.

———

At nine-thirty the next morning, Matt visited Pastor Boyle's office to ask him about Larry Rowland. He told his supervisor he'd reviewed a few of the annual reports to gain a better understanding of Hacienda's operations. Specifically, he wanted to know why the department chairs changed annually, except for Rowland. Pastor Boyle glared as he looked up from the paperwork on his desk.

"Do you know how difficult it is to ask for money? Finding a member who will lead a stewardship campaign is next to impossible. You'll learn, Beringer. Not only did Larry Rowland step forward when asked, but he's done an outstanding job. Rowland can remain the head of the Finance Committee for as long as he wants. End of discussion."

Dissatisfied with Boyle's answer, but without enough time to continue his inquiry, Matt hurried on to his next meeting at ten o'clock with members of the Foundation Committee. He was unhappy with himself for his poorly planned conversation with Boyle. At eleven-thirty, Matt met Pastor Staley at his invitation to discuss plans for his first sermon in November. The rest of his day was spent attending meetings of the Outreach Committee, which was planning an auction, and the Long-Range Planning Committee. Except for the Education Committee, which supervised programs for both youth and adults, none of the other committees were connected to youth education, but Staley had recommended that he attend their meetings to broaden his understanding of how the church functioned.

As he pulled into his apartment garage, he pondered what to do with his information about the second account. Maybe it was time he shared his findings with Boyle and Staley. It would be risky because Boyle might be another thief, given his check-signing authority. "Were Boyle and Rowland partners? Was Staley guilty of other sins, too? Were any of them, or all of them, murderers?"

15

Toward the end of September, bright tinges of red, yellow, and orange appeared on the leaves of the deciduous trees in San Lucas. Matt had been at Hacienda for seventeen days, and had held two meetings with the middle school leaders from the five other San Lucas churches about organizing the boys' and girls' basketball leagues. He wanted to start the program in mid-October, with games in the gyms of Hacienda Presbyterian and St. Joseph's Catholic Church. Matt prepared a tentative schedule, which he hoped to circulate to the other youth leaders for their review and approval within a few days. That would allow him to publish the list of games in the *Bell Tower* for the month of October, take sign-ups for the teams during the first week, and have at least one week of practices before the season began. The timetable called for a break between Thanksgiving and New Year's, resuming play in January.

He continued to wrestle with what he should do about Larry Rowland and the second account. It would be playing with dynamite to accuse one of the church's highly visible leaders of wrongdoing. Such a claim would cause a major upheaval within the congregation and would be devastating to the church's reputation. He decided to follow the chain of command in reporting his findings. He would share the information with Boyle, and let him pass along the news to Staley.

On Tuesday morning, Matt arrived a half-hour early before the weekly staff meeting in the senior pastor's office. He stopped at the office to check his mailbox, whose contents included a copy of the community newspaper, the *San Lucas Weekly*.

Mrs. Kirby stepped out of her office and walked to the counter. "Sally Rowland wants to speak with you before the staff meeting. She's in the Amigos Room. Seems to be in a bad mood."

"Thanks," Matt said, leaving the office for the large room next door where the coffee hour was held on Sundays. When he entered, he saw Sally Rowland sitting at the head of a long table in the center.

"Have a seat," she said.

Matt walked across the tile floor and sat down next to her.

"Who gave you permission to do this?" she asked, holding up a *Weekly* article and shaking it at him.

"A reporter came to my office over a week ago and asked for an interview. She heard about our basketball program and wanted to write an article about it."

"You weren't hired to be the church's marketing agent," Sally said, raising her voice.

"I thought it would be good PR for our middle school program."

"I've been fielding distinctly negative phone calls at home since the article appeared yesterday. People are asking me why the church is promoting basketball rather than the Bible. I don't need this kind of publicity. I don't need this!"

"I thought it would bring people to the games. I'd like to fill the gym."

"I don't care if anyone attends the games. Maybe some parents will attend, but we're just trying to keep the kids busy."

"People might come to the games and decide they want to join the church."

"The basketball program is not an outreach program to attract new members. You were hired to supervise the middle school group, not sell the church to the community. You overstepped the bounds on this one. Next time, you speak to me before you talk to anyone at the *Weekly*."

"Will do," Matt said.

"I'm very unhappy about this article," she said, tapping her finger on the *San Lucas Weekly* on the table.

"I can see that."

"Maybe I'm being a little hard on you, but it's been unpleasant dealing with the phone calls. Let's leave it at that for today."

Matt returned to the office for a cup of coffee. At her desk, Mrs. Kirby peered at him over her glasses.

"How did your meeting go with Sally?"

"Not very well," Matt said. "She's unhappy with the article in the *Weekly* about the middle school basketball leagues."

"I think it's a nice article. The middle school program hasn't been featured in the *Weekly* in years."

"She said I should have asked her permission before giving the interview."

"Don't let her bother you. She scolded me last week about not having enough sugar packets and creamers beside the coffee machine."

"There's something deeper that's bothering her, but I can't put my finger on it. Call it my sixth sense."

"You didn't tell us you had extrasensory perception," Mrs. Kirby said, smiling.

"Nobody asked me," Matt said, grinning. Walking to the door, he turned to Mrs. Kirby. "Mrs. Rowland is rather intense. You were right when you told me the members here have high expectations."

"It was a word to the wise."

Matt left the office and headed for the staff meeting. He wished he'd learned more about Sally Rowland from Jancy, and maybe Carlo. She seemed as controlling as his supervisor.

Following the staff meeting, he attended a board meeting of the Worship Committee at ten o'clock, followed by a Missions Committee meeting at noon, which included box lunches. He'd scheduled a meeting with Boyle at two-thirty, and would sit in on a Community Life Committee meeting at four.

After the Missions Committee meeting ended, he worked in his office until his two-thirty appointment. Arriving at Boyle's office, he knocked and waited for the invitation to enter. Boyle was leaning back in his chair, reading a copy of *Theater Review*. Matt sat down, and Boyle launched into a commentary on the magazine as the preeminent U.S. publication on plays, reviews, and related gossip.

"I read the monthly issue from cover to cover!" Boyle said. He said the magazine contained a schedule of performances at the major theaters across the country, and he enjoyed planning trips to New York, Washington, D.C., and Los Angeles. "I especially like summer theater experiences," he said, "such as the Oregon Shakespeare Festival in Ashland." When Boyle had finished his soliloquy, he leaned across his desk, and looked at Matt over his reading glasses. "But you didn't come to my office this afternoon to hear stories about the theater, did you, Beringer?"

"No, not exactly," Matt said, "but it's fun to hear people talk about their interests. You obviously have yours."

"You're right about that! As you know, outside of this church, I have two favorite pastimes: the theater and the Oakland A's. What's on your mind today?"

"I've uncovered a problem," Matt said. "And if I'm right, it's going to require a great deal of attention and sensitivity."

"Okay, okay," Boyle said. "What are you talking about?"

"You're my supervisor, so I'm sharing my observations with you first. However, I think the problem is bigger than both of us, and we'll want to turn the matter over to Pastor Staley." He paused. "And…perhaps even the police."

Boyle pulled his chair close to the desk and narrowed his eyes, looking decidedly uncomfortable. "What is it?" His voice had a lower pitch, from deep in his chest.

"Before Richard Finley died, he told me he thought someone was stealing from the church. So I decided to do my own investigation."

"And...," Boyle said, with an irritated tone.

"I think it's Larry Rowland."

"What?!" Boyle yelled, pushing back his chair.

"I've reviewed the last ten annual reports," Matt said. "In particular, the financial reports."

"And he confessed in one of his reports that he's a thief?" Boyle interrupted.

"No."

"Well, what are you saying?" Boyle said. "Our revenues have grown each of the past five years he's chaired the Finance Committee. Our finances are in great shape!"

"I think I've found a problem."

"That's highly unlikely. We have a successful businessman managing our financial activities."

"I agree there may be a correlation between the business skills of the members and how well a church manages its money. At the same time, how do ministers evaluate the members, given their own lack of financial training? My dad was a C.P.A., so I've had some exposure to balance sheets and income statements. However, seminaries don't offer courses on how to analyze financial reports."

"We take a leap of faith, Beringer, a leap of faith." Boyle's eyes revealed he was not liking where Matt was going with the accusation. "Our members include business executives in high positions in prestigious companies, and we rely on their help, especially when it comes to finance. Larry Rowland is one of those high-profile volunteers."

"You may know the resumes of your leaders," Matt said, "but who monitors their work?"

"There are periodic audits," Boyle said.

"In the five years prior to Rowland's term, audits were conducted annually, but they appear to have stopped five years ago." Now Matt sat back in his chair. His feet were securely planted on the ground, steadying himself.

"I'd say this church is running like a well-oiled machine," Boyle said. "We've never been stronger financially. Larry Rowland has been a financial workhorse for us."

"The financial strength of the church is not in doubt, but I do have some questions about Larry Rowland. There's a pattern in the offering revenues that concerns me."

"Like what?"

"In the five years before Rowland became chair, the check and cash receipts grew at the same rate. During the past five years, check receipts have continued to grow, but cash receipts have remained flat. I think there should have been some growth in the cash receipts the past five years."

"I don't have an answer for you, Beringer," Boyle said. "It's all ancient history by now."

"The lack of growth in cash receipts suggests to me that someone could be skimming money from the offering."

"Your assertion has no merit," Boyle said. "Our revenues have been growing, whatever way you want to look at it."

"The no-growth pattern of the cash receipts coincides exactly with Larry Rowland's term as chair of the Finance Committee," Matt said.

"Look, I don't know why you're so concerned about our cash receipts when our total revenues are booming." Boyle softened his tone. "Our cash receipts are less than ten percent of our overall revenues, an insignificant amount."

"That percentage still amounts to thousands of dollars."

"It's still peanuts compared to our overall budget. Larry's done an outstanding job for us."

"Isn't it a little unusual for him to chair the committee for five years in a row, especially when the other committee chairs have held their positions for one year?"

"Beringer, I've told you that fundraising is the one area where we have a tough time finding volunteers. Most people don't like asking other people for money. Our annual stewardship campaign is one of the most time-consuming projects of the year. Rowland has done a remarkable job helping us increase our budget. He has rolled up his sleeves and done the work."

"Then why haven't there been any audits the past five years?"

"I have no idea." Boyle's jowls were turning red.

"I believe Larry Rowland has been stealing money all that time."

"Now wait just a minute," said Pastor Boyle. "I'd be very careful with your accusations, young man. Larry Rowland has been a member in good standing for over ten years. He's served on the Session in multiple leadership roles. He chaired Building and Grounds. And he headed our Outreach Committee, trying to attract new members. The past five years, he's run the Finance Committee because he's a successful businessman. If you're going to accuse him of stealing, you're going to have to provide something much more substantial than mere speculation."

"I've found some troubling evidence."

Boyle loosened his tie and leaned forward. "Look, our finances have never been stronger. If you're suggesting that he's taking money from Hacienda, it's ridiculous. Also, I'll bet very few churches have regular audits."

"I've attempted to learn a little about our account at the Bank of San Lucas by speaking to the branch manager."

"Beringer, have you lost your senses?" Boyle's face turned red. "These activities are way beyond your job description. You went to our *bank*?!" Boyle's voice grew loud. "I don't think Jim Staley would appreciate hearing this one bit."

"Before I visited the bank, I asked Pastor Staley if I could discuss the Hacienda account with Mr. Washburn, the branch manager," Matt said.

"You did?!" Boyle snorted, and then collected himself. "Well, Jack Washburn has been a member at Hacienda for a long, long time. I doubt you found anything wrong."

"You're right," Matt said, "but I decided to follow Larry when he picked up the Sunday offering to take to the bank. Before he stopped at the Bank of San Lucas, he made a deposit to a Hacienda account at the Fremont Community Bank. The branch manager told me there is only one signer on the account." Matt paused, mostly for affect. He had Boyle on the edge of his seat. "It's Larry Rowland. And the account address? An Oakland post office box."

Boyle's mouth opened, and his face filled with anger. "You followed Larry Rowland in your car? Like some private eye? That's outrageous! And why would the bank in Fremont disclose this information to you? You have no official status here." His words picked up speed. "They shouldn't have told you anything!"

"Perhaps, but I visited the bank in person and told the branch manager we had misplaced our most recent statement. I told him I was on the staff and showed him my business card," Matt said. "He had no reason to suspect I was fishing for information. He was very cooperative, and I conveyed no alarm over the account. I'll bet no one at Hacienda knows about this second account."

"You're an intern, not permanent staff! What you did was completely out of line," Boyle said.

"What if I told you that the balance of this unofficial...let's call it a secret account...unless you're aware of its existence...is $30,000. There's every reason to believe those dollars came from Hacienda's offering plates."

"You don't know that!" Boyle said. "I'm sure there's an explanation, and I'm going to find out."

Boyle rubbed his chin, and his eyes darted over the surface of his desk. Frowning, he appeared to be sorting the information he had received as if he had heard his next theater performance had been cancelled. "Did Boyle know about the account?" Matt wondered. "Would he try to protect Rowland?"

"Listen carefully, Beringer," Boyle said slowly. "You're meddling in areas that are none of your business. We didn't hire you to analyze our finances. Let me also tell you that your accusations could be very damaging. If our members learn that Larry Rowland is suspected of stealing church funds, there would be an uproar from the congregation, the likes of which we have never seen. This kind of publicity would ruin us. The backlash from the members could cost me my job, and I'm not about to let that happen." As he rose from his chair, he stumbled and had to steady himself by grabbing the desk. "I'm sure there are good reasons why Rowland opened that account. If he hears you're accusing him of stealing, he could leave Hacienda in an instant and take half of the congregation with him to a neighboring church. And make no mistake, Beringer, as the perpetrator of these lies, you'd be fired so fast it would make your head spin. Not to mention a controversy that would stain your record for years. We can't afford this! I am ordering you to stop your investigation, immediately!"

"I understand your position," Matt said, "but I'd like you to discuss my findings with Pastor Staley, and then I'll be glad to leave the matter with the two of you. I've uncovered a pattern in the cash receipts over the past five years that's concerning. When combined with this second bank account, I think it requires some attention. I don't think it's my role as an intern to resolve this matter, but I'll need to know how you and Pastor Staley plan to deal with it."

"You're right about your role here! You need to stay out of the church's finances! You're playing with fire, Beringer. I'll take over from here." Boyle walked toward the window, scratching the back of his neck.

"After you speak with Pastor Staley, will you let me know what happens?" Matt asked.

"I don't think so," Boyle said, with his back to Matt. "Jim and I can deal with it ourselves, just as we do with other gossip. Our meeting is finished." Boyle spun around and stormed from his office, charging down the hallway toward the church office. Matt stayed behind. His reflection in the window of Boyle's office, with his arms crossed, showed his determination.

His meeting with his supervisor had just reconfirmed Jancy's comment that the man doesn't handle stress well. "I should have gone to Staley first and bypassed Boyle," Matt thought. Instead of feeling relieved by sharing his findings, he felt uneasy. He looked at his watch. One more meeting.

Around five-fifteen, after his last meeting, Matt returned to his office. He thought about how much he had packed into his day's schedule. Several members of the committees had children in his middle school group. He made a point to greet them and shake their hands, happy for their involvement in leading the church.

Before leaving for the day, he left a message on Jancy's voicemail, saying that he'd like to see her. He had been invited to Mike and Jean Jensens' home for dinner, a few blocks away from the church. Jean was on the Education Committee that had selected him for the internship, and he looked forward to becoming better acquainted with the family. After an enjoyable time with the Jensens, Matt returned to his office. There were no meetings at Hacienda that evening. In the church, deserted and dark, he sat quietly in his chair, slipped off his shoes, and propped his feet up on the corner of the desk.

He wanted to look at the annual reports one more time. His conversation with his supervisor that afternoon continued to bother him. Boyle's reaction confirmed his own thoughts about how explosive these suspicions could be if they became known to the congregation. The second bank account couldn't be denied, but Matt was aware that the pastors could choose to say they knew about it all along, that he had drummed up false accusations, and make him the scapegoat to preserve congregational unity. If Staley wanted to discredit his findings, Matt could serve as the sacrificial lamb.

Matt jumped at a firm knock on his door, and quickly dropped his feet to the floor. "Come in."

The door opened, and Larry Rowland stepped in from the dark hallway. His stocky torso almost filled the doorway. He stood there with his hands on his hips, and Matt could tell from his body language that he hadn't come for a friendly visit.

"Welcome, Mr. Rowland," Matt said. "How can I help you?" He slid a magazine he'd received in the morning mail on top of the annual reports.

"I want to talk to you," Rowland said, and closed the door. He walked over to one of the chairs facing the desk and sat down. "I'll get right to the point, Beringer. I've heard you've been asking about me. I don't know what you're trying to find out, but, if you have any questions, you come see me. Right? I'm telling you for the first and last time, if I hear about any more of your nosing around, I'm going to contact Jim Staley and have you tossed out of here."

"Who told you I've been asking questions about you?"

"None of your business," Rowland said. "Word travels fast at Hacienda."

Matt thought of Boyle, and possibly the branch manager at the Fremont Community Bank. Mrs. Kirby may have mentioned his interest in reading the annual reports to any number of people. However, he ranked Boyle as most likely.

"I've been reading the annual reports to learn as much as I can about how the church functions," Matt said. "The more I know about who the leaders are and how the committees operate, the better prepared I'll be for ministry when I graduate from seminary. Yours is just one of many committees I've been studying."

"I'm not sure you heard what I just said," Rowland said with a sneer. "I don't want you talking to anyone but me about my work here. You were hired to work with the youth, not to snoop into our church business. If I hear any more about your prying, I'll take my complaint to Staley. He'll have you out of here in a heartbeat. I'll bet that wouldn't look too good on your seminary record, would it?"

"Look, Mr. Rowland, I think you're placing too much importance on my reading of the annual reports," Matt said. "If I have any specific questions about your committee, I think you'd be the person best qualified to answer them. As I said, right now, I'm just trying to learn how the church works."

Rowland rose from the chair. "I've said what I came to say." Then he pointed his finger at Matt. "This is my only warning to you. If you have questions, you come see me. No more meddling, Beringer. If there is, you'll pay."

It took all his composure for Matt not to say, "You mean like Pete and Richard?"

After Rowland left, Matt gathered himself as best he could, but his hands felt cold and clammy. "Who'd spoken to Rowland? Had Boyle betrayed his confidence?" Placing the annual reports in his desk drawer, Matt stood to leave. He wanted to put Larry Rowland's visit behind him.

As he left the office, he realized he needed to discuss the Fremont bank account with Staley as soon as possible. Matt suspected that Boyle had contacted Rowland rather than Staley about his findings, which made him no longer trustworthy.

In bed that night, Matt considered the impact on Hacienda if Rowland were found guilty of theft. But, if Boyle had spoken with Staley and he had sent Rowland to scare him off, then all three may be implicated. His review of the annual reports should have been beyond criticism. He had only shown an interest in becoming acquainted with the church and its operations. On the other hand, his discovery of the second bank account had been a turning point in his investigation. Deep inside, Matt knew he had been prompted all along by the concerns of Pete and Richard. He wasn't just curious. He was downright suspicious, and he was determined to find some answers.

He'd have to step gingerly in dealing with Staley, hoping the senior pastor would see his activities as well-intentioned. Yet he couldn't let go of what he had found in Pete's journal. The profile of Staley that emerged was one of a philanderer. Pete's comments, coupled with the newspaper article he had discovered about Staley's ministry in La Jolla, hardly suited a member of the clergy. Matt suspected it was only a matter of time before Staley's womanizing would be discovered at Hacienda. However, before that happened, if Staley felt that Matt knew too much about him and threatened his position at the church, he could simply terminate him.

On the other hand, the dangers of accusing Larry Rowland of stealing from the church could cost him his internship and more. What worried Matt was that he knew he wasn't going to get away with just being fired. He could lose his life in the process. "Carlo will not be happy to learn what I've been doing," Matt said to himself, as he fell solidly into an uneasy but deep, deep sleep.

16

Boyle's outrage over Matt's revelation that Larry Rowland could be stealing from the church, plus Rowland's subsequent threat, pushed Matt to schedule a meeting with Pastor Staley as soon as he could, which happened to be Thursday, two days later.

"I found a Hacienda bank account at a bank in Fremont with over $30,000 in it," Matt said upon entering Staley's office, before even sitting down. "The address on the account is an Oakland post office box."

Pastor Staley looked up slowly from his reading. "How did you discover it?"

"I received a letter from Richard Finley," Matt said. "He suspected that someone could be stealing from the church. I never had a chance to discuss it with him before he drowned. He was an accounting major in college, so he was interested in finance and suspected some foul play. All of this led me to conduct my own investigation, and I've been studying the financial reports of the past ten years. I think Rowland is depositing money from the Sunday offering into a second account."

Matt sat down when Staley, oddly calm, motioned him to a chair. "Because some of Rowland's numbers in the financial reports raised a red flag," Matt said, "I recently trailed him when he picked up the Sunday offering. His first stop was not at the Bank of San Lucas, but at a bank in Fremont. I later met with the branch manager. Rowland is the only signer on the account."

"Have you told anybody else about your findings?"

"Just Pastor Boyle."

"What was his response?"

"He didn't believe it. He thinks I'm way off base. But he said he'd discuss it with you," Matt said. "Has he?"

"Very briefly. He said he needed to talk to me about some accusations you were making about Larry, but we haven't had a chance to discuss them."

"I'm disappointed he hasn't shared them with you. Don't you think Rowland's behavior is unusual? Enough to warrant an investigation into possible deposits of church money in a secret bank account?" Matt's speech was more animated than he'd intended.

"In all my years of ministry," Staley said, "I've never had an embezzlement case on my hands. First, I can't believe that Larry would do something like this. He's been one of our most faithful church leaders as Finance Committee chair. Second, he's a wealthy and successful business owner, as far as I can tell, and doesn't need money." Staley paused. "I don't want to put our members through a scandal if I can help it."

"Well, I'm not an attorney," Matt said, "but isn't theft a criminal offense? We're not talking about taking pens from the church office."

"All I'm saying is that I have a big decision to make. Starting an investigation based on your findings could be igniting a powder keg. What effect it might have on our church, if word about it leaked to the congregation, is unthinkable. You agree?"

"Of course, but—"

"I'd like to avoid any publicity, if at all possible. Larry may have a good reason for the separate account, and I will speak to him about it. I'll bet it's for a special mission project, or something like that. You can appreciate that I need to proceed with caution. He's a proud man and, if he thought

I suspected him of stealing from the church, I don't know what he'd do. This matter could be very damaging. Our members see him and his wife as leaders here. If the media got ahold of this story, it would take us years to recover."

"I think it's important to ask Mr. Rowland about the Fremont bank account. Don't you agree?"

"Perhaps I should speak to our attorney first," Staley said, "to get his advice."

"That sounds like a good place to start. I'd appreciate it if you'd keep our meeting confidential. Please don't mention it to Pastor Boyle. He became upset and very defensive when I told him of my suspicions. I wasn't sure he would share my findings with you, although he said he would. I'm disappointed he hasn't spoken to you."

"He's probably worried about the potential fallout for our church, if your suspicions are true," Staley replied. "I'm sure it all came to him as a big surprise."

"And then I had a disturbing visit from Mr. Rowland in my office," Matt said.

"You did?"

"He confronted me two nights ago after I spoke with Pastor Boyle. I asked Pastor Boyle to keep my findings confidential, except for telling you, but Mr. Rowland surprised me when he showed up at my office and was very angry about what he called my snooping around. I'd sure like to know how he heard about my concerns."

"What did he say to you?" Staley asked.

"He told me to stop asking questions about his activities as Finance Committee chair or I'd pay for it. Given the recent deaths of Pete and Richard, Rowland's threat has made me very uneasy. He said he'd take his complaint to you and have me run out of Hacienda."

"That's pretty strong language. Are you sure you didn't share your thoughts with anyone else?"

"I borrowed the annual reports from Mrs. Kirby. She knew I was trying to learn something about Hacienda's history. Maybe she mentioned it to someone. I think any intern might ask to see some annual reports. I felt I owed it to Richard to continue his investigation into the church's finances. So I don't know who could have told Larry Rowland besides Pastor Boyle and Mrs. Kirby. Maybe it was the branch manager at the Fremont bank."

"Do you have some physical evidence of the account with you?" Staley asked. "Like a copy of a recent statement?"

"Yes," Matt said, pulling an envelope from his shirt pocket and handing it to the senior pastor. "There were only two or three checks written on the account in the past month. The largest item is a payment to the El Dorado Apartments in San Leandro. What does that mean?"

After looking it over, Staley put it on his desk. "I've heard of these things happening before, but I never expected that it might occur on my watch. Larry Rowland is not someone I'd suspect of doing something illegal. Leave the matter in my hands for now, and I'll try to develop a plan to address it. I'm disappointed that Richard, and now you, felt the need to look into our financial operations, since it's outside of your job description, but I understand your concerns because of Richard's death. Perhaps you've uncovered something. I'll let you know what I decide to do."

After the meeting, he tried to put himself in Staley's position. The money in the Fremont bank account was relatively small in relation to the church budget. Whatever the reasons for Rowland's questionable behavior, they certainly didn't create a financial crisis for the church. On the other hand, a scandal over theft would be devastating to the congregation's morale. The media would have a field day over crime at a prominent San Lucas church.

Since the account had been open for five years, Matt believed Rowland had been taking money from the church throughout that time period. Given the Rowlands' affluence, he wondered why Larry Rowland wanted a secret account. Did he need an expense account that his wife couldn't see? Was the account supporting extra-marital activities? In any case, it appeared that Rowland also had a hidden agenda when he became chair of the Finance Committee five years earlier.

Back in his office, Matt cleared his desk before leaving for the day. He was surprised Jancy hadn't responded to his message of two days ago, so he gave her a call.

"It's good to hear your voice," she said. "How are you?"

"I've been busy. I've attended a lot of meetings this week. But I've missed you."

"You called on Tuesday, and I left a message on your cell phone the same day. Did you get it?"

"I may have, but I've been distracted. I don't think my cell phone is charged right now. Sorry about that."

"Are you okay?"

"Yeah, I'm all right. To be honest, I may have made matters worse."

"What do you mean?"

"I've come across some financial problems. When I told the pastors, it didn't go well."

"Sorry to hear that. I've been worrying about you."

"I really want to see you. I have things to tell you. Could you have dinner with me tomorrow?"

"Friday? Sure. Shall we meet in the Hacienda parking lot?"

"No. I'll come pick you up at your apartment. I don't want you to drive home by yourself after dinner. Pick a place to eat in Berkeley. I'll come by at six o'clock."

"Perfect. I'll think about a restaurant and make reservations. See you tomorrow."

After scheduling dinner with Jancy, Matt placed another call to Detective Miller. "Ben, this is Matt Beringer."

"I'm glad you called," he said. "I'm still working on the deaths of Rockwell and Finley. How are you?"

"I'm still alive, which is good, and I have some important news for you."

"Tell me about it."

"I found a secret church account at a Fremont bank that uses an Oakland post office box, and Larry Rowland's the only signer on the account. The plot thickens."

"Are you writing a novel about your experiences? It could be a best seller."

"That's funny. My next occupation, perhaps. I might be a better author than a minister, the way things are going. I just seem to be making enemies. It's been a little scary."

"What's in the account?"

"Over $30,000."

"Okay."

"I believe Larry Rowland is skimming money from the church's Sunday offering. I've spoken to the senior minister about him, but I think he may be afraid to investigate. Rowland is right in the center of all this. We know that one of his trucks was involved in the death of Pete Rockwell. And he threatened me the other night for looking into his activities."

"Listen, Matt, I need to digest this information. Right now, I have to go to a meeting," Ben said, "but I want you to call me every evening and leave a short message on my voicemail about your activities and that you're okay. You may be in danger, and we need to find some answers. Stay home in the evenings for a while, will you, unless you have a meeting or a professional obligation?

"Does that include going out on a date?"

"That should be okay," he said, lightening up. "I'm not asking you to become a hermit. But do try to be careful."

"Okay," Matt responded. "I'm not looking for trouble."

"I hear you. I'll call you in a few days."

Matt breathed a sigh of relief. He didn't feel quite as alone as he did before his calls to Jancy and Ben Miller.

17

The next day, Matt stood in front of Boyle's closed office door prior to an eleven o'clock meeting he'd scheduled to update him on the basketball program. He wondered what kind of mood his supervisor would be in after their last meeting. After knocking, Matt heard Boyle say, "Come in," so he opened the door. Boyle looked at him, but pointed to the phone at his ear. "I'm on hold. Come back in a five minutes." Then he wheeled in his chair, turning his back to Matt, and resumed his conversation on the telephone. "Yes," he said, "I'm calling to ask if you can switch my seats for tomorrow night's performance." Matt closed the door and walked down the hall to the office for a cup of coffee.

He spoke briefly with Mrs. Kirby about her vacation plans to visit San Diego in a few weeks, and then checked his mailbox. Sipping his coffee at the counter, his thoughts returned to Boyle. He guessed his relationship with his supervisor would be strained for a while. Boyle's rebuff moments ago, when he arrived for their meeting, conveyed a petulance that fit his supervisor's emerging personality profile—someone who is easily agitated. Finishing his coffee, Matt returned for his appointment. He knocked again at the door, and this time was invited in and offered a chair. The associate pastor pushed back his chair and crossed his legs.

"What's on your mind today?" Boyle asked. Matt might need to interject a comment or two about the Oakland A's to thaw his supervisor's chilly demeanor and turn their conversation around.

"I want to tell you about the basketball leagues," Matt said. "Also, I heard yesterday from Jimmy Matthews that his family is moving to Denver. Do you know they're leaving San Lucas?"

"No, I haven't heard a thing. That's too bad. We'll miss the Matthews. They've been faithful members for five or six years. Steve Matthews works for a company in San Francisco that makes packaged-food products for supermarkets, and he drives a beautiful, dark green BMW sedan. He must have it washed every day."

Matt thought to himself, "Boyle doesn't change his stripes. What a bizarre thing to say, describing the guy by the kind of car he drives." He would finish his report on the Matthews. "Jimmy told me his dad is receiving a promotion," he said, "and is moving to headquarters."

"Good for him. Look, Beringer, about your basketball program. Make your report short. I need to run some errands."

"Okay. The basketball program is on schedule. We'll start the leagues in mid-October."

"That's fine. Any other bombshells to drop in my lap?"

"Well, I did want to ask if you and Pastor Staley have decided what you're going to do about the Fremont bank account."

"We're moving cautiously on that matter. That's all I can tell you."

————

Later that day, Matt met again with Pastor Staley.

"Have a seat," Staley said, as Matt entered his office. "I'd like to talk to you about your internship."

Matt suddenly felt anxious. He wondered if Staley was going to terminate him because of pressure from Boyle and Rowland. The question crossed his mind, "Would Staley use me as a scapegoat?"

"How do you find Pastor Boyle as a supervisor?" Staley asked.

"He's given me considerable freedom to run the middle school program the way I want, and I'm glad of that. He said it's important to keep him informed, so I plan to leave notes in his mailbox and schedule regular meetings with him. I do sense that the middle school program isn't one of his top priorities."

"I don't think his heart is in youth ministry," Staley said. "He does enjoy calling on our members and supervising adult education. No minister excels at every responsibility in his job description. Charles tends to keep things close to his vest. His ministerial career has had some ups and downs, and I think he's just trying to protect himself."

"Pastor Boyle has been the least of my worries. I've been dealing with some other things. I don't know how much you've heard," Matt said, "but I've survived two murder attempts in the past two weeks. I was almost killed by a hit-and-run attempt in front of my apartment, and then I almost drowned when a member of my Y basketball team drove us off a pier in Hayward. I'm not used to being a murder target. And I'm beginning to think that the deaths of Pete and Richard are connected. All this could be part of a larger murder plot." He waited to see Staley's response to his statements.

"Mrs. Kirby showed me the newspaper article about your incident at the Hayward pier, and I've been meaning to discuss it with you. Pastor Boyle was on call that night, and he told me he visited you at the hospital. I haven't heard about your hit-and-run incident. Tell me about it."

"A car tried to run over me in front of my apartment one evening."

"Do the police have any suspects?"

"The San Leandro police don't think I was the intended target. They think it was drug-related, and the driver tried to run over the wrong person."

"It sounds as if you've had more than your share of trouble since you started with us. I don't know what's going on, but I hope you'll work closely with the police to learn who may be trying to harm you. The past month has been a nightmare for me, as well. But I haven't had my life threatened, like you have. While I can't offer much help to you about these police matters, I'd like to try to be supportive during your internship with us," Staley said. "I've asked Pastor Boyle if you could help me with some projects that may expand your view of ministry."

"What did you have in mind?" Matt asked.

"I'd like you to meet with some former members to learn why they left. This is an unusual strategy, something I've never tried before. Churches never contact members after they stop attending or transfer their member-ships, and these people could share some valuable information that might help us improve our ministry as well as member retention. You and I will decide what questions you'll ask these folks, but you'll discover a lot by just being a good listener. Then I'd like you to give me a written report of what you learn from each appointment."

"That sounds like an interesting project," Matt said.

"One other thing. I can't attend all of the meetings I'm invited to in our community and don't want to attend them all. I'd like you to be my representative at selected meetings where a church staff member should be present, and give me short reports in writing. That way, you'll learn about what goes on in San Lucas."

"I'd like to do that, too," Matt said. "I have the time."

"You may find some of these community meetings to be very boring, as I sometimes do, especially the evening meetings. I'd rather be home watch-ing TV or reading a book. But these meetings keep our church in touch with the community, so I think attending them is really quite important."

"Some of our committee meetings I've attended have been slow-mov-ing," Matt said, "so I appreciate your honesty in telling me that meetings can be tedious. I guess I need to be more patient."

"We all need to be more patient. This church is served by volunteers on their own time. It's not like they're our employees. One final matter," Staley said. "After your November sermon, I'd like to schedule another one for early next year, so you can better appreciate the time a minister gives each week to preparing them."

"Very good," Matt responded.

"Okay," Pastor Staley said. "Let's meet next Tuesday at eleven, and we'll discuss the ABC's of calling on former members. Then I'll give you names of some people to contact. We'll also discuss community meetings I'd like you to attend, and we'll plan your schedule. How does that sound?"

"Terrific!" Matt said. "I look forward to our next meeting."

"On the subject of your personal safety," Pastor Staley said, "I'd like you to keep me posted about what you learn from the police. After the losses of Rockwell and Finley, I don't want anything to happen to you. I want you to have a safe and enjoyable internship with us."

"Thanks for your concern. I'll let you know what I hear. Could I ask you something?" Matt had planned to ask this question for days.

"Sure," Staley replied.

"I had the mother of one of my middle school kids visit my office the other day. She's worried that her daughter is hanging around with the wrong crowd. She's an attractive woman, and I thought she was being a little flirtatious. We were alone together for about an hour. What if she claimed I made a pass at her? It would be her word against mine, and I think a jury would side with the woman. How do ministers protect themselves against that situation?"

Staley leaned forward, placed his folded his hands on the desk, and stared at Matt for a few moments. "That's a very good question, and relevant," he said. "After my last ministry, I earned a master's degree in pastoral counseling, partly because I enjoy it and partly because of a problem I had in my last church."

Matt resisted filling the silence with a comment.

"A woman at my previous church reported to the Session that I had made passes at her during counseling appointments with me. I was stunned, but I think it was an attempt to gain some attention from her husband that she wasn't receiving and, possibly, a desperate attempt to rekindle their marriage. I strongly objected to the charge, but she and her husband had been members for many years and had more political clout than I. In any case, I was asked to resign from my ministry there. It was a humiliating experience, to say the least. I thought my career as a minister might be over."

"What did you do?"

"I did a lot of soul-searching, and decided to continue in ministry, if a church would have me. I also determined that I would never counsel another woman without having a third party involved. I learned the hard way that I might need a witness to support me against false accusations. Since I've been at Hacienda, I tell people I counsel, at the very beginning, that Mrs. Kirby will be acting as a witness. Mrs. Kirby sits at her desk, with the door between our offices open, and can hear everything that is said at my counseling sessions. You might want to follow the same procedure."

Matt nodded, grateful to the senior pastor for sharing his personal tragedy. Perhaps he had been too judgmental about Staley.

"I didn't mean to shock you with my story," Staley said, "and I'd appreciate it if you'd keep our conversation between the two of us. We want to be able to trust our church members. At the same time, we're vulnerable to criticism because everyone has such high standards for us. It isn't always possible to deliver what they want. Plus, members may have different agendas than we think, which is what happened to me in La Jolla. I paid a dear price for not understanding the potential risks in counseling members of the opposite sex."

"Thanks for telling me about your experience and what you learned from it."

"One other item. I'm close to calling in the police because I haven't been satisfied with the conversations I've had with Larry Rowland about his secret bank account."

"Thanks for telling me." After he closed the office door, Matt pumped his fist over Staley's progress in dealing with the financial deception at Hacienda.

———

That evening, Matt and Jancy enjoyed Indian food at a restaurant in Berkeley. She was amazed to learn about the Fremont bank account, and believed it was further evidence of Larry Rowland's central role in the murders of Pete and Richard. Matt felt badly that he hadn't seen her in a week, but he was doing the best he could under the circumstances. He hoped she knew that. Their date ended on a high note when she invited him for dinner at her place the following evening. He was pleased that their relationship continued to grow.

18

When Matt arrived at Jancy's apartment for dinner, they greeted each other with a kiss and a long hug, and he handed her a bouquet of flowers. It had splashes of orange, red, and purple blossoms, combined with eucalyptus shoots, capturing the autumn mood. She guided him into the living room and returned to the kitchen. He had enjoyed a cup of coffee in her apartment before, but receiving this dinner invitation provided some proof that their relationship was deepening. Jancy's caring support had been a welcome gift, especially in light of the recent threats to his life.

He sank onto her sofa, admiring the interior furnishings and decorations. Shelves hung on the wall in front of him, filled with books and a collection of small, glass vases of various colors. Matt recognized framed prints on the walls by Renoir and Degas.

"I wish I had your artistic abilities," he said. "I really like what you've done here. My apartment has a bunch of rented furniture and not much else."

"But I've been here for two years," Jancy replied, "and you've been in your apartment for what—a month? I don't think decorating is a guy thing, so don't be too hard on yourself."

She brought him a glass of red wine, they toasted the day, and then she returned once more to the kitchen. The aromas coming from the stove told him that he would like the finished product. After several minutes, Jancy reappeared.

"I've been meaning to ask you about your decision to attend the seminary," she said. "You were heading to business school before your parents' accident. I'm glad you came to the Bay Area because otherwise we wouldn't have met. Are you happy you changed directions?"

"It was the right decision. When my parents died, I felt like the rug had been pulled out from under me. I needed to put my life on hold and regroup. Studying business didn't seem as important to me at the time."

"I would have felt the same way," she said.

"I spoke with my pastor, and he suggested that I consider going to seminary. That idea appealed to me. He's a Calvin alum, so I applied and was accepted."

"Has your seminary experience been helpful?"

"It has. I've appreciated the time I've had to read and study the Bible because I've learned some principles that will guide me for the rest of my life."

"Have you found some peace regarding your parents' accident?"

"I wondered why my parents had to die in that accident. The truth is, we all have to deal with losses. Courses at the seminary have made me realize that suffering can help us better understand ourselves and what's important in our lives. For example, my own suffering has prepared me to comfort others who suffer."

"That's true."

"There is a type of suffering that is beyond our understanding, and I believe mine falls into that category. At the same time, God is always reaching out to us in love. He will give us the strength to endure our suffering."

"God's love for us may be the central message of the Bible," Jancy said. "What a gift!"

"One of the biggest blessings of coming to the Bay Area has been meeting you, Jancy. I wasn't looking for romance, but I think I'm falling in love with you."

"I feel the same way about you, Matt."

Their eyes met as he rose from the chair. He walked toward her, and they held each other.

"I want you to be part of my life," Matt whispered into her ear. "When we're apart, I think about you all the time."

"You make me happy, Matt," she said.

After they shared a long kiss, Jancy said she needed to check the meatloaf. Smiling, she returned to the kitchen.

Matt sipped his wine and looked at a magazine on the coffee table, and then walked to the bookshelves in front of him. "You're a fan of C.S. Lewis."

"Yeah, he's one of my favorite authors," she responded, stepping back into the room. "My dad started reading his children's books to me when I was ten. I fell in love with his Narnia series, and started collecting his other books as well. His books have provided many, many fond memories for me. Have you read *Mere Christianity* and *The Screwtape Letters?*

"I've wanted to read his books, but never have. I feel sort of incomplete because of it."

"He was a prolific writer, with over thirty books, and led a very interesting life."

"Science fiction is another genre that I've never explored. I think sports and crossword puzzles have cut into my reading time, and I need to do some catching up."

"You could start with the Narnia series, which you might incorporate into your ministry to young people. Borrow one of my books. Why don't you try *The Lion, the Witch, and the Wardrobe?* If you like it, you can read the other six books when you have time."

Matt reached for the book she recommended. He opened it in the middle and saw the words, "White Witch." Holding the book, he joined Jancy in the kitchen. "Who's the White Witch?"

"I don't want to ruin it for you, so I won't tell you much," she said. "The book is about children who are transported to the land of Narnia by way of a wardrobe in a professor's house. They help a talking lion save Narnia from the evil White Witch, and that's all I'll say."

"Tell me a little more about the White Witch," Matt said. "Witches have always scared me, like the witch in 'The Wizard of Oz.' "

"That's exactly what they're supposed to do! Basically, the White Witch is a sociopath. Also, she's beautiful, proud, cruel, and tempts people with candy. Sound interesting?"

"I do like candy. And I'm easily tempted."

"If you feel vulnerable, maybe you should wait to read C.S. Lewis," Jancy said, chuckling. "Hey, are you hungry? Dinner's ready."

They ate at a table in an alcove adjacent to the kitchen, in front of a window that overlooked the neighborhood. From the third story, her unit offered a partial view of Berkeley, facing west. The sun was beginning to fall toward the San Francisco Bay.

"What an amazing sunset," Matt said. "Look at the colors!"

"No matter what kind of day I've had," Jancy said, "a sunset always makes it good."

"Getting back to the White Witch, the guy who drove me off the pier might also be a sociopath," Matt said, "or maybe a sociopath hired him to do it."

"Have the police found the driver?"

"I haven't heard a thing."

"Could he have been hired?" Jancy said.

"I have that feeling. He said he's a construction worker. I had never seen him until we started to play basketball together. What motive did he have? I've narrowed the suspects to Rowland, Boyle, and Staley, but what's their motive? My gut tells me it isn't Staley. I've had some good conversations with him recently, and I don't think he's an evil man."

"The deaths of Pete and Richard appear to be connected. What do you and Pete and Richard have in common?"

"We've all worked at Hacienda. Boyle and Rowland may want to conceal their stealing because they think their activities have been uncovered. I'm not so sure Staley's the womanizer I thought he was."

"It's disturbing to think that any one of those guys is a murderer."

"I had a good conversation with Staley yesterday. He told me about a problem with a woman at his La Jolla church who accused him of making a pass at her, and he was forced to resign. Now he says he counsels women with his door open and Mrs. Kirby as a witness. Maybe I misinterpreted the comments about Staley in Pete's journal. Also, our custodian, Carlo Barone, thinks Boyle is a decent guy. Not without issues, but basically harmless."

"Pastor Boyle seems overly interested in worldly comforts," Jancy said. "He may be trying prevent people from learning about his stealing."

"You could be right, but the guy who troubles me the most is Larry Rowland. Power and wealth can corrupt people. The police traced Pete's accident to Rowland's truck. My teammate who drove me off of the pier might be one of his truck drivers, just like that guy Kenny Cole."

"Do you think the police are investigating that angle? That your teammate is associated with Rowland?"

"I sure hope so."

"Without any proof," Jancy said, "these two murders could be viewed as random events."

"Rowland's secret bank account might be incriminating evidence."

"You may be right."

"He appears to be paying for someone's apartment. Could the secret bank account be supporting extramarital activities?"

"If it is, I feel sorry for Sally," she said.

"Hey, let's change the subject! I don't want to bore you with my problems. Your meatloaf is delicious! And I like the veggies, too."

"My mother trained me well."

"May I have seconds?"

"You bet." Jancy took his plate to the counter and returned with a generous serving. "Returning to Pete and Richard," Jancy said, "we need to solve these murders. It sounds like Rowland is your primary suspect."

"Thinking outside the box just a little," Matt said, "could there be a White Witch involved here?"

"What? You must be kidding. Women are seldom murderers. I'd hate to think one of the women at Hacienda could do such a thing."

"Maybe Sally Rowland is trying to protect her husband," Matt said. "Maybe she knows he's stealing from the church and wants to protect their reputations. They could be partners in crime."

"That trucking company was started by her grandfather and expanded by her father," Jancy said, "and I know from talking to her that she's proud of what they accomplished. The company could go up in smoke if Larry is convicted of murder and theft. Could she be helping him?"

"I wish I knew. Their family would be destroyed if Larry's found to be guilty." Matt said. "Could Liz Canfield be trying to prevent an affair with Staley from being discovered?"

"I can't believe Liz would be involved in murder."

"That may be true, but I need to find some answers."

19

On Wednesday morning, Matt placed a phone call that might save his life.

"Detective Miller."

"Hey, Ben, this is Matt Beringer. I thought I'd check in and see if you have any news for me."

"I'm afraid I don't have much. I did learn that the CHP has finished their work on the Rockwell death. They've called it a random murder by a guy on drugs. I don't see it that way. To me, it looks suspicious. The truck driver, Cole, had a clean record since moving to the Bay Area, so I find it hard to believe he would use drugs on the job. He had been busted before, but it was for recreational drug use only. Also, it's an amazing coincidence that a truck from Hannifin Trucking was traveling to Sacramento on Interstate 80 at the same time as Rockwell. But it's impossible to question a dead man, so without talking to Cole we'll never know what happened. The CHP has spent more time on this murder case than I have, so I have to defer to them on this one. I think they want to close the file and move on."

"Do you know how thoroughly they investigated Cole? Did they speak to people who knew him? Other truck drivers at Rowland's company? I wonder how much pressure Rowland and his law firm put on the CHP to limit their investigation?"

"The CHP thinks Cole was operating alone."

"In my opinion, that view is open to question. Have they found Tom Dawson, the guy who took me for a dip in the bay?"

"I haven't heard. But I've left a couple of messages with the Hayward Police. They know I'm looking for information. Let's have lunch tomorrow and review these murders. We have a killer running around the East Bay, and you may be his next target. Can you come to my office at noon?"

"I'll be there."

———

The next day, Matt met Ben Miller at his office, and they went to a restaurant in Jack London Square. Before taking a seat, Miller loosened his tie and draped his sport coat over his chair. "I'm sorry it's taken so long for us to get together to discuss your situation. I don't know where the time goes. My quarterly reports are due in a few days, and I haven't even started them. I've been swamped the past couple of months. But I've thought about you, and I don't think your recent swim in the bay was an isolated event. That makes two attempts on your life, and I have a hunch that Larry Rowland is our man."

"Maybe we should make it three attempts. When I drove to the church last month, a semi started chasing me after I crossed the Bay Bridge. I didn't get the license number, but, you know, I think it *was* a yellow truck. I hadn't even started my internship. Could I have been a target that day?"

"It fits the pattern."

A waiter came to the table with two glasses of water.

"If I'm connected to the other murders," Matt said, "I'd like to figure out the motive and identify the killer before I become the third victim."

"That's what bothers me. I can't figure out why Rowland would murder the two previous interns and attempt to murder you over a secret bank account with a grand total of $30,000 in it. Even if he's worried about being uncovered, it would be his word against an intern. Would anyone believe the opinion of a seminary student over Rowland, a church leader and respected businessman? Rowland could have made up just about any excuse for why he opened the second bank account. The senior pastor would have sided with him to avoid a scandal."

"Yeah, all that over a $30,000 bank account seems insane."

They gave their food orders to the waiter who had returned to their table.

"Any news about Dawson?" Matt asked.

"I'm still investigating your basketball buddy," Miller said. "I did learn that another driver at Hannifin Trucking has disappeared. He seems to fit the description of Dawson, but I still have some work to do."

"Very interesting. Another pattern is emerging. Maybe Dawson was hired to do a job, just like Kenny Cole. It would confirm that Pete's murder wasn't a random event, after all." Matt shook his head. "I didn't think my internship would be this exciting."

Miller pulled a lined yellow tablet from his briefcase. "I spoke again for some time with the California Highway Patrol. I actually talked to the officer who discovered and reported the Rockwell accident. A Sergeant Ron Parks. Our department was asked by the CHP for help in impounding the Hannifin truck they traced to the accident. It appears that Cole had traded routes for that trip the night he ran Rockwell off the road. However, drivers at Hannifin often trade routes for one reason or another. Unfortunately, Cole's death in that shoot-out prevents us from ever knowing why he took that trip. He was also driving on 80 at a later time than he should have been, but we don't know why. The Hannifin truck was due in Sacramento at ten o'clock that evening, but it arrived around one in the morning. The CHP really leaned on Larry Rowland, but they ultimately decided he wasn't involved with Cole. They couldn't find any evidence that Rowland and Cole acted together. However, I still have questions about Rockwell's murder."

"Ben, I think Larry Rowland knows more than he's telling about the deaths of Pete and Richard," Matt said. "I told you that he threatened me the other night, probably because Boyle told him I had found his secret bank account. The guy's a loose cannon. I'm convinced he's a thief, and quite possibly a murderer."

"I agree," Miller added. "You keep leaving messages for me every night on my voicemail."

"Will do," Matt said.

"Kenny Cole used drugs," Miller said, "but that's all. And he was supporting a wife and two kids who live on the East Coast. On the other hand, if he needed drug money, Larry Rowland could have hired him to run Rockwell off the road. The way I see it, Rowland's our guy."

"You think Cole was working for Rowland?" Matt asked.

"Yeah, man, I do," Miller said.

"What if Pete and Richard had some damaging information on the Hacienda ministers? Did the pastors know it and want them silenced? Maybe Rowland was carrying out a plan he developed with Staley and/or Boyle."

"What information did they have?" Miller asked.

"I found some notes in Pete's journal that suggested the senior pastor, Staley, is having affairs with some of the women in the church, although I'm less convinced of it today. I know Pete and Richard suspected Pastor Boyle of theft. Could either Staley or Boyle or both of them be involved in the two deaths because they feared that Pete and Richard knew about their activities?"

"That's what we need to find out. It's hard to believe that either minister would murder Rockwell and Finley, but truth is stranger than fiction."

Matt leaned forward. "I also keep returning to Rowland."

"The stuff that's been happening around you is very strange," Miller said. "I'm convinced that you're going to be a target again, and I'm worried that you may be in Larry Rowland's crosshairs. I thought folks who went to church behaved themselves."

"So did I," Matt said.

"Be very careful," Miller said. "You hear me?"

Matt nodded.

"I wouldn't work at the church past five. You leave when the staff leaves. Get yourself excused from evening meetings until we figure this thing out. Drive home during daylight hours. I want you to survive this internship."

"Okay."

"When you leave the church every day, continue to give me a brief summary of your day's activities on my voicemail," Miller said. "If you meet with a committee or an individual, tell me about it."

"I will," Matt said. "My aunt and uncle in Spokane don't know about this stuff because I don't want to worry them. I've shared much of it with the woman I've been dating, Jancy Nichols. But I feel it's important for at least one person to know everything I've experienced, in case something happens to me. I'm sorry I've dragged you into this."

"Hey, it's my work. This is what I do, so you're talking to the right guy. Plus, I want to help a friend."

When their food was delivered, their conversation shifted to sports. At one-thirty, Miller said he needed to return to his office for a two o'clock meeting. Before they left, the detective paid the bill. "When you get a job, I'll let you take me to lunch," he said with a smile. "Let's continue to gather information," he said, "and talk by phone at least once a week. I want to attend your seminary graduation, not your funeral."

20

The next morning, shortly after nine, Matt went straight to Carlo's room when he arrived at the church. When silence answered his knock, Matt headed to his office to spend some time preparing Sunday's middle school lesson. Opening the door, Matt spotted an envelope on the floor. When he opened it, he found an article from the *Oakland Tribune* about the drowning of Richard Finley. "Why would someone want me to see this today, when it happened almost four weeks ago?"

Matt went to the church office and spoke to Mrs. Kirby. "Someone slid an envelope under my door this morning. Do you know who might have done it?"

"I saw Sally Rowland walk past the office about a half hour ago," she said.

"Okay, thanks," Matt said. Puzzled, he returned to his office.

In an hour, he returned to Carlo's office next to the gym and knocked again. When Matt heard, "Come on in," he opened the door.

Carlo sat at his desk, looking at a bulletin board with the week's schedule of upcoming events. As custodian, he needed to know about certain activities because he helped make them happen, like setting up and taking down folding chairs, providing a cart with a coffee maker or two, and supplying other equipment, such as a flip chart or podium.

"I need to speak to you," Matt said, "if you have time. I'd like your opinion about something."

"Fridays are busy because I'm getting things ready for Sunday. How much time do you want?"

"Fifteen minutes? I probably need an hour or two, to tell you the truth."

"That's an interesting request, my fine-feathered friend. I can give you fifteen minutes now or an hour early next week."

"I'll take fifteen minutes now."

"You got it. Have a chair. What's percolating today in that overactive mind of yours?"

"I think Richard Finley's death is very suspicious. How does an expert sailor drown? What if he was poisoned?"

"What's that?"

"What if Richard was poisoned?"

"When did you dream that up?"

"Ever since his death, I've been wondering if he was murdered."

"You have an active imagination. I'd say your guess is as good as mine. Was there an autopsy?"

"I don't know."

"I have no idea about Finley," Carlo said. "The deaths of Rockwell and Finley, happening so close to each other, are troubling."

"As in...you think they might be connected?" Matt glanced away, giving Carlo a moment to consider what he already believed to be true. "It sure seems that way to me." He waited.

"I don't know who would want to kill Rockwell and Finley," Carlo said, "if that's what you're asking. The truck driver is dead, and nobody knows how Finley fell in the water. There are a lot of questions to be answered."

"What do you think about Larry Rowland?"

"He's a bit of an odd duck. At times he struts around like a rooster, and at other times he seems moody and withdrawn. I've seen him flirting with various women when his wife isn't looking. Other times, I've seen him sitting by himself with a frown on his face. My take is that he's not a happy person, and being pushy is a cover-up for an insecurity. I don't know what he's hiding. He has everything going for him—a good-looking wife, nice kids, successful business, beautiful home." Carlo rose from his chair and paced in the small office. "They lost a kid in the canoeing accident. Maybe he's still trying to recover from that. What do I think? He's battling demons. Big time!"

"One of them was a Rowland kid?" Matt asked. "I didn't know. That had to be devastating."

"Yeah. Really tough."

"What other families lost kids?"

"The Canfields and Jensens.

"I wish I had heard more about it. You said Pastor Staley didn't want it discussed."

"Yeah. Thought it would hurt morale."

"Did I tell you I found a secret church account at a Fremont bank? Larry Rowland is the only signer. It has $30,000 in it. He could be taking some money from the Sunday offerings."

"Larry Rowland? I doubt it."

"Rowland showed up at my office one night and threatened me after I told Boyle about the account. He said he didn't want me snooping into his business."

"Having a secret bank account sounds very strange because he doesn't need the money. He owns a great business."

"I know this sounds crazy, but could he have murdered Rockwell and Finley?"

Carlo stopped pacing and eased into his chair. "Hard to say, but I doubt it. Why would he commit murder?"

"Both Pete and Richard thought someone was stealing from the church. They both suspected Boyle. When I told Boyle about Rowland's secret bank account, he blew his top. Maybe Boyle and Rowland are working together, sharing the money in the secret bank account. Maybe they thought Pete and Richard knew what they were doing and decided to take action. They hired drivers at Rowland's trucking company to run Pete off the road and poison Richard."

"Anything's possible, but I can't believe Charlie could murder somebody. He likes money, don't get me wrong, and he also enjoys what money can buy. But I don't see him doing all that for a few extra bucks. If he went to jail, he wouldn't be able to go to the theater and see the A's play. Besides, he inherited some money from a rich aunt several years ago."

"What about Rowland?"

"Same sort of answer. Why does he need to risk his position in the community? I'm surprised to hear about the secret bank account. I wish Rowland's truck driver was still alive. He could clear up a lot of things."

"One of his drivers may have driven me off the pier a week ago."

"I read about it. Could your incident be connected to Rockwell and Finley?"

"Yes, and before that, I was almost run over in a hit-and-run attempt in front of my apartment one evening. I definitely think I'm a murder target."

"Matt, my friend, I don't want you to worry, but I think you may be part of some kind of plot that's unfolding, whether you know it or not. Something doesn't fit here, but I can't get my head around it. Earlier, I told you to mind your own business while you're at the church. Now, I think your detective work may be essential for your own safety. You could be in danger, especially since Larry Rowland has already threatened you. Have you told the San Lucas police what you know?"

"No, but I've told everything to Detective Ben Miller at the Oakland Police Department."

"You've had an awful start to your internship. Have you talked to the pastors about all this?"

"They know about the attempts on my life. And I've told them both about the secret bank account. Detective Miller asked me to leave a message on his voicemail at the end of every day, telling him about my daily schedule. He also believes I'm in danger."

"Be sure to leave those messages."

"Definitely."

"Let me know what else you learn. I'll keep my eyes and ears open."

"Thanks. I'm a little stressed these days. See you later." Matt closed the door behind him and returned to his office.

21

A fog clung to the San Francisco hills after sunset. The city lights glistened and sparkled in the moist air. In late September, with students back in school, the pace of life had quickened. People hurried around corners and darted across streets on shopping missions. Their quick steps became eighth notes and staccato-like in the symphony of human street activity. It had been a sunny day, but in the late afternoon clouds rushed into the San Francisco Bay from the Pacific Ocean through the mile-wide, three-mile-long channel spanned by the Golden Gate Bridge, wrapping the city in a misty blanket.

Matt drove across the Bay Bridge around six, right in the heart of the rush-hour traffic on Friday evening. He had been invited to the Canfields' annual wine tasting party at their Nob Hill condo. Liz said she and her husband tried to stay in the city at least one weekend each month, and he used the condo whenever he had a long day at the medical center or an early meeting the following morning. She'd asked Matt to arrive around seven, and added that she would serve food as well as wine, so he didn't have to worry about dinner. Wanting to bring a small gift, he planned to shop downtown before driving up to Nob Hill.

He'd expected heavy traffic, but not the bumper-to-bumper commute he encountered, as people started their weekend activities. Finally reaching the commercial district, he spotted a candy shop and decided to buy a box of chocolates. Luckily, a car was pulling out of a parking place right in front of the store.

Matt emerged from the shop with a white box of twenty-four chocolates and caramels, wrapped with a red velvet bow. Driving to Nob Hill took forever, and he appreciated the Canfields' offer that he use one of their two parking places in the garage. Taking an elevator to the fourteenth floor, he was greeted by Liz at the door. She smiled when he handed her the wrapped box. Undoing the paper, she purred with pleasure when she saw the candies, and patted his arm in appreciation. "I love the salted caramels. They will be gone by the end of the evening," she said.

"Could this woman be guilty of murder?" Matt wondered.

He followed her into the spacious kitchen, where she popped a caramel into her mouth. She placed the box on a counter and motioned for him to take a candy as well. The kitchen looked toward the bay and connected to an open living room whose windows offered a view of downtown San Francisco.

"I read the article in the San Lucas paper about your basketball program. Are you enjoying your contacts with the other San Lucas churches?" she asked.

"Yes. I've met some good people who've been very helpful, and I'm looking forward to starting the season."

"It will energize your middle school group."

"I agree," he said. "I think the more we can improve relations between the churches, the better."

The doorbell rang. He was curious to see who else had been invited to the Canfields' party.

"Matt," Liz said, "would you help me by answering the door until Steve arrives? You can put our friends' coats on the bed in the den down the hall."

Mike and Jean Jensen were the first to arrive. Ryan, their son, was going to be one of the better players on the boys' team. Matt had already seen him shooting baskets in the gym.

"Hey, Matt," Mike said, "It's good to see you! Ryan is really looking forward to playing on the team. He thinks you're a pretty neat guy. What's the magic formula?"

"I'm not sure," Matt said, taking their coats. "I'm a pretty good shot, so maybe he thinks I know something about basketball. We have a good group of kids this year. It'll be fun, and I think they'll grow closer to the church because of it."

"Keep up the good work," Mike said, as he swept by Matt and walked toward the kitchen. "I'm ready for dinner."

"We'll be seeing you tomorrow morning," Jean said.

"I'm looking forward to it," Matt said.

After depositing their coats in the den, Matt was about to join the Jensens in the kitchen when the doorbell rang again. Opening the door, he greeted the next guest, Daniel Kincaid, who had grilled him during his initial interview with the Education Committee. Matt managed a smile for Kincaid, who turned to Liz as she walked toward him. After exchanging hugs, Liz returned to the kitchen.

Kincaid paused in front of Matt before following her. "I read the newspaper article about your basketball program," he said. "A skillful piece of marketing on your part."

"The reporter asked for the interview, not I."

"Don't forget we want our kids to study the Bible. Shooting baskets won't help them get to heaven," Kincaid said.

"But it might help them grow closer to Hacienda. It could cause them to bond to the Church for the rest of their lives. That's not a bad outcome, is it?"

"They can find a gym anywhere."

"Probably not a gym where a game starts with a prayer."

Kincaid shrugged and walked toward the kitchen.

Ten minutes later, Liz joined Matt in the living room. "I heard some of your conversation with Daniel. He means well, but he isn't always tactful. Don't take his comments to heart. Beneath his gruff exterior, he cares about the church and wants our programs to succeed. Let his words roll off your back."

Then the front door opened. "Sorry, I'm late, dear."

"I was wondering where you were," she shot back, smiling at Stephen Canfield, M.D. "Matt has been helping me with the coats."

"Hi," Steve said. "I'm glad you could join us tonight."

"Thanks for inviting me."

Matt retreated to a spot next to a Steinway baby grand piano in the corner, where a hired pianist had begun to play. He watched the Canfields greet their other guests, including Pastor and Mrs. Staley, Pastor Boyle, Evelyn Kirby, Larry and Sally Rowland, and a handful of other couples and individuals he didn't recognize. On a long table in the living room sat open bottles of Napa Valley wines along with an abundance of hors d'oeuvres. The guests converged on the table and filled their glasses and plates. As they passed the piano, he tried to speak with as many as possible.

Matt went to the kitchen for a glass of water and found Liz instructing the caterer to replenish the trays of food in the living room.

As the caterer left the kitchen carrying a full platter, Matt said, "Didn't I see you and Pastor Staley at Angelo's the other night?"

"Maybe so," Liz said. "We own the restaurant, and I often go there during the dinner hour to check on things. I've been in counseling with Pastor Staley since our daughter drowned over a year ago. Sometimes he drops by to see how I'm doing."

"I'm sorry to hear about your loss."

"It has been a crushing experience for us, and we're trying to deal with it."

Matt was caught off guard by her response, and didn't know what else to say. After an awkward moment, Liz said, "I need to take some more wine to the living room. Maybe you could help me." Matt followed her holding a bottle in each hand.

By ten-thirty, all of the guests had left, and Matt was sitting with the Canfields in their empty living room. He had been told they would go to the Mark Hopkins Hotel for coffee and dessert, even though dessert had been served to the guests. The plates and wine bottles had been cleared from the table.

"Let's head over to the Mark Hopkins," Liz said.

"I'm ready!" Steve said. "Matt, a few years ago, we started going to the Top of the Mark for a snack after our guests left. It's become a tradition."

"Sounds great," Matt said.

A chilly night had settled over San Francisco, so they all put on jackets. On the two-block walk to the Mark Hopkins, they passed other partygoers. Entering the hotel, they saw a line of cars and taxis leading to the front door, typical for a Friday night. They walked into the lobby and headed toward the elevators. As an elevator door opened, three couples emerged, the men wearing tuxedos.

Matt straightened when he saw Jancy Nichols.

"What a surprise, Matt! It's good to see you," Jancy said, standing next to a man he assumed to be her date.

"You all look great," Matt responded. "Have you been to a party?" He tried to cover his shock at seeing Jancy with someone else. He'd assumed she wasn't seeing anyone, but he'd miscalculated.

"We went to an auction and dinner dance to raise money for the homeless," Jancy said. "Then we came here to have dessert."

"Aren't you going to introduce me to your friend," Jancy's date asked her, slurring his words.

Jancy looked embarrassed. "Matt, this is Tom Robertson. Tom, this is Matt Beringer."

Tom didn't look very steady, and they had an uncomfortable moment trying to shake hands. As he turned to leave, Tom stumbled and fell to one knee. The other young men helped him to his feet, and Matt decided to intervene.

"Jancy, would you like to join us for dessert?"

"I'd like that." She turned quickly to Tom. "Thanks for the evening, and I hope you get home safely."

The other two couples standing next to Tom wore surprised expressions when Jancy entered the elevator with Matt and the Canfields. Before he could introduce Jancy, she had greeted the Canfields, having known them from her year at Hacienda. When the door opened on the 19th floor, they found a table next to the windows. Their sweeping view looked south, across the illuminated skyline to the Bay Bridge.

"Thanks for rescuing me," Jancy whispered to Matt. "Tom was a blind date. The auction was for a worthy cause, but all of them had way too much to drink."

A waiter approached their table, and they ordered dessert and coffee.

"Jancy, were you at the church when Pete Rockwell was the intern? Steve asked.

"No, I was there during Richard Finley's internship."

"We've been reading that Pete may have been run off the road by one of Larry Rowland's trucks," Steve continued.

"Pete's death worries me," Jancy said, "and so does Richard's death. Matt and I were going to have dinner with him the day he drowned. We arrived at Lake Chabot and saw him face down in the water. Matt swam out and brought him back to the dock, but it was too late. We're wondering if the two deaths are connected."

"Let's change the subject, shall we?" Liz said. "I want to talk about happier things."

Their conversation moved from food to travel and finally to books. Liz also reminded Matt and Jancy that they would see them in Napa Valley the next day. After dessert, they walked back to the Canfields' building. In the lobby, Matt and Jancy said goodbye to their hosts and took the elevator to the garage.

"You were a lifesaver this evening," Jancy said, as they were driving across the Bay Bridge. "I was feeling a little desperate."

"Glad I could help. Blind dates can be unpredictable."

"One of the women was an old high school friend who asked me if I would go to the auction with a blind date. I haven't seen her in a couple of years. I had never met the others."

"I should have invited you to the Canfields' party tonight, but I thought you might be uncomfortable interacting with that group. I've been thinking about you a lot the past week." Matt reached over and took her hand.

"That's good to hear. I've been thinking about you, too."

"I recently had lunch with Detective Miller of the Oakland Police Department. Miller thinks the guy who drove me off the pier could be a Hannifin truck driver who's recently disappeared, just like Kenny Cole."

"I don't think Cole wasn't acting on his own, like the police think," Jancy said. "Someone wanted both Pete and Richard dead. I believe you may be on that list, and we need to find out whose list it is."

"But I don't want to involve you in my problems."

"Please don't keep any secrets."

"All right."

"I can't get to know you if you don't tell me things."

"I hear you," Matt said. "I had such mixed feelings seeing you in the elevator tonight."

"Why?"

"It was great seeing you, but I wanted to be that guy standing next to you. And, to be perfectly honest, I wasn't happy seeing you with someone else. I'd like to be the only man in your life."

"I'd like that, too."

"With all that's been going on, I haven't been the best communicator. It's totally my fault. Maybe it's an only child thing. I tend to keep information to myself because I don't want to bother other people."

"If we're going to get to know each other, we need to share the good and the bad."

They were approaching Jancy's apartment. "If you're interested in another cup of coffee, I'd like to hear more about your conversation with Detective Miller," Jancy said.

"Coffee sounds great. Something warm will hit the spot."

Matt pulled in front of Jancy's building and parked at the curb. He opened her car door and, when she got out, he drew her into his arms for a long kiss and embrace. She held him tightly, which signaled to him that they were on the same page. They held hands as they walked toward the lobby entrance. Taking the elevator to her third-floor unit, Matt felt at peace, happy that they were together. While having a cup of coffee, they discussed his lunch with Detective Miller and their plans for the next day.

Two weeks earlier, Matt had invited Jancy to join him on a picnic with the Jensens and Canfields in Napa Valley. He had called her earlier that day to confirm their date. They would be riding with the Jensens, who would pick her up at nine-thirty. After a hug and a kiss, Matt drove his car back to San Leandro, pulling into the apartment garage as his dashboard clock said one-twenty in the morning. He looked forward to seeing her again in eight hours.

22

Before coming to the San Francisco Bay Area to attend the seminary, Matt had never visited Napa Valley. He knew about it because his parents had honeymooned there. They would occasionally reminisce about the wineries, picnics under shady trees, and their mud baths at a Calistoga spa. It sounded like a magical place. They agreed to take Matt there after his college graduation. However, their deaths two months before that ceremony meant that Matt would have to visit Napa Valley on his own.

After spending the summer in Seattle following graduation, Matt needed to arrive at Calvin Seminary in late August for an intensive course in Hebrew that started the academic year for first-year students. He decided to stop for a few days in Napa Valley on his drive to San Francisco. Under blue, cloudless skies, he visited several wineries selected before the trip, and ate some leisurely meals at recommended restaurants. Enjoying the warm weather, Matt celebrated how relaxed he felt in spite of the strenuous studies that awaited him. He only wished he could have shared Napa Valley with his parents, so he left the wine country with bittersweet memories embedded in his heart and mind.

———

When Mike and Jean Jensen invited him to join them and the Canfields on a picnic in Napa Valley on the first Saturday in October, he'd accepted with mixed feelings about the place he had never visited with his parents and yet had enjoyed two years before on his way to the seminary. He asked if he could bring Jancy, and they wholeheartedly approved. The Jensens picked him up at nine in the morning, and then stopped at Jancy's apartment on their journey north. The drive to the Robert Mondavi Winery would take about an hour and a half.

Heading north on I-80 in the Jensens' SUV, they left the freeway at Vallejo and worked their way west to the south end of the valley. Going north on Highway 26, Mike took the exit into downtown Napa for some groceries. Driving through town, he sang a few lines of a pep song from his days at Napa Union High School. He had grown up in the town of Napa, so this picnic outing allowed him to recall his youth and, for his sake, they made a series of traditional stops to mark the occasion. First, they visited the Butter Crème Bakery for donuts and maple bars. Then they found Lawler's Liquor Store to buy some gin, tonic water, limes, ravioli, and garlic bread. The final destination was Vallerga's market for a few more picnic items that Jean hadn't packed, such as soda and plastic utensils.

Mike owned an insurance agency in San Francisco. Jean had served for three years on the Education Committee, and they had been members at Hacienda for five years. The Jensens had invited him to join them for their annual picnic in Napa Valley to celebrate Mike's birthday, which coincided with the October grape harvest. They also said it was to thank him for his leadership of the middle school program.

As they drove to their picnic site at the Mondavi Winery, at the southwest entrance to the valley, Matt saw workers in the nearby fields, picking grapes. On the side roads, crates of the fruit filled the backs of pickup trucks. In the autumn, activity accelerated in the wine country, when after months of care and attention, the grapes would tell their worth, starting with the harvest and crush.

The Canfields were waiting in their car after eleven when Mike pulled into the winery parking lot. Matt and Jancy greeted Liz and Steve, who joked about how long it had been since they had last seen them. They all unloaded the Jensens' SUV, and helped Jean spread a large checkered table cloth and blankets on the emerald lawn. Then each of them found a place around the picnic basket in the center.

Matt suspected his inclusion in the picnic had partly to do with the Jensens' and Canfields' interest in becoming better acquainted with the seminary intern in charge of their kids' Christian education.

Jean set out food and beverages. Mike and Jean mixed gin and tonics. Steve and Liz opted for glasses of Chardonnay. Matt and Jancy chose the Merlot. Lively conversation accompanied the ravioli, potato salad, garlic bread, and peach pie. By the time they finished their leisurely meal, Matt noticed that Mike had enjoyed two gin and tonics.

"Matt," Mike said, "I want you to aim for first place in the boys' basketball league. If you let my son play enough, you'll win some ball games." He was speaking in a loud voice.

"Mike," Jean said, "I'm sure Matt doesn't need another coach. The kids will have a great time. Matt can manage things on his own."

"Now wait a minute, Jean," Mike said. "This is important to me! After we lost Scott last year, I decided to become more involved in Ryan's activities. I want him to get the most out of his life."

Matt hesitated, knowing they were discussing a sensitive subject. "Mike," Matt said, "in my letter to the parents a few weeks ago, I mentioned that teamwork, giving everyone a chance to play, and learning how to be a good loser were more important than winning at all costs. But don't get me wrong. I like to win, too." He laughed, hoping to lighten the mood. "That's why we keep score."

"The Education Committee agreed, Mike, and signed off on those priorities," Jean said. "You know how little the gym has been used since we've been members. Our kids will improve their basketball skills and learn about teamwork. The program will be a big success."

"Our daughter, Julie, is looking forward to playing," Steve said. "You can count on one hand the number of times I've been in the gym."

"I'm not saying the program won't be successful," Mike said. "All I'm saying is the boys want to win, and the program should focus on that goal.

Losing is unacceptable." Mike reached for the gin and began to mix himself another drink.

"A year from now, it won't matter to them where they finished in the league standings," Jancy said. "They won't remember how many games they won and lost. But, hopefully, they'll have good memories of spending time at church and making new friends."

"I hear you, Jancy, but you only pass through life once, so you want to get as much out of it as you can. After losing Scott, I think the church owes us a little extra consideration," Mike said, crossing his arms. "Sometimes I wonder why we're still involved with the church." Then he stretched out on the blanket, looking up at the sky.

"Mike, take it easy," Jean said. "Matt had nothing to do with the canoe trip."

"He sure wouldn't be here today if he had," Mike said.

"Mike, we all still hurt," Steve said, "but we need to put our grief behind us. Julie is really looking forward to the games, and I've never seen her so enthusiastic about going to Sunday school. Her relationship with the church should deepen as she gets to know her teammates."

"Matt, I don't know how much you've heard about the church canoe trip a year and a half ago," Liz finally said, "but we, and the Jensens, and the Rowlands each lost a child when their canoe capsized. Their deaths have devastated our families." She paused. "We're still grieving. Every day, Steve and I think of our daughter who's no longer with us."

"I'm sorry for all of you. I've heard very little about the canoe trip," Matt said. "Shouldn't I have been told about it when I interviewed with the Education Committee?"

"You weren't told because Pastor Staley urged us to put the tragedy behind us," Jean said. "Staff wasn't supposed to discuss the incident. Pastor Staley worried that dwelling on the subject could permanently affect the health of the church."

"I understand," Matt said.

"We never imagined such a disaster could happen on a church outing," Steve said. "At first, we suspected a lack of proper supervision. We even thought about suing Hacienda. You can imagine how upset and angry we were. But we reviewed the trip, as did the police. It was well organized and had adequate adult supervision. Poor Pete Rockwell, our intern who planned it, was destroyed by the accident, and I'm not sure he ever recovered from it. Pastor Staley met with us often and persuaded us to stay involved at the church for the sake of our other kids. None of us planned to move from San Lucas, so he counseled us that trying to move forward with forgiveness was better than harboring bitterness. We three families made a decision to stay at Hacienda. But our pain will probably never go away."

"What went wrong?" Matt asked.

"The trip was given a green light by the Education Committee," Mike said. "There were four adults and eighteen kids. As I understand it, the Russian River was moving slowly, and the kids were having a great time. Somehow, our kids' canoe fell behind the others."

"Maybe they were hurrying to catch up," Steve said, "but their canoe veered toward the shore at a curve in the river. It ran into the tangled root system of an overhanging tree. The canoe overturned and trapped them under water. By the time someone realized a canoe was missing, the others were a fair distance down the river. When the adults came back and found the kids, they had been under water for several minutes. They must have been so disoriented they couldn't free themselves. It was a freak accident that probably couldn't happen again in a million years. Autopsies showed that all of them drowned. The accident has left deep scars."

"What a painful experience for all of you, " Matt said.

"Jim Staley has been a wonderful friend to all three families," Liz said. "He's spent countless hours meeting with us. I don't know how we could have worked through our pain without him, especially us mothers. He has been available whenever we've needed him."

"Has Pastor Staley met with the Rowlands as well?"

"Yes," Jean replied. "Sally has mentioned that he'll drop by their house in the afternoon and have a cup of coffee with her."

Matt suddenly realized he'd been wrong about Pastor Staley. The notes he'd discovered in Pete's journal had led him to the wrong conclusions. Staley hadn't been a womanizer after all.

"Hey," Liz said. "We didn't invite Matt and Jancy to Napa to talk about the canoe trip. Let's go enjoy some wines. We came to celebrate Mike's birthday, so let's do it!"

The six adults rose from the picnic blankets and agreed on two nearby wineries they would visit before returning to San Lucas. Matt felt much closer to the three families who had lost children, and he hoped his day with the Jensens and Canfields had increased their trust and confidence in him as the church's middle school leader. The group of six spent the next hour comparing wines and enjoying the agreeable Napa Valley weather. On the way home, Jean drove the Jensens' SUV.

23

Learning on the picnic about the pain the three couples had experienced made a powerful impression on Matt. Did he have the counseling skills to help them? Perhaps his best contribution might be to be a positive influence on their kids in his group. If the Canfield, Jensen, and Rowland kids enjoyed their middle school activities, maybe he could play a role in the healing process. He had gained a new respect for Pastor Staley, who had been a faithful caregiver to the families after their losses. After the day in Napa Valley, Matt removed him from his list of suspects.

At the same time, he had to remain vigilant. Even though he no longer considered Staley to be an adversary, he still needed to identify the killer before he became the third victim. Matt kept asking himself, "If Pete and Richard were murdered, what was the motive?"

He took stock of his internship. Sunday school attendance was good, much better than Boyle had expected. Sign-ups for the boys' and girls' basketball teams were encouraging. "Maybe they're okay with my leadership," he reflected.

Among various invitations from church members, Matt had received a note from Sally Rowland, inviting him dinner. He promptly called her to accept. To Matt's relief, she said Larry wouldn't be home for the evening barbecue because he had to entertain some customers. The prospect of a home-cooked meal and interacting with the Rowland kids, one of whom belonged to his group, sealed the deal. She also suggested he bring his bathing suit. At the right moment during dinner, he intended to tell her how sorry he was over the loss of their oldest son, Derek. After he hung up the phone, he slipped her note into his middle desk drawer.

———

The Rowlands lived in a large, two-story stucco house on one of the highest streets in San Lucas. Their residence on the west side of Alta Avenue offered a 180-degree view of the San Francisco Bay, stretching from Palo Alto north to the Golden Gate Bridge. Because of their spectacular setting, the Rowlands hosted numerous church gatherings, especially youth groups that could take advantage of the heated swimming pool.

Matt arrived around five-thirty on a Monday evening in early October, with sunset fast approaching. The air felt warm. Sally and Larry's two children, Susan, age eight, and Ricky, age twelve, greeted him at the door. Ricky had joined the boys' basketball team, which would begin practices in the next week. Susan looked up to her older brother and liked to follow him around.

Sally showed Matt the guest bathroom for changing into his swimsuit. "Burgers won't go on the grill for a half hour," she said, "so you have time for a short swim. The kids are heading for the pool, too. It's down there," she said, pointing toward the nearby staircase, "and through the door."

Wearing his swimsuit and carrying his shirt, Matt found his way out. He walked barefoot across the stone surface of a large patio to steps leading to the lower level. The kids were already in the pool.

"Jump in, Pastor Matt," Ricky squealed. "The water's warm!"

"You're not trying to fool me, are you?"

"No, honest. You'll like it. I promise."

Matt put his shirt on a chair sitting on the tile border encircling the pool. As he slipped in, he saw a bracelet of lighting around the pool's edge which made the blue-green water glow. Commuters were making their way home from jobs in San Francisco, streaming across the Bay Bridge and Golden Gate Bridge, their cars spreading outward on highways like the glittering tentacles of an octopus.

Sally Rowland appeared at the pool's edge wearing a terrycloth robe of pastel shades, partially covering a two-piece bathing suit. "What a great evening for a barbecue," she said, slipping off her robe.

"You have a fabulous view, Mrs. Rowland," as he leaned against the side of the pool and looked west at the expansive vista.

"Glad you like it." She stood at the edge of the pool, with her hands on her hips.

"I've had a long day, and this really feels good," Matt said. "How could anyone tire of this view," he thought to himself. He wished Jancy were standing next to him.

Sally dove head-first into the pool, glided half the length under water, and surfaced just a few feet from him. She ran her hands along both sides of her head, squeezing the water from her shoulder-length hair.

"How long have you lived here, Mrs. Rowland?"

"Call me Sally," she said. "I like to be on a first-name basis with my friends at church. You're part of our church family now, whether you like it or not." She ended her comment with a short laugh.

"Okay," he said. Matt estimated that she was in her late thirties. As head of the Education Committee, she had been instrumental in hiring him and was no doubt evaluating his work with the middle school group.

"We've been here for a little over ten years. After Larry and I married, we lived for three years in San Leandro and dreamed of a home in San Lucas. With a lot of help from my parents, we were able to move here."

The kids giggled as they slapped water at each other at the shallow end of the pool.

"Time to start dinner," Sally said. She swam to the other end and climbed out of the pool, put on her robe, and started across the patio to turn on the barbecue. "I'll call you in a few minutes," she said.

Matt turned to Susan and Ricky and challenged them to a game of Marco Polo. He would close his eyes and try to find them. When they heard Sally's call, Matt and the kids joined her on the upper patio. Mixing a tossed salad on a glass-topped table with a wrought-iron frame, she motioned for them to each take a hamburger and put it on the grill. Matt slipped into the house and dressed, stuffing his wet swimsuit in his duffel bag. He returned as Sally was serving the hamburgers.

"Do you enjoy wine with your dinner, Matt?" she asked.

"Sure."

"Do you prefer white or red?" she asked.

"Whatever is open. Red, if you have it."

"I do. That's what I'm having."

After a moment, Matt said, "Did you grow up in the East Bay?"

"No. I'm a Delta girl," she answered. "My Dad was a farmer near Sacramento. I grew up near Vacaville north of here, off of Highway 80. Do you know that area?"

"Not really," Matt said. "I've driven to Lake Tahoe a few times, but I've never explored the Sacramento area. What's the Delta like?"

"Lots of farms. A nice place to grow up, I guess, but I always enjoyed our trips to San Francisco. After high school, I came down to attend U.C.-Berkeley and stayed."

With the warm evening breeze caressing his face and the lights of the Bay Area twinkling in the background, Matt thought for a moment he'd died and gone to heaven. The sun continued its decline toward the horizon and the sky became darker. As the four of them sat around the patio table, he gazed at the distant lights encircling the bay.

Having dinner with the Rowlands, minus Larry, was a welcome break from TV dinners in his apartment or meals at East Bay restaurants. He liked Ricky, a quiet boy who didn't say much. Susan filled any silence with chatter about a wide range of subjects, including the Big Dipper and her favorite television programs. Both kids seemed well mannered and comfortable around adults.

Following ice cream sundaes for dessert, Sally reminded Ricky and Susan that it was time they walked to her sister's house down the block to spend the night with their cousins. They scurried from the table. "Don't forget to take your tooth brushes," she called after them.

All he could hear was the hum of traffic on the Nimitz far below. Sally suggested to Matt that they go sit by the pool. "You bring the wine and I'll bring our glasses," she said. At the pool, Sally motioned for him to sit in the chair beside her. He set the bottle of wine near the wine glasses on a small table next to Sally.

Looking at the panorama of lights to the west, Matt savored the beauty of the evening. He felt just a twinge of envy at the comfort of the Rowlands' lifestyle. It seemed they had achieved the American Dream, with their castle on the hill. He was baffled as to why Larry Rowland needed to steal from the church and might be connected with the murders of Pete and Richard. If he was supporting a mistress, he certainly didn't need the money. Why did he have to cheat on his wife? Matt thought Sally was very attractive.

Ricky and Susan ran to give their mother hugs and kisses before dashing off to their cousins' home. "I'll pick you up tomorrow after breakfast and take you to school," Sally shouted to them as they ran up the steps.

She broke the silence after the kids left with a question that caught him off guard. "Matt, how have you been doing since you lost your parents a couple of years ago?" She poured some wine into a glass and handed it to him.

"Quite honestly, it still hurts," he said, glancing past her to the blue-green water glowing in the pool. "I think about them every day."

"How did it happen?" she asked.

"I think you asked me the same question during my interview," he said, taking a sip of wine. "They were hit by a drunk driver speeding in the wrong direction on a one-way street. Our doctor said they died instantly."

"You must feel alone at times," she said.

"Yes. There are times I feel very lonely," Matt said. "As an only child, I sometimes resisted their support and guidance, wanting to solve all of my own problems. When I went away to college, I began to realize how important they were to me, and they were starting to relax a little and not worry so much about me. We always had a close relationship, but we were relating to one another as adults. I'm afraid I took them for granted for many years, and now that they're gone there's so much I'd like to share with them. I try to make sense of why it all happened, but there are some things that are beyond my understanding."

"When Larry was thirteen, he lost his father due to a heart attack," Sally began. "That left a big void in his life, and I think it still haunts him. I know how you must be feeling," she said softly. "I apologize for getting so personal, Matt."

"It's okay," he sighed, and scanned the dark sky in search of a few stars. "How did you and Larry get into the trucking business? It appears you have a very successful company." Matt drank more wine, enjoying the full-bodied taste.

"My grandfather started the trucking company as a second business when he was a farmer in the 1950s. He saw the need for the transportation of crops on the Delta as the area grew. Farming boomed because of the expanding irrigation system. He eventually spent most of his time transporting his neighbors' crops to wherever they needed to go. The trucking business was simply in the path of explosive growth in farming around Sacramento, and he did very well with it. My dad took over from grandpa and grew the company. I'm the oldest of three daughters, so dad was happy when I married Larry. I think he would have liked to have had a son, but he trained Larry to take over the business. When dad died, we moved the headquarters from Vacaville to Oakland."

Matt sensed a profound sadness in Sally as she spoke about her youth and family. Maybe she missed a simpler, less stressful life on her parents' farm. Maybe the death of her oldest son continued to trouble her. She looked down at her glass of wine, as she slowly swirled its contents. He was getting close to expressing his condolences over her loss.

"You must have been stunned by that guy Kenny Cole running Pete Rockwell off the road in one of your trucks."

"I'd prefer not to talk about that disaster," Sally said. "Let's talk about something else." She reached over and placed her forearm on top his, so her hand cupped the top of his. He was aware she was looking at him. And he was beginning to feel the effects of the red wine. A warm, relaxed calm surrounded him, while at the same time not knowing what to think about Sally's touch. Also, he wondered why she had dismissed his question about Pete's death so quickly. "Matt, I appreciate all the good things you're doing at Hacienda."

"Thanks," he responded. "I'm very sorry to learn that you lost a son," he blurted suddenly. "I heard about the canoeing accident last Saturday, on a picnic with the Jensens and Canfields." Sally removed her hand from his forearm. "I wish I had been told about the incident when you interviewed me, but I heard Pastor Staley didn't want the subject to be discussed."

"Why?" she turned quickly toward him and leaned in. "What good would it do?"

Matt was surprised by her tone, which was nearly aggressive. "I'm sure your children are still coming to terms with the tragedy," he said. "It would have helped me be a more understanding youth leader." He was slowly becoming aware that his words were beginning to slur.

"Hey, before the wine goes to my head," she said, "I'm going for a swim!" Sally stood up from her chair and dropped her robe at her ankles. She walked to the edge of the pool and then turned to face him. "Will you bring me my glass of wine?" she said.

He was just about to rise from the chair when his head went woozy and his vision blurred, and he suddenly felt very tired.

"Matt, Matt?" A woman's voice was speaking to his face. Up close. He couldn't make it out. What was happening? "Are you…."

24

Matt awoke on the floor of a moving vehicle, his mind cloudy and confused. His face rested sideways on a carpeted surface, and a strip of duct tape covered his mouth. He felt more duct tape around his wrists, bound behind his back, as well as encircling his knees and ankles. The size of the area where he lay told him he was in the back of a van. "Have I been kidnapped? What's going on?" Beyond the van's windows, he saw only a black sky. Trying to recollect the evening, the last thing he remembered was Sally standing at the edge of the pool.

He heard the tires' thump-thump, thump-thump as the vehicle changed lanes, and he noticed lights from highway lamps appear and disappear as the vehicle pushed through the darkness. Now and then, lights from shopping centers filled the sky, like an artist splashing yellow paint on a dark canvas. The left side of his head ached, and his left cheekbone stung, like he had scraped his skin on a rough surface. Rolling onto his back, he scanned the interior. He must have blacked out at the Rowlands' house. "Did someone strike me from behind?" he asked himself. "Did Sally Rowland put something in my wine glass?"

His left knee hurt, and his head throbbed. The duct tape around his wrists, knees, and ankles immobilized him. Whoever had kidnapped him meant business. Matt tried to recall the last moments before he lost consciousness. He remembered having a glass of wine with Sally by the pool, but nothing more. While his head cleared, he pretended to be unconscious. Then, with sudden clarity, he thought about Pete and Richard. "Am I going to be the third victim?"

He heard a man's voice coming from the driver's seat. It sounded like Larry Rowland. And a woman's voice. Sally? Larry must have come back early from his evening meeting with clients, if there even was a meeting, which Matt now doubted. Had Larry hit him on the head?

"Take the exit to my parents' farm," Sally said. "Davis Road. I want to go to the Weyand Canal."

"Okay," Larry said.

He couldn't believe that Sally would be trying to harm him. "This doesn't feel like some kind of sick joke," he thought. On the other hand, perhaps Larry had forced her to carry out his orders. "Was I right about Larry's plot to murder Pete and Richard, and now me?! Why? What is the motive? Did Sally drug my wine?"

"We'll dump him in the canal," Sally said, "and no one will ever find him. Take Davis Road. It's four exits before Dixon."

"Yeah, I know. You already told me!"

"Larry, I'll tell you something else," Sally said. "After we dump Beringer in the canal, I'll feel a big weight lifted off my shoulders. Then our Derek can rest in peace, along with Linda and Scott."

"They may rest in peace," Larry said, "but I'm not so sure we will. We're talking about three murders here. Do you know what you've done?!"

"Relax," Sally said. "Those interns deserved what they got. An eye for an eye is the way I feel about it. Every time I think about that church, it makes my blood boil. Pete Rockwell was totally negligent! If they had been paying attention, the accident would never have happened."

"It did happen," Larry said, "and we can't bring Derek back!"

185

"But we can get even."

"You could get life or the chair for what you've done. Have you lost your mind?"

"You're part of this, too, so get down off your high horse."

"Wait a minute."

"You'll go down with me," Sally said. "I have your fingerprints all over these jobs. The truck that killed Rockwell was from the company you manage. I told the guy who gave me the poison that you wanted me to find a chemical to kill rats. The cement weight we'll tie around Beringer's waist belongs to Hannifin Trucking. The police might even look at you as the kingpin behind all of this. It would be my word against yours, so I could blame it all on you. Any way you cut it, you're just as involved as I am."

Matt's head swirled with fear. "They're really going to kill me."

"What if we're caught?" Larry asked.

"They'll never catch us, if they haven't yet. They won't even suspect us. You deflected Rockwell's death pretty well."

"That's because I didn't know anything about it!" Larry shouted.

"Calm down. We won't even show up on their radar screens. We're pillars of the church. We're successful."

"How'd you happen to pick a canal?" Larry asked.

"It's close to one of my favorite make-out spots in high school."

"Yeah, sure."

"It's the truth," Sally said, "but that's not why I chose this place. It's because of the siphon. Did you ever look at the siphon when we visited the folks' farm?"

"No."

"That's one of the differences between us, Larry. You're a city slicker. You don't have a clue about what happens on a farm."

"And I could care even less at this point."

There was silence. Matt tried to imagine what was going on between them. And he was coming to realize he had it all wrong. "Is it possible Sally was behind it? Behind it all? Pete? Richard? Nobody will suspect her." His fear made him sweat from his forehead, and the back of his shirt was damp. "How am I going to get out of this alive?"

"What's the big deal about the siphon?" Larry asked.

"The siphon is a remarkable piece of construction. It takes water from an irrigation canal, under a road, and brings it out on the other side, into a lower canal. The bottom of the siphon is a perfect place to hide a body. The noise and power of the water plunging into the siphon used to scare me as a kid. In high school, I grew to admire the engineering behind it. Nobody went there, so it was a great place to make out after a dance."

"I'm beginning to think there's a lot about you I don't know. And I'm not liking it."

"Shut up, Larry. We don't have time for that. Wake up! We've got Beringer in the back, and we've got to complete this whether you like it or not."

"All right, all right."

"We'll tie that cement block around his waist, dump him into the canal, and he'll get sucked into the siphon. He'll end up at the bottom of it. His body will decompose there, and no one will ever find him."

"You've thought of everything, haven't you?" Larry said.

"You bet," she replied.

"And just one final detail I'm sure you've thought about. Are you certain he didn't tell anyone he was visiting you and the kids tonight for a barbecue?"

"Beringer isn't married and lives by himself. From what I've observed, he's a bit of a loner. I invited him to dinner with a note, which I regret, and I need to go to the church tonight and retrieve it."

"You know," Larry said, "I've bent the rules on our tax returns and taken a higher salary from the company than maybe I deserve, but I've never thought about murdering someone. What pushed you over the edge?"

"Those kids are all I've got," Sally said. "That's all I'm going to say about it. Derek was my favorite, and losing him tore my heart out."

Lying on the floor of the van, Matt listened to the Rowlands' conversation. His kidnapping had been Sally's idea. "If she masterminded the murders of Pete and Richard, how had she done it? Did she drive the truck that ran Pete off of Interstate 80? Of course not. Did she poison Richard's sandwich? Absolutely."

"But why try to lessen your pain with murder?" Larry asked.

"After Derek died, my life turned upside down. You know that. I had big plans for our Derek. He was going to run our trucking company. I was so angry at Rockwell for planning the canoe trip. I decided it was time the church paid for the death of my son. They thought I was a hero for asking to chair the Education Committee, in the midst of my grief. They applauded my efforts to put Derek's death behind me and stay busy. But I knew it was the way I could get my revenge. I'd murder three seminarians to avenge the three kids who died. You have to admit, my plan was clever. Taking care of Rockwell was easy. As chair, I had the dominant hand in choosing the interns who followed him. I spoke with the Calvin Seminary dean about possible applicants. When I heard that Finley was an expert sailor, I chose him. He would give classes at Lake Chabot, but his sailing expertise disguised the real reason behind his selection. I learned that his father was dead, and his mother was in poor health and lived all the way up in Idaho. If Finley were murdered, there was little chance his mother would start an investigation into her son's death."

"What about Beringer?"

"If you spent more time at home talking to me and less time fooling around, you'd know what I've been up to, but we'll talk about that later."

"What did you say?

"Let me finish! I used the same strategy with Beringer. He was an even better fit. Both of his parents were killed in a car accident a couple of years ago. Remember Jancy Nichols? You told me she was kind of cute, as I recall. She urged me to make better use of our gym at church. When I learned that Beringer played basketball at Princeton, I picked him to follow Finley as our next intern and organize boys' and girls' basketball leagues for the San Lucas churches, using our gym. Since Beringer's parents are dead, it's unlikely his relatives will investigate his death. That was part of my master plan to get rid of three interns."

"Didn't anyone on your committee think you were being a little controlling when you wanted both Finley and Beringer?"

"No. The committee liked my idea to have sailing classes and basketball leagues. I had urged the seminary dean to have Finley and Beringer apply for our internship, and they were clearly the most qualified applicants we had. Most importantly, however, these seminarians had virtually no parental support. Also, Staley's instructions to the staff and Session to avoid speaking about the canoe incident allowed me to operate without anyone thinking too much about Derek's death. I'm sure it's never crossed anyone's mind that I, the mourning mother, might be connected to the deaths of Rockwell and Finley. They think I've been a big supporter of our interns. Besides, the committee felt sympathy toward me, so they've pretty much let me have my way."

Matt couldn't believe the devious thinking Sally had used to weave her web.

"You lied to Finley and Beringer about why they were chosen for the internships. The sailing and basketball programs were ploys to help you select a couple of vulnerable victims."

"Right. The sailing and basketball programs appealed to their male egos. My strategy worked perfectly."

"How did you arrange to have Rockwell murdered using one of our trucks?"

"I asked your driver, Kenny Cole, for some assistance."

"I'm surprised he offered to help you."

"Money talks. He had a drug habit, you know."

"Well, I didn't know. But the media found out and made a big deal about it."

"He told me about his habit at one of our Christmas parties, and he asked me if I was interested in doing drugs with him."

"He what?!"

"He'd had a few too many drinks, and started getting friendly. I told him I thought he was good-looking, and he said he wanted to start seeing me."

"I'll bet he did."

"Getting him to murder Rockwell was easy. When you told me they found truck paint on Rockwell's car, that made me nervous."

"*You* were nervous! I was panic-stricken because I had to face the police and the media. You put me through the ringer on that one, having to defend myself. I never dreamed you'd hired Cole. You lucked out when he shot himself and the police concluded he'd acted on his own. If they'd taken him alive, he would have spilled the beans, for sure."

"You mean *we* lucked out, Larry. We're partners in crime. Yes, we're lucky Cole killed himself."

"How'd you kill Finley? The paper said he drowned."

"I poisoned him. I called a family friend, Bob Walker, who has a farm near the folks' property, and told him you'd seen a rat in our yard. He suggested that we use succinylcholine, so I drove to his farm one afternoon and picked up a small bag of the chemical from him. I did some research and learned it's hard to trace. It's a white powder. He mixes it with peanut butter to kill rats. I invited Finley to our house one Saturday, ostensibly to ask him some questions about our new intern, Beringer. When he said he planned to go sailing after our meeting, I offered to pack a sack lunch for him. However, he already had a lunch and asked if he could put it in our refrigerator while we met. I sent him out to our patio with a glass of lemonade. Then I was able to add some poison to his tuna fish sandwich. The rest, as they say, is history."

"And now, Beringer."

"He's been the hardest to kill. I hired someone to run him over and, when that didn't work, I asked the same person to drown him."

"Who was it?"

"Al Agnew."

"Agnew! You hired Al Agnew?! How'd you manage that?"

"Another Christmas party conversation. After having one too many, Al mentioned he had a ton of gambling debts. I filed that information away. A few months ago, I offered to pay off all his debts in exchange for his services."

"You sure made connections at our company Christmas party. I'm stunned that you would involve our drivers in your murder plots."

"He was very grateful to get out of debt. I thought Al would have a better chance of running over Beringer than I would. But the hit-and-run failed, and I had to put up some more money to fix the side of his car."

"So he was the guy who drove Beringer into the bay."

"Exactly. When the hit-and-run didn't work, Al and I came up with Plan B. I gave Al a new name. He became Tom Dawson. I learned from that witch Kirby at church that Matt had joined a Hayward Y basketball league, so Al joined Matt's team using his new name. One night after a game, he drove Beringer off a pier in Hayward in a stolen truck, but unfortunately he survived."

"I read about it in the newspaper, but I never dreamed you and Agnew had a hand in it. You came up with quite a plan."

"When Plan B didn't work, I took matters into my own hands. This time we'll succeed."

"Do you know that Agnew recently asked for time off? We don't know where he is. What if he talks to the police?"

"I suggested that he take a short vacation. He'll be back. Al and I plan to have coffee in a few weeks to discuss his finances. But I may have to poison him, too. The police might connect Rockwell's death with Beringer's disappearance and start interviewing your drivers."

Matt shuddered at what he'd just heard. He was glad he had left a recording for Ben, telling him that he was having dinner at the Rowlands' house. But Ben couldn't help him now. He needed to develop an escape plan. Fast. He tried to loosen the duct tape around his wrists, but it wouldn't budge. The tape around his knees and ankles bound his legs together tightly, yet he was able to gain some movement. If he could free his legs, he might be able to outrun Larry and Sally when they opened the back of the van.

"What do we do after tonight?" Larry asked. "A couple of plane tickets to an exotic island for an extended vacation?"

"First, I have to find the dinner invitation I sent to Beringer. I don't want anyone to find evidence that he was at our house tonight. I should have invited him by phone."

"Okay, but what do we do tomorrow?"

"In general, Larry, I think we'd better do our best to act as if we know nothing about Beringer's disappearance," she said. "We got our revenge. Now we pretend we didn't have much involvement with our last three interns."

"Right," Larry said quietly.

Matt was piecing it together. It hit him between the eyes that Derek's death had pushed Sally into some kind of madness. Her grudge against the church over the death of their son had caused her to conspire with the devil. Larry, whether he knew it or not, was probably going to be her next victim.

"Do we go home tonight?" Larry asked. "Tomorrow, will it be business as usual?"

"I have us going separate ways, to be perfectly honest."

"You mean one of us leaves town for a while?"

"Not exactly," Sally said. "What I mean is, our charade of a marriage has taken its final curtain."

"You mean split up?"

"Yes. I don't want to be married to you anymore."

"When did you come to that conclusion?!" Larry shouted.

"Months ago. Scotch tape and paper clips have held our marriage together for so long I can't remember when it began to fall apart."

"Now wait a minute, Sally," Larry protested. "I just helped you kidnap Beringer, and you want me to say sayonara?"

"I don't plan to file papers right away. I may wait six months until Beringer's disappearance dies down."

"What about our kids and our company?"

"My sister can help with our kids until we get our lives sorted out," Sally said. "The trucking business is in a trust, so the revenues will go to the kids in case we have to leave the country."

"Leave the country?! What do you mean by that?" Larry stammered.

"If the police suspect us, I don't plan to wait around for them to arrest me. I have money in an offshore account, so I can stay away indefinitely. In a couple of weeks, I'm catching a plane to Costa Rica, where an old friend has invited me to visit him on his ranch. You can confer with your mistress, Joanie Prentice, and decide what you want to do with the rest of your life."

"How do you know about Joanie?" Larry asked.

"You've been seeing her for the past two years," Sally said. "I've had a private eye trailing you off and on for several years, and I must say I haven't been very impressed by your choice of talent."

"You've had someone following me?" Larry asked.

"You heard me," Sally said. "I could feel your interest in me ebbing years ago. You had a fling with Lilly. Or was it Lila? It doesn't matter. Then there was your secretary, Paula, who thought you might divorce me, but left you after a couple of years when it didn't happen. Hiring a private eye isn't cheap. Fortunately, I could afford it. I grew so tired of hearing from you that you were working late at the office or entertaining clients."

"Who's the guy in Costa Rica?"

"He's my high school boyfriend. He called me a year ago. He sold his parents' farm a few years ago and made a killing. He now lives six months in Palm Springs and six months in Costa Rica. He's gone through a couple divorces, so maybe he's also learned a thing or two."

Larry slumped in the driver's seat, looking straight ahead at the highway.

"I can't understand," Sally said, "why you'd risk your marriage for a string of girlfriends."

"I like to keep my options open."

"That's a pretty feeble excuse. You married into a pretty sweet arrangement. My dad treated you like a son and trained you to manage a successful company that you didn't build. I've been holding the marriage together for the kids' sake. Derek was growing into such a fine young man. But, when he was taken from me, I felt completely alone. My anger grew, and I wanted revenge. I wanted someone to pay for my pain!"

"You seemed to withdraw from me."

"Why wouldn't I?! Like a lot of women, I dream about being with a man who wants only me. I haven't been that woman for you, and now it's time I follow my own dreams. I regret that it's taken so long to reach my decision. You've never been very supportive, so Derek's death made me feel lonely and very angry."

"Will you give me a second chance?"

"I'm not thinking of anything else right now except dumping Beringer in the siphon. We're operating in treacherous waters right now, and we need to keep our cool. Let's go finish our job."

25

The conversation between Sally and Larry ended, and the van ride continued in silence for miles. When the vehicle slowed, Matt thought they were leaving the highway. After coming to a stop, it turned left and proceeded down a long road. It slowed again and turned right onto some gravel that soon changed to dirt. The engine labored on the soft soil and stopped.

"Back it up to the canal," Sally said. The van made a u-turn, stopped, and then reversed. It moved backward until she said, "That's close enough. Turn off the lights."

Matt heard the rumbling sound of surging water. He guessed they had arrived at the siphon. He needed an escape strategy. Time was running out.

Larry and then Sally opened their doors and walked to the back of the van. The three of them were surrounded by the roar of water tumbling into the siphon. As Larry opened the rear doors, Sally asked, "What time is it?"

"About nine-thirty," Larry said.

"Let's move fast."

"Beringer is a load. Couldn't you have picked someone smaller?"

"He was the right guy," Sally responded. "No parents. We can do this."

Matt continued to fake his unconsciousness as they pulled him out of the van. He offered no resistance to their tugs, and his limp body hit the ground hard. When his left knee hit the dirt, Matt gritted his teeth in silence. As they pulled him toward the canal, he uttered some low groans. The duct tape around his wrists, knees, and ankles had restricted his blood circulation, and his arms and legs tingled.

"Tie the cement block around his waist," Sally said. "I wonder if I should shoot him first. I think the siphon noise would hide the sound."

"You have a gun?" Larry asked.

"Sure," Sally said. Matt sensed Larry's uneasiness escalated with the news. Surely he must realize she could shoot him as well. He wondered why Larry had ever offered to help her with a third murder, when he wasn't connected to the first two. "I bought it several months ago," she continued. "It's in my purse. What if my meetings with Cole and Agnew went badly? Let's say they wanted more money. I could shoot them and claim self-defense."

"Well, I think you should leave the gun in your purse," Larry said. "All we need is the police out here at this hour."

"Okay," Sally said. "Go get the block."

Matt hoped that was the last he heard about Sally's gun. He didn't want to join Larry in being shot to death. The more he thought about it, Larry was more valuable to her alive than dead. If the police ever suspected her of multiple murders, she could blame them all on him. It would be her word against his. When Sally paused and pulled a flashlight out of her purse, Matt's heart skipped a beat. He didn't have much time left to resist. She turned it on and laid it on the ground in the direction of the canal. Light in a starless night.

The sound of rushing water falling into the siphon sent shivers through Matt. Larry went to the back of the van and carried the cement block to the edge of the canal. Matt could hear him breathing heavily. He dropped the block and returned to the van to find the rope.

"Is there a chance someone might inspect the canal tonight and find us?" Larry asked, as he tied the cement block to Matt's waist.

"I'm sure they don't visit the canals at this hour. Take my word for it, no one is watching. Let's push him into the canal."

They dragged Matt a few feet to the edge of the canal. A cyclone fence on both sides of the siphon prevented the Rowlands from dumping their victim closer to it. With his eyes closed, Matt couldn't see the warning signs posted on the fence. The loud noise of the cascading water heightened Matt's fear, and he wondered how he could withstand its force. Bound, gagged, and afraid, he somehow had to avoid being sucked into the funnel and certain death.

"After we shove him into the canal, let's get out of here," Larry said. "Beringer is a dead man, and I don't like being near dead people."

"Relax, Larry," Sally said. "I want to savor the moment. Three interns have been silenced, and I feel good about it."

"I don't know how you can feel so good about a third murder. You sure picked a strange gravesite for Beringer. I wonder what else is at the bottom of the siphon."

I heard they cleared it last year, so it will be another year or two before they do it again. By that time, his body will have decomposed, and nothing will be left."

"Let's hurry," Larry said. "I'm feeling very uncomfortable."

Matt's adrenaline was flowing. He didn't want to die this way. He had to act, so he rolled onto his left elbow and eyed Larry Rowland.

"Larry, he's awake!" Sally yelled.

Matt swung his bound legs toward Larry, hoping to knock him off his feet and into the canal. He struck a glancing blow, causing Larry to stagger backwards and fall to the ground. Sally dropped to her knees and wrapped her right arm tightly around Matt's neck in a strangle hold.

"Help me!" Sally said.

Larry scrambled to his feet. He leaned over and swung at Matt's face, hitting his jaw in a glancing blow. Matt pretended to be dazed, worried that Sally might grab her gun and shoot him.

"Let's push him in," Larry said, gasping for breath.

They shoved Matt and the cement block into the irrigation canal. After a splash, he disappeared into the dark water below. The Rowlands returned to the van and drove away. Sally Rowland had completed her revenge plot.

26

When Matt hit the cold water in the canal, a jolt of terror struck him. His body, bound by duct tape, plunged beneath the water's surface, but he soon began moving his legs back and forth to hurry his ascent. At last, his head and shoulders emerged from the water, and he breathed deeply through his nose, duct tape still covering his mouth. "Larry miscalculated!" Matt thought to himself. "Thank God!" Wanting to submerge Matt in the ten-foot-deep canal, Rowland had included more rope than necessary in tying his waist to the block. It had not dragged him to the bottom of the canal as planned.

Matt looked toward the ledge where the Rowlands had pushed him into the canal, but they were gone. Floating on his back, he looked up at the night sky. Then he heard the crashing sound of water hurtling into the siphon, and he knew he had to act quickly before it swallowed him.

Looking around, Matt assessed his situation. "What can I do to avoid being sucked into it?" Moving his bound legs back and forth, he attempted to propel his body toward the far wall, fighting the current. Maybe he could find something to hold onto and stop his movement toward the siphon's opening. He tried to stay hopeful as he reached the wall and searched for anything to grip. It was a challenging maneuver, since his hands remained bound by duct tape behind his back. His back scraped along the surface, moving slowly with the current, until he bumped into what felt like a cyclone fence. The flowing water pressed his body against the wire mesh, and his feet found support on the wall beneath it. The chain-link barrier stretched across the entire width of the canal. His heart soared. "This fence has saved my life!"

Standing sideways on the wall, with his head and shoulders above the water, he held onto the wire behind his back and steadied himself. He turned and rubbed his chin on the protruding hooks along the upper border of the diamond-shaped mesh. Forcing the duct tape on his mouth over one of the prongs, he pulled the tape away from his lips. Now he could breathe better. He decided not to waste his energy by calling for help in the middle of the night.

After moving his arms like pistons, resting, and repeating the action, the duct tape finally loosened around his wrists and he was able to free his hands. Matt ducked under water and worked for minutes to untie his knees and ankles. He'd been saved by a cyclone fence installed to prevent objects from being drawn into the siphon's mouth. Apparently, Sally had not known about this feature, and her oversight proved to be Matt's salvation.

He removed the rope around his waist that was attached to the block. Its forward movement had been halted by the cement wall supporting the cyclone fence. Gathering strength, he moved toward the wall from which he had been pushed and pulled himself out of the canal, rolling onto the dirt at the edge of the waterway. He lay there, under the dark sky, exhausted, and grateful to be alive.

Matt rose to his feet by the edge of the canal. His arms and legs felt like lead weights. His hands were numb. He ached all over, as if he had been beaten up by a couple of thugs. In fact, he had been assaulted by two criminals masquerading as church leaders. Sally Rowland had stolen the lives of two young ministers and, with Larry's help, intended to make him her third victim. But she had failed, and there, in the middle of farmland, he'd escaped from her clutches. His wrists and ankles throbbed, but he was too relieved to care about the pain.

He shivered in his wet clothes as a soft wind brushed his skin. He wanted to rest, but he had to find a house or get to the road and flag a car for help. Starting to take a step, he hesitated. "I have to lie down for just a couple of minutes." Then he would find the strength to walk and find some aid. Just a couple of minutes. That's all he needed.

Images of Sally and Larry Rowland interrupted his sleep, and he awoke from his nap. How long had he dozed? He had to call the police and tell them about the Rowlands. Straining to get up, his eyes searched the darkness. He spotted a lighted farm house across a large field and started walking. After a short distance, he had to stop and rest. Catching his breath, he continued moving toward the two-story structure with a wide front porch. Matt wanted to run toward it, but his body wouldn't respond. When he finally reached the house, he trudged up the steps. After several knocks, a man appeared in his pajamas and robe.

"Hello," Matt said. "I'm sorry to bother you at this hour. My name is Matt Beringer. I'm a seminary student at Calvin Seminary in San Francisco. I was kidnapped last night in San Lucas, tied up, and driven here and thrown into the canal over there, by the siphon. Somehow I managed to escape." Matt realized he was short of breath. "Can I use your phone? I need to call the police."

"Come on in. That siphon is dangerous. I'm amazed you survived. The phone's over there on the table." The porch light outlined the man's face, tanned and wrinkled, with strong features and clear eyes.

Matt's wondered if his watch was accurate. "What time is it?"

"Almost ten-thirty. I was just about ready to hit the hay. My wife's asleep."

"Where am I?" Matt asked. "Near Sacramento?"

"You're about twenty miles south of Sacramento, near Dixon on Interstate 80. To be exact, my farm sits right next to the Weyand canal, which is part of the Solano Irrigation District. I'm Bob Walker."

"I'll call 911," Matt said, as he reached for the phone and dialed the number. "Hello? My name is Matt Beringer, I'm an intern at Hacienda Presbyterian in San Lucas. Last night I was at the home of some church members, Sally and Larry Rowland, and they drugged me, tied me up, and drove me up here near Dixon and threw me into an irrigation canal. They tried to murder me."

The voice at the other end asked for his location.

"I'm at Bob Walker's farm on...."

"8945 Davis Road, by the Weyand Canal," Walker interjected.

Matt was also asked about his condition. "I'm okay," he said, "but I want to speak to the police as soon as possible." He was told a California Highway Patrol car would be dispatched to the farm. Matt hung up the phone and stared into the darkness of an adjacent room. Facing death by being swept into the siphon had been a terrifying experience.

Walker broke the silence. "Did you say Sally and Larry Rowland? They tried to kill you?"

"Yeah, they attend the church where I'm interning."

"I know the Rowland family. Sally grew up a mile down the road. She came to visit me a couple of months ago. Said her husband needed some rat poison."

"She used it to murder the intern who worked at the church before me. And she arranged to have another former intern run off the road near here, about a month ago. She hired a driver who works for their company."

"You must be kidding. Sally?"

"She planned to make me her third victim."

"That's unbelievable. I remember reading about the car accident. A young minister from Sacramento. The first police report said the guy fell asleep at the wheel. The next thing I heard, the CHP said one of the trucks from Hannifin Trucking was involved. They said the driver was probably high on cocaine or something because he had a history of drug use. Larry was cleared of any charges."

"Sally planned it."

"I'm shocked. Sally came from a good family. I knew her parents well. Why would she murder someone?"

"I think losing her son on a church canoe trip a year and a half ago pushed her over the edge. She's a very angry woman."

"I knew they'd lost Derek, but I can't believe it would cause her to do something like that. When she came here, she seemed okay to me."

"She hid her anger from everyone."

"That's really sad. I've known Sally since she was a little girl," he said, shaking his head. "Hey, you need to get out of those wet clothes. I'll go find something for you to change into." Walker went upstairs and returned with an armful of clothes. "You can use the bathroom around the corner. I'll give you a plastic bag for your wet clothes."

"Thanks," Matt said. "I'm soaked."

Within ten minutes, a California Highway Patrol car pulled into the Walkers' driveway. Matt opened the front door and walked down the front steps toward the approaching officer. He had never met anyone from the CHP.

Walker followed him out the door.

"I'm Officer Martinez." Looking at Matt, he said, "You must be the guy who called 911. Can I see some I.D.?"

"I don't have any," Matt said. "The people who kidnapped me took my wallet."

"Okay. You can tell me what happened on the way to the station," Martinez said. "We need to find the people who tried to kill you."

Before Matt opened the car door, he went over and shook hands with Bob Walker. "I'm sorry for keeping you up tonight, but I'm sure glad you were home. I'll return your clothes to you. Thanks for everything."

"You're welcome. I'm glad you're okay and getting some help."

Officer Martinez nodded at Walker, and then returned to the patrol car. On the way to the CHP's Vacaville station, Martinez drove Matt back to the siphon, and he showed the officer where the Rowlands had dumped him into the canal. As they pulled into the station parking lot, Sergeant Ron Parks walked out to meet them, eating a sandwich.

"What do you have?" Parks asked the officer.

"This is Matt Beringer. He was tied up and thrown into the Weyand Canal near the siphon next to Bob Walker's farm."

Inside the station, Matt again summarized his kidnap and escape for Sergeant Parks' tape recorder.

"You've had a pretty exciting evening," Parks exclaimed, turning to Matt.

"You can say that again. This is more like a movie than real life."

"We see a lot of crazy things in our work," Parks said, "so nothing really surprises us."

"I expected my internship at the church to be calm and peaceful," Matt said. "It's been just the opposite."

"Larry Rowland was cleared in the Rockwell death on Interstate 80," Parks said. "I found Rockwell's car in the ditch after the accident. At first, we thought he fell asleep at the wheel, but later we found some yellow paint on the car that matched the color on Rowland's trucks. Given the truck driver's history, we concluded that Rowland's driver was using drugs and acted on his own. Now you tell us that Rowland's wife planned the murders and hired the truck driver to run Rockwell off the road. Larry Rowland may not have had anything to do with that murder, but it wasn't a random act."

"That's true," Matt said.

"Church work, huh? I'll bet this isn't what you expected," Parks said.

"You're right."

"I'll call the San Lucas police," Parks said. "Hopefully, they can find the Rowlands."

"It's hard for me to believe that Sally Rowland masterminded all of this," Matt said. "She's the one who hired me at the church, but she was definitely directing traffic tonight."

27

Sergeant Parks asked Officer Martinez to drive Matt back to San Lucas. The Rowlands had to be arrested ASAP.

"Will you call Detective Ben Miller at the Oakland P.D.?" Matt asked Parks. "He's a friend, and I've told him all about the recent attempts on my life. Would you ask him if he can meet us at the Rowlands' house?"

"I'll do that. I just sent a report to the San Lucas police. I've alerted them that you two are on your way. I'll send my report to Detective Miller as well."

"I think Sally plans to go to the church to try to find her dinner invitation," Matt said. "She wants to destroy evidence that I went to her home this evening. However, I think she'll visit her sister first, where her kids are staying tonight, and fill her in on what's been happening. Sally plans to leave the country in the next couple of weeks, and she wants her sister to take care of her kids for a while. Maybe Ben and I can beat her to the church, while the San Lucas police hold Larry."

Matt was wide awake as they sped along Interstate 80 from Vacaville toward the East Bay, with the patrol car's roof light flashing. The traffic moved quickly to the right-hand lanes. For the first time, he felt the scales were tipping in his favor as they drove through Oakland on the Nimitz Freeway. Leaving the freeway at the San Lucas exit, Matt noticed a few pedestrians staring at the unfamiliar police car speeding through the village. He guided Officer Martinez up the hill to Alta Avenue, where he switched off the roof light. As they turned onto the tree-lined street, Matt wondered what was in store for them. Pulling in front of the Rowlands' house, he saw Larry's Mercedes in the driveway. Two San Lucas police cars were parked at the curb, with an officer seated in the one in front. Across the street sat his own car and a plain white car he assumed belonged to Ben Miller.

Matt and Officer Martinez stopped to greet the San Lucas police officer. "We have Mr. Rowland inside," he said. "I'm watching for Mrs. Rowland. We don't want her to see us and try to escape." They hurried up the front steps, and Martinez knocked on the door. Miller's voice boomed from within, "Come in!"

They entered to find Larry Rowland sitting on the couch while Detective Miller and a San Lucas policeman occupied large leather chairs facing their suspect. When Rowland saw Matt, he gaped.

"Hello, Larry," Matt said. "Surprised to see me? Alive?"

Rowland slouched, unable to speak, staring at Matt as if he had seen a ghost. Then he leaned back and focused on the ceiling, slowly shaking his head. His face went ashen.

"I didn't mention that you were coming," Miller said. "I thought we'd surprise him."

"It's great to see you, Ben," Matt said. Then he turned toward Rowland. "Where's Sally?"

"I haven't a clue," Rowland mumbled, still staring at the ceiling. "I don't know where she is."

"The San Lucas police are watching for her," Miller said. "We know she's driving her silver BMW," Miller said. "We're pretty sure she'll eventually return to San Lucas."

"I overheard her say that she planned to go to the church," Matt said, "to find the dinner invitation she sent me. She wants to destroy evidence that I was here tonight. Should we head to my office?"

"Sounds like a good idea," Miller replied.

"Can I mix a martini?" Rowland asked, now sitting on the edge of the sofa, ready to stand.

"No, because you're under arrest," Miller said, "but I'll follow you into the kitchen and watch you have a glass of water. That's about all you can drink tonight."

As Rowland moved toward the kitchen, he looked again in wonder at Matt. "How'd you escape from the siphon, Beringer? I can't believe it."

"Yeah, with no help from you."

"You got lucky, that's all l can say."

Matt felt sore, had scratches on his hands and arms, and was exhausted, but he knew he'd dodged yet another bullet. He heard Miller question Rowland in the kitchen. "Not including your verbal threat to Matt two weeks ago, did you know that he had at least two other attempts on his life the past month?"

"No, I didn't," Rowland said, reaching into the refrigerator for a pitcher of iced water.

"Would you or your wife know anything about the hit-and-run in front of his apartment?"

"No."

"How about the guy who drove him off a pier?"

"I don't know anything."

"Sure you do," Matt said, walking into the kitchen. "I heard Sally tell you in the van that she hired Al Agnew to kill me. He was driving the car that tried to hit me, and he drove the stolen truck off the pier with me in it."

"Yeah, but I knew nothing about those incidents before tonight. I wasn't involved in any of that stuff. You'll have to ask Sally for the details."

"Tell us where she is tonight, Mr. Rowland. It might help your case," Miller said.

Rowland didn't respond as they walked back into the living room, but he appeared to be weighing the offer. Holding his glass of water with both hands, he leaned back in the sofa.

"When your message said you were going to the Rowlands' house for dinner," Miller said, turning to Matt, "I became concerned. I drove by and didn't see anyone here. I smelled a rat. I was relieved to finally hear from Sergeant Parks that you were okay. How'd you avoid the siphon?"

"I had some help. There's a cyclone fence in front, to keep debris from being sucked into it. The fence saved me."

"Back to you, Mr. Rowland. One more time. Where's your wife?" Miller asked.

"I tell you, I don't know. Maybe she's at her sister's place, checking on our kids. She likes to spend time with her sister. She definitely wasn't interested in being with me. Our marriage is finished. She told me tonight she plans to file for divorce."

"You won't be seeing a lot of each other in the coming months," Miller said. "It's likely you'll be spending jail time apart from one another, for quite a while."

"Listen, if I give you some information, you say it could help me?"

"It could, Rowland," Miller replied. "What more can you tell us?"

"My wife is a very sick woman. She told me tonight that she hired Kenny Cole, one of my truck drivers, to murder Pete Rockwell. Then she told me she poisoned Richard Finley. I didn't know anything about those murders until tonight. And, yeah, she told me she tried to kill Beringer a couple of times. She hired another of my drivers, Al Agnew, to do the hit-and-run and drive him into the bay. Those attempts didn't work, but she was determined to kill Beringer, so she made me help her kidnap him. She threatened to frame me for the other two murders if I didn't help. I've learned through the years that it isn't wise to say no to my wife. Besides, she carries a gun these days, and I feared for my life if I didn't help her."

Matt stood beside Officer Martinez, who leaned against a bookshelf next to the fireplace. The San Lucas policeman remained seated in the leather chair. Miller stood near the sofa. They waited for Rowland to continue.

"Look, I know I should have called the police when she told me about her plans to kidnap Beringer, but I was scared," Rowland said.

WHAT LIES CAN DO

"Why did your wife murder these two previous interns, and then try to murder Matt?" Miller asked.

"A year and a half ago, we lost our oldest son, Derek, on a church-sponsored canoe trip. He was Sally's favorite of our three. She had big plans for him. I thought Sally was doing all right, but she was hiding a lot of rage. Our son was a great kid. Bright, good-looking, and ambitious. A lot like her. She adored him and wanted him to manage our trucking business one day. She hid her bitterness from everyone else, including me. I guess she blamed the church for Derek's death and decided to get revenge. She kept her pain bottled up inside her, but she must have snapped."

"I thought Christians are all about love and forgiveness," Miller said.

"We're supposed to be, but Sally couldn't forgive the intern in charge of that canoe trip. She told me that killing three seminary interns would help her get even for the three kids who drowned. An eye for an eye. I think her anger poisoned her, and she went over the edge. Believe me, she's one sick lady."

"Did you know about the canoe trip, Matt?" Miller asked.

"I found a newspaper article, but nobody told me about it when I was hired. I heard that the senior pastor didn't want the staff to discuss it with anyone because he was concerned about its effect on the members."

"Sounds like they weren't being completely transparent with you," Miller said.

"I also learned that I wasn't chosen for the internship because of my basketball experience. Sally lied to me. She chose me because my parents died in a car accident. After she killed me, she wanted the chances to be slim to none that my family would start an investigation into my disappearance."

"She had quite a scheme," Miller responded.

"What about the secret bank account, Larry?" Matt asked. "Did you really need the money? Were you paying for someone's apartment rent?"

"It's none of your business. I used that account to help some friends. I'm planning to pay back the church. No big deal."

"As a church leader," Matt said, "you used very bad judgment. You broke the law and abused the church's trust, and I think Pastor Staley plans to contact the police about it."

"I doubt it. It's small potatoes, Beringer. Stay out of it!"

Turning to the Officer Martinez and the San Lucas policeman, Miller asked if they would stay with Rowland while he and Matt drove to the church. They both nodded. "Sure, I can stay a while," Officer Martinez said, smiling. "Maybe Larry and I will talk about sports."

"Matt, let's beat Mrs. Rowland to the church," Miller said.

"You took the words right out of my mouth."

"My wife mentioned buying an airplane ticket to Costa Rica," Rowland said. "She might try to leave the country sometime soon."

"What's her sister's address?" Miller asked.

"It's 260 Alta Avenue, a couple of blocks south."

Miller asked the San Lucas policeman if he would visit Sally's sister and tell her Sally is wanted by the police. Then he and Matt left the house, jumped into the unmarked, white police car, and headed south on Alta Avenue toward Hacienda. No silver BMW sat in front of the sister's home.

Continuing their drive to the church, Miller called the Oakland P.D. and asked his staff to learn what flights were leaving the Bay Area for Costa Rica over the next two weeks and from what airport they were departing. He asked that officers be assigned to cover those flights and intercept Sally Rowland if she appeared. Maybe Sally had gone to the Oakland Airport to book her flight to Central America.

After midnight, Miller parked on the street behind the church, and they found their way to Matt's second-floor office through the entrance by the gym. They left the ceiling light off as they waited in the dark for her. The courtyard lamp below supplied enough visibility for them. Papers from two projects covered Matt's desk—the schedule for the boys' and girls' basketball leagues and next Sunday's lesson. Matt confirmed the presence of Sally's invitation in his middle drawer. Sitting at his desk, Matt winced as he remembered that the basketball program had been her smokescreen to draw him to the church as her third victim. In her eyes, his deceased parents were a far more important qualification for the Hacienda internship than his college basketball experience. He and Richard had been duped. They had been recruited to die. Their internships had been designed with plenty of deception, and they had been lured into a murderer's trap. Sally had told them no ordinary lies.

Miller sat on the leather sofa against the wall. After several minutes, Matt began to drowse in his chair. A long half hour later, they heard a key in the lock. Miller reached for the gun strapped to his chest. Matt's heart raced. The office door opened slowly, and a hand reached around and flipped on the light. Sally Rowland stepped into the room and saw Matt sitting at his desk. Her jaw dropped and her eyes widened.

"What are you doing here?" she asked.

"Waiting for you, Sally," Matt said. "I might ask you the same question. You thought I was lying at the bottom of the siphon, didn't you?"

"I don't know what you're talking about," she said.

Sally walked toward Matt's desk and stood in front of it, glaring at him.

"Have a seat there by the desk, Mrs. Rowland," Miller said. "We've been expecting you."

"Who are you?!" she shouted, looking at the man on the couch.

"I'm Detective Ben Miller of the Oakland Police Department. Your husband is being detained by San Lucas police at your home right now and is cooperating fully in our murder investigation. You're going to be charged with the murders of Pete Rockwell and Richard Finley, and the attempted murder of Matt Beringer."

Matt pulled Sally's invitation from his center drawer and held it up in an outstretched hand. "Is this what you're looking for?"

"Give me that!" she shrieked, as she lunged toward Matt, reaching for the piece of paper. He pushed back his chair from the desk, avoiding her grasp.

"I had dinner at your house tonight, Sally, at your invitation. Remember?"

"You're crazy! Larry and I had dinner in Jack London Square."

"I told you to sit down, Mrs. Rowland," Miller repeated.

She stood in front of Matt's desk, focused on the seminarian. "I'll sit down when I'm good and ready," she snarled.

Matt motioned for Sally to do the same, but she ignored him.

"I can't believe you tried to kill me tonight," Matt said. "This isn't what I signed on for when I accepted your internship offer."

"You're out of your mind," she grumbled.

"I heard what you told Larry on the ride to the irrigation canal," Matt said. "I wasn't unconscious like you thought. I heard it all."

"You shouldn't believe everything you hear."

"Your fingerprints are all over the murders of Rockwell and Finley," Miller said, "but you failed tonight in your attempt to kill a third intern. Your husband's testimony, coupled with what Matt heard in the van, prove your role in a plot to murder three persons. We think that Al Agnew should also provide some convincing testimony."

"You'd believe Larry Rowland?! You've got to be kidding. You can't trust anything he says. He's lied to me most of our married life!"

"He's not lying tonight, Mrs. Rowland," Miller said. "You're in big trouble."

"You have no evidence!" Sally yelled.

"I've read Matt's police report and heard your husband's confession. So we have two witnesses who heard you describe your involvement in the Rockwell and Finley murders," Miller said. "And Bob Walker told Matt you asked him for some rat poison that you used to murder Richard Finley."

Sally looked around the room like a caged lioness. Fury filled her eyes. Matt wondered if she would reach for the gun in her purse. She had nothing to lose.

"You still can't prove I did any of it," she said.

"I want you to sit down, Mrs. Rowland," Miller repeated, "and put your purse on the desk."

"Sally," Matt said. "No one's to blame for Derek's death. It was a tragic accident that nobody intentionally caused."

"My Derek and the two other kids drowned, and God could have prevented it from happening."

"We can't explain why innocent lives are taken. You know that. Illness and accidents happen. Suffering is part of the human experience. God is aware of all of these events, but He doesn't cause them. God feels our pain. If we cause our own suffering, He wants us to change our ways. If others cause us to suffer, He wants us to turn away from them. God was deeply saddened by your son's death. Think about how He must have felt when His own son died."

"Okay, okay, stop it!" she growled, slumping into the chair in front of Matt's desk.

"Why did you want to murder the three interns?" Miller asked.

Sally seemed to be making some mental calculations before she spoke. "Rockwell was responsible for killing my Derek and two other kids on the canoe trip. I heard an inner voice telling me to get even."

"I think you heard Satan tempting you," Matt said, "and you fell for the trap."

"You think so?!" she screamed. "Wait until you lose a child and see how you feel!"

"I'm sorry about your loss," Matt said, "but Pete Rockwell didn't cause the accident. He was devastated by it. He felt responsible for all three of those kids."

"Then why did God let it happen? He could have prevented it. Why was my Derek taken and not some other kid?"

"Sometimes bad things happen, and we suffer. The deaths of the kids on the canoe trip just can't be explained."

"Derek was a special child to me. He was my favorite. We were very close. I wanted him to run the company after Larry retired, but that dream was shattered."

Silence filled the room as Matt and Ben Miller considered her words.

"So God lost me when Derek died," Sally added.

"That's a shame because God loves you," Matt said. "He will never leave you, and He's always there to help you if you reach out to Him."

"Don't preach to me, Matt," Sally said.

"We know you have a gun in your purse, Mrs. Rowland," Miller said from the sofa. "I want you to put your purse on the desk."

Sally held her purse with her right hand, keeping it on her lap. She looked weary and defeated. "Okay, Beringer, you win. I tried to kill you over and over, and you survived every attempt. I thought for sure we had succeeded tonight." She paused. "When Derek died, it hurt. It really hurt."

Matt let her comment hang there for a while. After what seemed like a minute, he responded to her. "I know. I lost both of my parents. Killed by a drunk driver. But I don't hold God responsible for their deaths."

"I didn't deserve to lose my son!" Sally said.

"I'm sure the hurt will never completely go away," Matt said, "but you should bury your hate. It hasn't brought your son back and has already destroyed two innocent lives."

Matt could see the wheels turning inside Sally's head. Again, she looked like a cornered animal, confused and angry but weighing her situation. He thought, "Please don't let her open her purse! Please!"

Sally leaned her head back against the top of the chair and stared at the ceiling.

"I'm tired" Sally whispered. "I thought God betrayed me when Derek died. Maybe getting even isn't as important as I thought."

"Mrs. Rowland, you need to put your purse on the desk," Miller said, one more time. "I know you have a gun in it. I don't want to shoot you."

"I don't want to," Sally said.

"Why did you take me to the siphon?" Matt asked, buying time.

"They'd never find your body."

"Did you ever worry about being caught?" Matt said.

"No. I had it all figured out. Killing Rockwell and Finley was easy. You've been the problem."

"What are you feeling right now?" Matt asked.

"Depressed," Sally said. "I thought revenge would be sweet, but now I have a bitter taste in my mouth."

"Did you think about talking to someone about how you were feeling?" Miller asked. "Like your pastor?"

"Staley came to speak with me after Derek's death, but he didn't understand. I thought about talking to my sister, but she's weak and it would have scared her. There aren't many people I've trusted in my life. The one guy I really loved married someone else, and Larry has cheated on me for years."

"Seeking some professional counseling might have helped, Mrs. Rowland," Miller said.

Scowling at Matt, Sally said, "You've really messed things up for me. Anyway, it doesn't matter now." She rose from her chair. "I just want to go home."

"Sally, why don't you sit down?" Matt said. "I'd like to hear your side of it."

"No, I'm leaving. I want to see my kids."

"No, Mrs. Rowland. You're coming with me," Miller said.

"No, I'm not." She stared menacingly at him and reached into her purse. Miller fired once. A deafening shot. Sally gasped and, almost in slow motion, sank to the floor in front of Matt's desk. As she collapsed, car keys fell from her hand.

28

It was October eleventh, five weeks since Matt had started his internship. He sat next to Jancy at Angelo's restaurant in San Leandro, where Pastor Staley had organized a luncheon for a small group of friends. They sat around a large round table in a private room, and a waiter had taken their orders.

"First of all," Staley said, "I want to thank Liz and Steve Canfield for hosting this luncheon today. Second, I'm glad that the Jensens were able to join us. I want you to know how much I appreciate each of you and your commitment to the church. We've been through an agonizing period, and it's a relief to see an end to all of the turmoil we've faced. We'll never forget Pete and Richard, and what they mean to our congregation, but I'm grateful to be moving beyond those days of danger and uncertainty. It's been sad to see one of our church families self-destruct, but it reminds us how far we can fall when we lose our faith. Matt has become a local hero for his role in the arrests of Sally and Larry, so I wanted to host a gathering to thank him for his efforts. We never intended his first month to be so action-packed."

Muted laughter rippled through the small group, as all eyes turned to the guest of honor.

Staley continued, "It's incredible that Matt was involved in a murder plot, while the rest of us never imagined it could happen. His work with Detective Miller ultimately led the police to the Rowlands. Matt, we're sorry for what you've been through, but we appreciate all you've done. I'm confident that your future with us will be much more enjoyable. Would you like to say a few words?"

"Thanks, Pastor Staley, for organizing this luncheon. And thanks to Liz and Steve for inviting us to their restaurant. I'm also relieved that we have ended a challenging period for the church and can return to normalcy. It was a scary experience to be a murder target, and I know I'll sleep much better in the weeks ahead. Through all of this, I've grown closer to Hacienda, and I want to thank each of you for your wonderful support this past month. Jancy, I couldn't have made it without you, and I am so blessed to have had your support through it all. Mrs. Kirby, Pastor Staley, Pastor Boyle, Ben, Carlo, Liz and Steve, and Jean and Mike, thank you for being here today and for caring enough to get to know me. Your friendship helped me cope with all I faced in the past few weeks. I'm grateful that you'll be part of my life as I continue my internship."

A few moments of silence followed his remarks.

"Matt, you can drop by my office anytime for a Coke," Carlo said, grinning.

"The last one I had with you was especially refreshing," Matt said with a wink.

"I gave you a pretty hard time when you first joined us, Matt," Mrs. Kirby said, "but I've become a big fan of yours. I'm looking forward to having you around for the rest of the year."

"Thanks. I've enjoyed working with you, too."

"Mrs. Kirby tells me you have excellent handwriting," Boyle interjected. "She says my writing is practically unreadable."

"They say handwriting clarity is inversely proportional to intelligence," Matt said, "so you must be bordering on genius, Pastor Boyle."

"Sure, sure," Boyle said. "Flattery will get you everywhere, Beringer."

"Before I forget," Matt said, "I want you all to know that I've had several telephone conversations with Mrs. Finley, Richard's mother. I've updated her on all that has happened. She continues to grieve over her son's death, but she's grateful to have some answers."

"It's been a difficult time," Staley said. "As the Rowlands' pastor, I take responsibility for not staying closer to them after Derek's death. I counseled them, but obviously it wasn't enough."

"Don't be too hard on yourself, Jim," Liz said. "We appreciate all of the support you gave us. None of us understood that Sally had such deep emotional problems."

"Thanks, Liz," Staley said. "I've had second thoughts about my decision to restrict conversations about the canoe accident. I wanted to put it behind us, but that approach may have caused Sally to bury her sadness, and it surfaced later in hatred and anger toward the church and our interns."

"This congregation is prospering under your leadership, Jim," Boyle said. "The way the Rowlands became separated from God had nothing to do with you."

"Okay," Staley said. "I'll conclude my comments by saying I've been told Sally is expected to make a full recovery from her gunshot wound. Also, I want you to know that Matt has been visiting Sally and Larry at the jail on a weekly basis, and I commend him for doing that."

"That's pretty generous of you, Matt," Mike said, "considering they tried to murder you. It sounds as if you've forgiven them."

"I have. The Lord's Prayer asks us to forgive. If we don't forgive others, our anger can lead to grudges, which is unhealthy. We need to live in the present and future, and not hold onto the past."

"Thank you for visiting them," Jean said. "I think most of our members have abandoned the Rowlands."

"I'd like to help Sally recover her faith," Matt said. "Larry's pretty scared about his future. He realizes he could have been a better husband and father. He tells me they've hired the best attorneys money can buy. Sally plans to plead not guilty by reason of insanity. Larry says he will plead not guilty, claiming he was coerced to follow Sally's instructions."

"I feel so sorry for the kids," Jancy said. "They're the ones who suffer the most when couples have problems. Visiting their mother and father in prison or at a mental health institution will be hard on them."

"Kids with arrested parents have a higher incidence of depression, anxiety, and withdrawal than other children," Steve said, "and an even higher percentage of attention problems and disruptive behavior. They will face the social stigma of having parents in jail, and they may experience teasing."

"The Rowland kids are staying with Sally's sister," Staley said. "They're in counseling, but I'm sure they're not having an easy time at school."

"I hope we can provide the kind of support Susan and Ricky will need," Jancy said.

"I'm always surprised to learn about these kinds of problems in wealthy communities, like San Lucas," Miller said, "but people can have issues and be in pain no matter how much money they have."

"Having money can be a curse," Steve said. "Some people treat money like their god. Money can interfere with leading the good life that God wants us to live."

"Ben asked me to leave daily messages about my activities on his answering machine," Matt said. "He worked overtime on my behalf, and I'm grateful that he was so concerned about my safety."

"You're like family," Ben said. "I'm glad I could help."

"Sally really fooled us on the Education Committee," Jean said. "None of us thought she was acting unusual."

"She wanted her first two murders to look like accidents, " Matt said. "If I had ended up at the bottom of the siphon, I would have been a missing person. She was confident no one would suspect her because she was a church leader."

"She almost pulled it off," Carlo said.

"Until you told me about them," Jean said, "I wasn't aware of the number of times Sally tried to kill you."

"Yeah, she was pretty committed to making me her third victim," Matt said. "Her revenge meter was really flashing. Fortunately, she wasn't successful."

"It must have been a stressful time for you," Liz said.

"There were some sleepless night," he said, "and it may take a while to process all that's happened. The murders of Pete and Richard were such evil acts. Who knew Sally was that unstable and that determined?! I'm lucky to be alive."

"We're glad you are, too," Mrs. Kirby said, "and we want you to know that we're here for you. I put your October basketball schedule in the current newsletter. You need to give me next month's schedule."

"I'll have it on your desk today," Matt said. "We have our first practices tomorrow afternoon, and the games begin next week."

"Our Julie is raring to go," Liz said.

There was a pause in the conversation, and then Matt said, "I think it's time to share a happy announcement with all of you. I've asked Jancy to marry me, and she's accepted."

Matt's words were greeted with cheers and applause.

"I knew from the day I met her that she's a very special lady. She's wearing an engagement ring I've given her, and we plan to pick a wedding date that is sometime after my seminary graduation in May."

"Maybe a June wedding?" Mrs. Kirby asked. "Jancy, we'd love to hear from you."

"This intern of yours is the best," she said. "Matt and I have grown so close during the past month, and I've seen his positive attitude and caring spirit in some tough situations. We clicked from the very beginning. I think the two of us will make a great team."

"We'll see what kind of a coach he is when the basketball season begins," Mike said, chuckling.

"Since I oversee church finance," Boyle said, "you two can have your wedding at the church for free!" He waved his fists in the air and broke into laughter, causing his jowls to redden.

"I second the motion," Staley echoed.

"In addition," Boyle said, "I have two tickets to a play in San Francisco this Saturday, if you'd like to use them."

"Thanks, Pastor Boyle," Matt said. "We'd enjoy seeing a play."

"Very generous of you, Charles," Staley said. "I'm glad we could have some conversation before our food arrives. Again, thank you all for your comments and for being here. In a week, the middle school boys' and girls' basketball leagues begin, so please attend the games as your schedules permit."

"I have an idea," Liz said, smiling. "As the new chair of the Education Committee, I think the church ought to consider hiring Matt full-time. That way, there won't be any interns left . . . to kill."

Her attempt at humor caught the group off guard. It was followed by several moments of silence.

"Hey," Liz said. "I was just trying to bring some closure to a serious subject. The worst is now behind us, and we can focus on the future. No harm intended."

"Liz," Matt said. "I like the way you're always looking out for my best interests."

Laughter followed, and Pastor Staley said, "Amen to that!"

Acknowledgments

The idea to write a mystery novel was born around the time I graduated from theological seminary in 1971. I have always enjoyed mysteries—high on crime-solving and low on violence—and I thought that using a church setting would provide a compelling backdrop for sinister activities. I started writing my story in 2001.

My wonderful wife, Judy, has been with me every step of the way. She has helped me find the right word, rephrase a sentence, redesign a chapter, and brought her valuable insights to my writing project. Without her love, understanding, patience, and support, I never could have finished my novel.

Doris Vinnedge and Priscilla Long offered suggestions and encouragement. Julia Young and Deborah Bianco provided helpful advice.

I appreciate the assistance I received from Dr. Darrell Clardy, retired forensic toxicologist from the Orange County Sheriff's Department.

Finally, a special thank you to my editor, Christine Breen, who offered constructive guidance and wise counsel.

About the Author

Erick Leithe was raised in Seattle, Washington. After graduating from college, he attended a theological seminary and earned Master of Divinity and Doctor of Ministry degrees. For the past 35 years, he has been a financial advisor for a major Wall Street investment firm. He and his wife, Judy, live on Mercer Island, Washington, near Seattle.

91787495R00128

Made in the USA
Columbia, SC
25 March 2018